Praise for
The Paper Stars Series

GOLD MEDAL WINNER Independent Book Awards

"Lyrically written, this powerful and at times painful read captures the reader and does not let go."
—*Booklist*, starred review

"The author imbues the story with a fable-like quality through her beautiful, lyrical, and poetic prose, full of rich metaphors and similes. Best read of the year so far."
—Books Direct

"This is THE book that most people, if not everyone, should read because it actually shows us a whole new meaning to understanding POC and also the stuffs that go on behind closed doors."
—*Once Upon a Story*

Hiro loves Kite

A Paper Stars Novel, Book 2

Lauren Nicolle Taylor

OWL HOLLOW PRESS

Owl Hollow Press, LLC, Springville, UT 84663

Hero Loves Kite: Paper Stars Book Two
Second Edition

First Edition — 2019 by Clean Teen Publishing

Library of Congress Cataloging-in-Publication Data
Hiro Loves Kite / L.N. Taylor — Second edition.

Summary:
Nora's struggles are just beginning, and she must now become Kite—a stronger, more independent version of herself. Kettle must accept that he is also Hiro: a Japanese American with every right to happiness and freedom. They must rely on each other, otherwise it's their future in jeopardy, the fates of the street kids in their care.

Cover by Pocket Hollow Designs

ISBN 978-1-958109-14-4 (paperback)
ISBN 978-1-958109-15-1 (e-book)

I'm sure this is weird, but I'm dedicating this book to myself.

You got lost for a while there,
but words have always brought you home.

Chapter One

Kite

The path gleams white as bleached bone. A small, black-board cottage. A bland neat garden. A road between that could be a pit of tar.

"She's in there." My voice is shaky, my throat salty from so many tears. When I close my eyes, the flash of a polaroid camera burns my eyelids. The photo we took. The tumble we made. The memory of my father, a statue, frozen in violence and pain. He waits for me on that landing. He's always right there. Waiting.

I swallow. *He can't reach me here.*

A warm hand graces my back and finds its way between hunched shoulder blades and quickly parting ribs. "She is," he says, serious, careful. No chirp to his voice.

Toes bunched, eyes scrunched. I want to move, but… *the guilt, the guilt, the guilt.* It's seven pirate coins stacked on my tongue. Hidden treasures with heavy consequences. Bitter. Nauseating. I lean into his touch, and his hand gives way so I'm no closer. *I want closer.* He won't give it to me. I dig fingernails into my palm. "What if she's…"

Kettle takes my hand, gently pulling my fingers apart one by one. "If she's hurt, we'll take care of her." *Patch her together with found buttons and lengths of string.*

"If she's…" *If she's hurt, I will never forgive myself.* I think of her eyes, dark blue rings around powerful irises. Blinking, I picture bruises growing around those irises like dark clouds trying to swarm her eyelashes.

Kettle turns me to face him, his calloused fingers brushing my skin. Sandpaper to smooth old pain. "Nor-- I mean, Kite." He's still getting used to my new name. His blue eyes lighten like gold glint in the sky. His mouth lifts. "You have to go." *I know.* "She needs you." *I know.* "I can't drag the house across the street for you," he says with a dusting of regret. Like if he could, he would.

Taking a small breath, I fill my heart with feathers. With clouds that make happy shapes in the sky. Checking for traffic, I limp into the street, feeling the loss of Kettle's touch the moment our skin breaks contact. He can't come.

I have to do this alone.

My feet crunch on glassy gravel. My leg throbs, and my body aches from the fall down the stairs. It's been six days. Six long and harrowing days. My elbows press against my sides when the sea wind blows, pushing a shadow into the corner of my eye. I feel watched. I feel like his fist is about to come down. I flinch and wobble.

I glance backward to Kettle sitting on a park bench, hands clasped, knees wide. Our eyes connect, and he nods. *I can do this. I have to do this.* The imaginary hands of lost boys and girls shove me in the back. *Be brave. Be a King.*

Biting my lip, I knock on the door. A dog barks, low and lazy, and I quickly straighten my skirt as I wait.

There's a scuttle and a thwack as the dog barks again and is chastised by its owner. "Humphrey, that's enough!" Cold boards, sharp banging noises, and then, "Frances, would you be a dear and answer the door?"

There are hot coals in my chest. Burning holes, puncturing what air I had left in my lungs. I clutch my ribs, trying to keep calm.

The thick wooden door creaks open, and shadowed behind a screen is my sister. My beautiful sister. "Nora," she whispers in her husky voice. Her head tips to one side, a small, doubtful smile touching the edges of her mouth. "You're here."

"Frankie." I sigh. She's intact. Taller. *How can she be taller?* Bewildered and acting fast, I open the screen door and grab her hand, pulling her from the doorway. Without a backward glance, I yank her along the path. But she's fighting me and trying to return to the house.

"Nor-ah, wait! I hef to say goodbye to missus Bee-Champ." She stares up at me with watering eyes, frowning. "It's rude. And Missus Bee-Champ has been lookin' after me." There's something pointed in her tone. A maturity that's grown there. Planted from a seed of trauma and neglect. She yanks her hand from mine and crosses her arms. "*I've* got manners. Manners is sayin' goodbye. Manners is tellin' people where you're going and not jus' disappearin'.'"

Splinters and saltwater spray my face, stinging.

I kneel, cup my sister's fretful face. "Frankie, we can't stay here." My eyes dart from left to right. "Do you want to come with me?"

Her eyes round and spill. She nods, but she doesn't answer my question. The door behind us whines on sea-rusted hinges. "You must be Nora." An old lady jams the point of a black umbrella in the doorway, eyes squinting. Frankie turns and runs to the woman, arms outstretched. She sinks into her bosom and sniffs loudly, wiping her snotty nose on the woman's dress. "I think you and your friend..." The old woman motions toward Kettle, now standing and looking concerned. "...better come inside."

Chapter Two

Kettle

This seems like a very bad idea. The old woman lumbers down a dark hallway, leaning heavily on an umbrella with a wooden handle. A dog, the size and dimensions of a ham hock, bangs into her legs, knocking her into the walls like an oversized pinball. Frankie's eyes are like soup spoons, scooping up every detail. She eyes me with fascination. No signs of fear or distrust. Just curiosity. As I steal looks, I'm picking out the Nora-ness of her. There's a lot.

We move to the back of house to a dingy living room with peeling wallpaper and not much else between us and the eleasZments that batter the leaning home. She points her umbrella at a piano stool lacking a piano and a dining chair. We sit when we really should just grab the sister and run. But there's something quiet and kind about the woman. Her face is like a history book with folded-down pages. I get the sense she knows things. She collapses heavily into a worn armchair with a sigh.

Kite's legs jiggle nervously, and I resist the urge to place a hand on her knee. These are things I shouldn't do. My jaw tenses. Frankie sits on the floor at the old woman's feet and pokes at a hole in the rug, pulling the thread and gathering it into a ball.

Clapping her hands over Frankie's ears, the old lady whispers, "your father is an awful, awful man." She shakes her jowls in disgust. This place smells like mildew and acres of dust. Scrunching my nose, I nod in agreement.

Kite draws in a shocked breath but I feel myself relax. Each tense muscle gives just a little, not all the way. Flight is my natural state. I'll always be ready to run.

Frankie stares at me. Her innocence feels foreign to me and I can't quite relate. My innocence was lost before I had a chance to recognize it, as it slipped down the drain with the bathwater.

Kite leans forward, head tipped just like Frankie's. Her pale lips part, and she pulls at a hair that's caught in the corner of her mouth. "Who are you?" Each word is a sword held out to guard her younger sister.

"Anita Beauchamp," she says, nodding her wrinkly head. "I was Rebecca's…" she clears her gravelly throat, "…your mother's governess." Her milk white eyes with inky irises look like boiled eggs, and they moisten at the mention of Kite's mother. The three females all seem frozen in bad memories. A triangle of grief I'm watching from the outer edge.

Kite's chest expands with air as if she's about to say something, but she holds it. I cough, and they startle. Frankie says," Bless you," with a voice like a dying engine. I smile, winning a return one as bright as the first star.

Kite recovers. "But how is this…" Her chin dips to her lap. "I don't understand."

"Your father knew I would do just about anything for Rebecca." Mrs. Beauchamp's head falls too, folds of wrinkles, falling over her stiff collar. "I should have done more…"

She can barely push the words from her mouth, but I see her square herself and I ask the dreaded question. "Did he hurt her?" My teeth clench, bracing for the bad answer.

The woman shakes her head. "No. Thank goodness. I wouldn't allow it. He only visited twice." Her eyes harden. "Twice too many."

Kite's demeanor stays tense, but a small sliver of the guilt she's been carrying seems to slide away. I see her catch it, though, storing it in her pocket for later torture.

Pointing her umbrella to the hallway, the woman croaks, "Frances, I think it's time you went back to your family." Frankie springs up. "Go pack up your things."

To us, she whispers, "You need to hide. You need to take your sister and hide from him. I can't protect her any longer." She touches her wrists. Dark bruises peek out from beneath the ruffle of her lace sleeves. She heaves herself up. Kite stares blankly as shock renders her mute and inactive. Mrs. Beauchamp flaps her veined hands anxiously. "You need to go. Now!"

Heaving a leather suitcase that's almost as big as she is, Frankie knocks down the hallway, huffing and puffing. Kite shifts on the old floorboards, swaying to music none of us can hear. Laying a palm on the green wall, I breathe in. She's beautiful even in her devastation. She is beautiful and unreachable. *In so many ways.* Her honey eyes glance my way. Heart heaving. Breath catching. They say, *I have questions.*

My eyes answer. *Your questions will have to wait.*

I jump as Frankie dumps the corner of the case on my foot. "Who're you?" she asks, peering up at me, small waves of wariness pouring from her stare.

I am... I don't know why I say it. I haven't used the name in years, but I extend a hand and say, "My name is Hiro."

Tiny pearl teeth with gaps like licorice in her smile. "Dats a keen name." She shakes her head and collapses on top of her case, legs swinging. Banging out a tune on the hard surface. "Are you Nora's boyfren?" Her hair lights a fire in this murky green room. Her words burn a hole through my chest.

I shake my head as Kite joins us in the hallway. "No. We're just friends." It's more, of course, but I don't know how to explain that to an eight-year-old. We're a part of each other. I also don't really want to say that out loud.

Woodenly, Kite taps Frankie's back. "We should go, darling."

"Do you need money?" the old woman asks, offering what she cannot offer as she struggles to get to the door. After holding it open for the girls, I pick up the case and we leave the darkness, stepping into the bright afternoon filled with salt and bashing waves.

A gull squawks and dips low, grazing the straggling treetops in the garden, and Kite's hands fly to her head. Frankie watches her sister with one of those expressions. The kind seen repeated on every face of a youth turned toward horror. It pains me. It pains me and links me to her instantly.

Kite told me her father never hit Frankie after the time he blew her ears. But sometimes, watching a loved one suffer abuse can be almost as bad. It does something to a person. Something dark and learned. A book they're forced to read. A permanent thing in ink and paper.

This woman is poor. She has nothing. Kite bows her head and says, "No, but thank you, Mrs. Beauchamp. You've done enough."

She takes her sister's hand, and we walk away from the cottage.

"I can't believe he brought her here," she mutters as we cross the road and head for the bus stop. I look around. Marooners' Cape seems like a pretty nice place. I shrug. Too nice for someone like me. I pull my cap lower over my eyes.

"Seems nice enough," I say, the suitcase banging against my leg.

Kite frowns, her eyes running along the coast and watching the elegant arc of waves crashing on the narrow beach. "You don't understand. When Frankie was five, we came here for a vacation. She waded out too far. Because she couldn't hear Mother calling her in, she kept going and fell over the sandbar into deeper water," Kite whispers over the top of her sister's head.

The path brings us closer to the water's edge, and I notice the change in the little girl's manner. Her shoulders migrate to her ears. Her eyes blink rapidly, and she clutches Kite's hand tight. The child is deathly afraid of the water.

"Heroes save people, don't they?" Frankie rasps, pinching her sister's arm.

I nod. Not feeling much like a hero right now, but I want to reassure her. "That's what I've been told, kid."

To herself, she whispers, "Heroes save people."

Kite's eyes are stony. She focuses on the bus stop and the road leading away from the water's edge. Her fists are tight and white. Pearls formed from anger. She drags her leg stubbornly, refusing assistance. I try to force the memory to the back of my brain, but it slips out like a forgotten photo left in the back of a frame. The image of her body hitting the stairs of the grand brownstone. The crunch, the thud. The fear that I was losing her. Rolling my shoulders, I shake it off. She's here. She's all right.

When we reach the bus stop, Kite lets out a long, hard sigh. After I put the case down, I lift Frankie onto the wall behind us. She giggles when I touch her under her arms. "Stay there," I warn.

Kite stares down the street, willing a bus to appear. I slip next to her, then take her fist between my palms. A precious stone. A fight still raging inside her. "We've got her now, Kite," I say, trying to sound comforting. Her hand clenches tighter. "Nora, look at me."

"Please, don't call me Nora," she says to the ground. Then she turns slowly. "I just can't... I can't believe how far he'll go.

Every time I think there's no lower he could possibly sink, he sinks even lower. He's like, like the lowest of the low. The dirt beneath your shoes. The, the…"

"The gum on the sidewalk. No, the gum under the gum on the sidewalk. Let's be straight, there's probably gum from the dark ages under there."

Maybe she'll smile. I can't believe how invested I am in *wanting* her to smile. Her hand relaxes, and she crosses her arms. "Yes. The gum under the gum under the gum." She gives me a brief flash of teeth. Like wiping fog from a window.

"But she's safe. She's here. It what's you wanted, right?" She's gift-wrapped tight. Arms like ribbons holding an amazing treasure inside. Her heart.

"Yes." Her words are snapped and blunt, but it's not because of me. It's exasperation with life and the bullets we have to take, over and over.

The bus pulls up to the curb and I reach for Frankie, helping her from the wall. She's light like a crumpled wing. Light but strong. "Where're we going?" She squints at the bus like it's a spaceship.

Kite and I say it at the same time. "Home."

"I'm hungry," she announces as we step onto the bus.

Chapter Three

Kite

id I just say home? Wedged between Frankie and Kettle, I feel like the loose page in a book. Just a rustle and my part in the story could be lost forever. I'm taking her to the Kings' home. I can't wait to show it to her, but at the same time I'm frightened of what she will think. She might love it. My lips quirk. *She'll probably love it.* But everything feels impermanent. We're torn wings on the wind. We're not sure where we'll end up.

The bus pulls away, rumbling and grumbling about the three-hour drive back to the city. I cross my legs and uncross them, staring down at the dressing Kettle applied gently and very competently over my skin. His hands supporting the weight of my calf as he brushed antiseptic over the wound, then blew on it to get it to dry faster. *His touch. His touch. His touch.* It's sunlight, and I'm the plant that bends to it. My heart scrunches and I put my nail in my mouth, chewing what's left.

Kettle leans his head against the window, his tanned face cut by the light. A man across the aisle stands up suddenly, gripping the cold metal poles to come hover over us. He clears his throat, and I look up into his young freckled face. "'Scuse me, Miss. If you like, I can trade seats with you. I mean, if you're feeling uncomfortable." His eyes land on Kettle, who slips down in his chair and pulls his hat so low it almost sits on his nose.

Raising an eyebrow, I frown. "Why would I be uncomfortable?"

The man shifts awkwardly, actually points right at Kettle. "Coz of that nip sitting next to you."

Drawing in a deep breath, I glance at Kettle, who gives me a stern, sharp shake of his head. "Leave it," he mutters between his teeth.

Frankie glances up at the man and smiles. "What's a nip?"

I touch my chest, mortified, then address my sister. "Nip is a derogatory term that uneducated and insensitive people use to refer to Japanese people."

"Derogg… ag… doggatory…" Frankie sounds out the word and quickly gives up, favoring poking the back of her seat repeatedly.

My eyes are fixed forward as I say to the man who's still staring at us. "I'm perfectly comfortable right where I am, thank you."

Next to me, Kettle tenses. He doesn't say a word to me for over an hour. And the man glares at us until he gets off at his stop, as do the surrounding passengers. Two men, angry for very different reasons. I shrug. I'm used to angry men.

"You shouldn't have made a scene," Kettle whispers tersely. "Drawn attention."

We're passing into the city now, buildings popping up like clashing continents. The scenery becomes more familiar. Frankie plays with her hair, complaining again about being hungry. The responsibility of it—*the cost of it*—weighs heavily on my mind. "I didn't make a scene. What was I supposed to do? Just allow him to talk about you in such a manner?"

He catches my eyes, shadows playing over his cheeks. "Yes. That's exactly what you should have done."

"People shouldn't say things like that." At this, he laughs bitterly. The bus bumps, and we all move with it.

"Since when do people care what they should and shouldn't do? Everyone talks to me like that. You better start getting used to it if you want to be with me." He stalls like an old truck. "I mean, be around me."

I roll my eyes. "I know what you meant. You know you… Ouch!"

Kettle leans forward, anger forgotten. "What? What's wrong?"

Frankie pokes a sharp finger into my stocking. "Frankie, that hurts."

"What heppened to yer leg?" she asks, going for another poke.

I grab her hand, holding her wrist strongly but gently. "I fell down the stairs." My lip threatens to quiver at the memory, but I hold myself together. For Frankie.

Frankie's eyes widen in terror, and she covers her mouth. I want to pull it back, but it's too late. I've already said it, and she's looking at me with such devastating fear and a film reel of memories unrolling in her eyes. "I'm swell. Really. I'm fine." I reach down, prodding the wound myself to prove it. "See." I turn to wince, so she doesn't see my expression.

Kettle watches us both like he's discovered a new and fascinating version of crazy. Until Frankie says in a matter-of-fact voice, "Mama fell down the stairs. She died. She's dead."

God. How do we get through this? How do we carve out something even remotely normal out of all this pain and grief? It seems… It seems impossible.

Kettle bends forward, talking over my lap to Frankie. "My mom's gone, too."

"Did she fall down the stairs?"

His smile is like flashes of gold at the bottom of the ocean. Ripples taking the light to the surface. "No. At least, I don't think so."

Yes. Definitely impossible.

"What about yer daddy?" Frankie asks, questions pouring like off-key music from a flute.

His tone is amber warm. No regret. No need to know. "I don't know what happened to my dad. I never knew him."

Then Frankie says something that breaks me into two uneven halves, a cracked marble rocking on its round sides. "I think dat would be okay. Dat would be okay with me."

Chapter Four

Kettle

I feel nervous. Like getting this skinny, electrically charged kid's approval is super important. She bounces around like she's got ants in her pants. And those ants have other ants in their pants. She's insatiable.

She also coughs and wheezes like she's used up all the oxygen around her. And the way she moves, I wouldn't be surprised if that were true.

We finally pull into the bus station, and I drag the suitcase down the stairs. Thump. Thump. Thump.

My body unwinds just a couple of lengths of twine. There are more people. More ways to blend in. Out there on the end thread of the long island, I felt as conspicuous as the Statue of Freedom. Just with the opposite kind of regard from the people staring at me.

Okay. Just put one foot in front of the other. I can tell Kite's mind is whirring. There is a lot to think about, which is why I'm not thinking at all. Trying to reel my thoughts back, I decide I'm not good with the future. The future was never good with me.

Feed the firecracker and get home. That's as far forward as I'm willing to go.

I have people waiting for me at home.

I tap Frankie on the shoulder. She crashes into my leg, her limbs like assorted crowbars wired together. "What do you want for dinner?" I ask.

Frankie clasps her hands as we walk toward the center of the city like she's praying. People suck us into the flow, just like always. At least the crowd is always welcoming. It doesn't notice skin color. With heads down, coats closed, scarves and hats covering our faces, we all look the same. "Can I hef roast beef'n'gravy?"

Kite glances at me apologetically. I laugh half-heartedly, understanding we have more than one challenge ahead of us. She comes from privilege. Roast meat on silver-rimmed plates. "How about a famous city delicacy?" She blinks expectantly. "Roasted mystery meat with red sauce?"

Kite covers her mouth as she giggles quietly. Frankie jumps, and I understand why Kite always seems at the ready when she's nearby. Like a boxer bracing for the next punch. Because Frankie's head connects with the underside of my chin. "Dat sounds good."

I stroke my sore jaw. "You're a walking hazard, kid."

I dodge the next angular attack and Kite smiles, elbowing me softly. "You're learning."

Reaching for her face, I almost tuck a strand of hair behind her ear. She gazes at me hopefully and leans into my touch, taking my reluctance away. "Always," I chirp. "We Kings have to adapt."

Paying for a hot dog in pennies and dimes is embarrassing. Being two pennies short and having the hot dog stand guy take pity on us was completely humiliating. We're skinny. I just hope the Kings haven't eaten everything we had stored away.

Without Kin and Keeps, there's been a little more to go around. My shoulders sag. Now there are more mouths to feed. My fingers scrape the insides of my pockets, searching for a coin that maybe got snagged in the seams. If I turn them inside out, I really will look like a street urchin. I'm the pirate who opens the treasure chest, finds he's been beat, and opens it again just to rub it in. I snort.

We wait for a large crowd to head for the subway and melt in. Frankie's eyes are as wide as a sliced moon as we weave and duck. Eyes on each other, hands gripped tightly.

Kite pushes Frankie's head under the turnstile as I pay with our last coin. She presses her back into me. The smell of faint perfume, the last of her old life, and salt from the new come from her hair. As I reach around her to push the stile, a two for one, her breath catches. I let my hand rest on her waist for a second. Let myself imagine we're a couple on our way home from a shopping trip, and then it falls like so many un-granted wishes into a fountain.

Leaning close to her ear so she can hear me, I hold my breath, thinking inhaling any more of her sweetness may actually kill me. "Ready?"

She nods. Her cheek brushing my lips.

We take our route to the secret door. To the home we now share like kids playing house, only far too real.

Frankie, to her credit, rolls with the punches. Punch one: Hot dogs instead of roast beef and gravy for dinner. Punch Two: Cheating our way through the subway. Punch Three... I knock on the King's door, and Krow answers. He looks us up and down, slick and distrustful for a moment, then breaks into a grin. "Kettle! Kite!" he shouts. "Kettle and Kite are home." He stares at my hands. When he sees there's no food—only a suitcase—he quickly looks away. But there's no hiding his disappointment.

Frankie squeezes her way through the doorway into the vast, abandoned subway tunnel. My home. My refuge. And now hers. Blinking, she stands on her tiptoes. Lip in teeth. "Holy hell!" she shouts, and several Kings look her way.

Kite flushes pink, then taps her sister's shoulder. "Frankie!" she chastises. "Language."

We step inside, and Frankie swings her head from side to side. "I mean tank you, holy hell."

We both chuckle, eyes connecting over the top of her head.

Punch three: "This is where we're going to be staying for a while," Kite's voice chases after a galloping Frankie as she jumps from bed to bed. She is the spokes of a traveling star. She is the light you can't catch.

Frankie doesn't hear her, and Kite runs to catch her sister. I drag the case inside, plonk it on Kin's bed. Now Kite's to share with her sister.

Finally, Frankie stops running and presses a palm to her chest as she wheezes. Kite rushes to her, and she puts both hands on her sister's shoulders. "Are you okay?"

Punch four is for me, and I feel it sock me right in the guts. As I watch them, I know. Like *really* know that I would do anything to help them. They are instantly and permanently part of this family. And it scares me.

Chapter Five

Kite

I watch my sister for signs of distress. But at the moment, the excitement is overriding any other feelings. She's asked every member their name, and she's given her opinion on whether she liked them or not. She does. Frankie glances at the arched stone ceiling every now and then, marveling at its scale and pointing at the cast-iron chandelier. She's taken by its beauty, and its potential to collapse.

She coughs, and I wrap her in a cardigan. *She's just excited.* Once she calms down, her breathing will do the same.

The suitcase sits on the bed like a tomb of the old life. Not really wanting to open it, I know we need to unpack her things. I unclick the buckles and fling back the lid. "Frankie, will you help me?" She's eyeing the others as they play cards. Kettle sits on his bed sorting through foodstuffs, shaking his head.

We need money.

Tiny socks. Little skirts and shirts. Her stuffed toys and of course, at the bottom, her bunny plate. I pull it out, the faded pattern no longer catching any light. The bunny family looks happy, picnicking in the English countryside. I trace the mother, thinking of Mrs. Beauchamp. I have questions I need answers to, but it's too much of a risk to go back there for scraps of the past. With a sigh like the last of an autumn breeze, stripping the leaves from the tree and letting them dance down the sidewalk, I know I have to let some things go.

Frankie crawls onto the bed as I carefully organize her things, leaving them in the suitcase but untangling the twirl of mixed-up items. "When're we goin' home?" she asks, pulling her knees up to her chest.

After I pull out a picture book, I hand it to her. I can't answer. "Don't you like it here?"

I find her hearing aid. The wires knotted, only a handful of batteries left. "Yes," she replies, tapping her chin. "I like it here."

Kettle casts a warm shadow over our bed. His expression a mixture of pride and wistfulness. This is Kin's room. I know it hurts him to see another taking up the space. "I haven't even given you the official tour." His voice is all serious and mocking. He offers a hand, and Frankie takes it. To me, he says, "You can pack away some of Kin's things if you want. Make it your own."

His eyes land on small things. Tiny cups. A comic book with the pages turned down. "I… I couldn't possibly."

"Please," he says, a small plea in his voice. "I insist." And I understand. He's asking me to do it because he can't stand to do it himself. I nod.

"Okay. Thank you."

He shrugs hard. "Don't mention it."

He leads Frankie away, and I run my eyes over the neatly stacked shelves. I treat each item like it's precious. They *are* precious. I lift the comic book and shake the dust from it, placing it carefully in a box. The corner of a bookmark pokes its way out from between the pages. I pull out an old photograph. Stern lines of Japanese women looking like they're in a school picture sit across bleachers with their hands on their knees. Young children sit in a row in the dirt at the women's feet. I handle it with care, though I ache to touch the face I know is Kettle, or Hiro as he would have been called here. His expression is lighter, but only by a shade. The weight balanced on his little shoulders must have been less heavy back then. But not by much. Kin grins beside him. The woman behind him with her hair curled precisely has her hand on his shoulder. Her clothes are neat, and she looks like a soldier. They all do.

I pat the photo in my pocket that I took a week ago. My father poised to punch one of the people he had vowed to help. I don't want to leave it out for everyone to see, but I do want it close. Taking it out, my eyes wander to Frankie and Kettle, hand in hand. Their shadows grow as they near the back of the tunnel. Her trust in him swells my heart. His intent care of her threatens to burst it.

Placing the incriminating photo inside the comic book, I cover it with Kin's things. It will be safe there, and I need good things over the top of it. I need a small amount of distance from that horrible, horrible day.

I stand as they return from the 'tour'. Frankie's nose remains scrunched from her introduction to the very basic bathroom facilities.

I tuck the photo of Kettle and Kin away. It feels like now is not the time. And selfishly, I want to hold onto it a while longer.

"Why do people call you Kettle?" she asks, still gripping his hand tightly.

I watch him mull over answers in his head. Most are too complicated to give to an eight-year-old. He leans down and speaks into her good ear, already learning her quirks. Her needs. "Kettle is my street name."

Frankie nods seriously. "Then what's Hiro for?" she asks.

He makes a show of looking around, making out like it's a big secret. Making her feel special. "Hiro is my secret name. I only give it to very, very special people."

She puffs up proudly. "Like me?"

He pats the top of her head. "Like you."

And me.

"Do I get a street name?" The idea both horrifies and fulfils me at the same time.

"Sure." He cocks his head at me to check that it's okay, and I nod. "What would you like to be called?"

She bends her legs, jumping as high as she can, and snatches at a moth that flutters past our eyes. "You can choose."

He taps his smooth chin. He is made of dark sweet things. He is damaged as I am, yet he can find joy. He can find the smile in the sky. The light hiding behind the gray. "How about Kricket?"

My chin falls, and I smile widely at the floor. Kricket. It's more perfect than I could have imagined. "Kricket!" Frankie spins around in a circle, skirts flying out like a parachute. "Kricket!"

I risk my hands to reach out to grab her. Folding her into my arms, I nuzzle my chin in her hair. Firelight and broken leaves. Tears prick at the corners of my eyes, weights on my eyelashes. She's here. She's safe. I will never let her go.

Kettle sees my face. A flash of pain crosses his features, but then is replaced with heart. His family is still incomplete.

The lights flicker above, and Frankie tenses. "It's okay, sweetheart. It happens all the time." I stroke her head, and she presses close to my chest.

Kettle claps his hands, and the others snap to him. "Time to cut the gas!" He puts a finger to his lips.

Frankie yawns loudly. It's been a long day.

After I undress her, I help her into her nightclothes. I change into one of Kin's shirts, which sweeps my knees.

Kettle shouts out a last call for the bathroom before shutting off the lights by pulling a fuse from a switch board. They switch off with a loud bang.

Sleeping with Frankie is like sleeping in a bed full of vindictive coat hangers. She seems twice as big as she should be, and squirms like a caged ferret. I've been pushed to the edge of the cushions, my injured leg numbed comfortingly by the cold floor. She rolls into a ball, then goes off like a bomb of legs and arms as she pushes out and finally expels me from the bed. I press my cheek to the stone and shiver. I know she needs the sleep, so I can't wake her. Her breathing has finally evened out after much puffing and panting.

Standing, I shake my head. She is the wind that fills a pirate ship's sails. Forceful. Magical.

The darkness is total, and it presses down on me. The dark was when father would come, fists tight, knuckles white, just aching to hurt me. I flinch, pulling my arms close to my sides.

He's not here. He's not here. He's not here.

I shuffle forward in the dark unable to shake the ghosts of past beatings. The feeling of a bruise flourishes up my side. It's just a memory, but the pain feels real.

It's not real; it's not real; it's not real.

The cold air between one bed and the next is like ice. I move fast, eyes closed. Hands hugging my ribs.

A crack. Skin breaking. Blood dripping.

I hurry, operating in a dream state. *A nightmare state.* My knees give, and I collapse at the foot of his bed. "Kettle," I whisper. "Are you awake?"

A grumble and a groan. A blanket opening like a door to a safer place. "In you get," he mumbles as he shuffles backward to make space for me.

I crawl under the covers. My back against his chest. The breath of deep sleep lulling me. The warmth of his body welcomes me. His hand slides over my shoulder. Rests over my heart.

I breathe in and out slowly. The pressure releasing. The fear easing.

And as I fall asleep, my last thought is, *This must be the worst feeling on earth. This safety. This pure comfort. Because it can't possibly last.*

Chapter Six

Kettle

How can something feel so natural, yet also feel like it's tearing shreds from my heart? As delicate as a cocoon, she feels dry, fragile, and easily crushed beneath my arms. She feels like she's meant to be there. Like there was already a space, just waiting for her to fill. Her breath pushes her skin closer to mine. Her heels stack neatly on top of each other and press into my shins. Letting my forehead rest in her hair, I allow myself to sink into this moment because I know it might be all I get.

This is going to destroy me.

At first, I thought she was Kelpie. She is very far from Kelpie.

The air sinks in temperature, like the heat is searching for the center of the earth, and she curls in on herself. I stroke her arm gently. I do all the things I shouldn't, but can't stop.

Kelpie's soft shuffling as he makes his way to me is the slide of reality. The flash of a camera. The crack of a whip. "Kettle," he whispers into the dark. "I cain't sleep."

I ease myself backward, leaving her, only to imagine her shivering from my absence even in her sleep. Then I curse under my breath. *What are you doing? This is not the way things go for you. The sooner you understand that, the better.*

I find the little King standing in the space between Kin's and my beds. I reach out in the dark to find Kelpie's head. "Come on."

I'm not sure what to do since I don't want to take him to my bed. And that feels selfish. *Is it okay to want something just for myself?* I'm not sure. It's not a feeling I'm used to.

He likes to sleep at the foot of my bed like a pup. I lead him to Kin's bed. "Frankie," I whisper. She snores loudly. Her feet barely reach halfway down the bed. She won't even notice he's there.

I pat the foot of the bed. "But there's a girl in there," Kelpie whispers, and I almost laugh out loud. There's a girl in my bed, too. As miraculous and yet completely ordinary as that may seem.

I lift the covers, ushering him onto the end of the bed. "She's a King, just like the rest of us, Kelpie."

He accepts my explanation, shuffling under the covers. Patting his head, I soon hear the small rumbles of him falling asleep. I back away until I'm standing between the two beds, hands on hips, wondering what to do.

My shadow leaves me. It's already folded under the covers, light hands on her waist. Feeling the expansion of her chest as she breathes. I want to go. But something stops me.

It's the press of the real world. The stupid, prejudiced real world that stops me. I scrunch my toes, staring up at the opaque ceiling I know by heart.

I curse again. To hell with it. This is my home and my own little handheld world. It spins at a different angle. It could be crushed, but not tonight.

Creeping back, I crawl under the covers and take my place next to the beautiful, brandy-eyed girl who climbed into my bed.

Chapter Seven

Kite

I feel a rumble like a soft landslide down my ribs as the morning trains speed through nearby tunnels. A struck match and then the softest golden light lays across his forehead like a kiss. He opens his eyes, dreamy, deep blue, and beautiful.

Our bodies make a heart shape. "Hi." His voice is crackly. He brings his hand to my face, his touch like the brush of fairy wings. Enchanted. Soft and charged.

I blink. Trying to freeze this moment. This idea of *us*.

"Hi," I mouth, not even wanting to speak. Speaking might break this moment. I want to press it behind glass. Hang it on the wall.

Children talking nonsense floats over the curtained walls.

"But if you were a bear, you couldn't live in a tunnel no more."

"Bears live in caves, silly. Dis is lika bear's cave."

"You talk funny."

Frankie blows a raspberry.

Reality throws lassoes around our shoulders and pulls us up. Kettle jumps. His hair spiked and rough. I stare down at my bare legs and pull them under Kin's shirt. Our eyes connect. Tracks of regret—of longing—are laid down between us.

But the world doesn't wait. It doesn't give us time to catch up.

I wrap the blanket around my waist and stand, too. We are inches apart in this small room. He looks up at the ceiling, at the flickering shadows that dance and wobble over the sandstone. Mouth pulled down. "I need to turn on the lights."

I nod sadly. But then he grasps my shoulder, squeezing gently. "I'm not..." He rakes a hand through his hair, staring at the floor for a breath. "I need..." The Kings are waking. Cursing, he leans his forehead against mine for the split breath of a second. "Sorry."

I'm not... I need... Sorry.

Beginnings of sentences he can't finish.

He leaves me and stalks to the back of the tunnel, and I rush across the floor to Frankie. The cold stones sting my bare feet. The unfinished-ness of the night hangs over me like a cloud about to open.

Frankie yawns loudly, stretching those rocks on rubber bands she calls arms. "What's fer brekfast?" She sits cross-legged on the mattress with Kelpie, cushions stacked in a wobbly tower between them.

Kelpie tips his head, scrunching up his little face. He's probably the same age as she is, but life has matured him. "You're kookie, Kricket. Food don't fall from the sky."

Frankie crosses her arms, fire building in her eyes. "I aren't kookie, and I know dat."

The lights flicker and crack on, pouring strong light down on us. We rub our eyes. Kettle rattles a box by the door and Kelpie springs from the mattress, sending the tower toppling. "Breakfast is whatever's in the box." He licks his lips.

The other Kings stream toward Kettle like chickens to feed.

Frankie's eyes widen, and I have to remind myself she's new to this life. She'll need to be eased into it like a foot to a new shoe.

She taps her head and rocks on the bed. "I cain't hear good, Nor-ah."

I lift her suitcase onto the bed and search for her hearing aid, sighing at the low battery count. "Get dressed and I'll help you in a second."

Unwinding the wires, I wonder whether Mrs. Beauchamp even made her wear it. Her language seems to have slipped a little. Dropped letters and sounds lie in piles around her jiggling feet.

I help her wiggle into a dress and put her shoes on. Her pale face pops through the head opening, and she grins. "Mornin', Hiro!"

Kettle puts a finger to his lips. "Sh! That's supposed to be a secret." He kneels, then presents us with two apples from behind his back.

"I like Kettle better anyway," Frankie says as she snatches the apple.

I tell her off. "Frankie! Use your manners."

She takes a large bite, juice pouring from the corners of her mouth. "Tank you."

I take the apple gingerly. Feeling a little shy. A little unsure how to act around him now.

I'm not... I need... Sorry.

I stare down at the wires in my lap, deciding it's probably best to put this on her while she's distracted. Kettle watches me closely. Studying my movements.

I start plugging in the leads, and he puts a hand out to stop me. I freeze. Frankie chews noisily behind me, chunks of apple falling on the bed. "Can you show me how to, er, can you teach me how to put that thing on?"

Maybe I've been shot. Because I feel this flooding of my chest, like warm blood is swirling around my heart. "What? Why?"

He smiles, carefully. No teeth. More of a gentle smirk. A dimple appearing on one cheek. "Well... I want to know how to care for her, you know, in case you're not here or something." The last part is mumbled, and he shuffles backward self-consciously.

I reach out to stop him like he might disappear. I'm taken aback and so touched by his interest and care.

Of all the things he could have said and done to enamor himself to me, this would have to be the worst. The absolutely worst. There is so much meaning in those words. My heart wants to jump from my chest and live between his palms. It is painful and wonderful, and I feel the world tipping and leaning into something new.

He takes my silence as doubt, beginning to stand. "I just thought it might be a good idea, is all."

I catch his leg, composing myself. "Kettle, wait." I stare up at him. "I think it's a wonderful idea." My voice runs out at the end.

While Frankie bounces around on the bed, I show Kettle how to attach all the wires, curl it around her ear, and tuck it into her sash. He listens and copies with the seriousness of a grad student.

I take it all off, then get him to do it by himself. He lets out a laugh when he's done it successfully. "At least that was easier than braiding hair."

I giggle, covering my mouth. "You've braided hair?"

There's that wistful expression again, as memories cross his face like weather patterns. "I have been known to... On occasion." He grins to cover it and stands, glancing at his watch, a band as scuffed as a workman's shoe.

"Do you have somewhere to be?" I ask, teasing.

He shakes his head. "No. Not today. But in a couple of days…"

Frankie inhales deeply. On the out breath, she sounds like her lungs have halved in size. We look to each other, concerned, but then she jumps up and runs over to the others. Tapping Kelpie on the shoulder and play fighting.

"What's in a couple of days?" I ask.

"Kin's eighteenth birthday," he says with pride and guilt mixed together.

Chapter Eight

Kettle

Kite smiles in a shy, secret, blushing kind of way when she says, "Kin," and I don't like it at all.

I shove my hands in my pockets and mumble, "I'll probably go visit him."

Hands clasped in her lap as Frankie pinches her shoulders and jumps up and down on the bed. They are the rose and the bee. Kite purses her lips, rolling her eyes at her little sister. "Can I come?" She knocks her head backward in the direction of the creature with invisible wings. "I mean… can we come?"

I shrug. "Yeah, I guess."

She ignores my reluctance, clapping her hands. "Peachy."

I snort. *Yeah, peachy.*

"Kettle," she asks, blinking sunflower eyes up at me. "What are we going to do for money?"

She needs that steady dependence. I bend my toe into the cracks between the stones. I don't know what that's like. "It's too late to go to the docks today." I glance at my watch again, knowing I should have left ten minutes ago. I raise my voice so the rest of the Kings can hear me. "Today's a dumpster day," I announce. The Kings nod solemnly, then fetch bags and sacks from their sleeping quarters.

Kite blanches, and Frankie looks confused. "Dumpster day?" I think Kite probably knows what it means but hopes she's mistaken.

Frankie tugs on my sleeve, Kelpie holding her other hand. "What's dumpster day?" and I don't know how to answer her.

Kelpie leads her to the door. "C'mon, Kricket. I'll show ya."

Kite's hand hasn't left her shocked mouth.

I reach for her, but the Kings are watching and my hand falls, empty as a starved stomach. "C'mon, Kite. You want to be a King? Well, this is part of it." I force cheerfulness into my tone, hoping she'll buy it.

We begin filing out in small drips like a barely working percolator. Bags tucked in our waistbands or clutched in our hands. We don't want to draw attention.

As we wait in the crawlspace, Krow clears his throat and taps my shoulder. I turn around, almost chest to chest in the tight space. "Er, Kettle, I… er, I found this yesterday." He presses notes into my hand.

I scrunch the money in my fist. "You *found* it?" I wish I could see him better. Check his face for signs of lying.

His hands fly up defensively. "I didn't steal it, I swear."

Frankie makes a loud clucking noise with her tongue. "You shouldn't swear. It's rood."

Krow sighs loudly, his feet hitting mine. "Just take it, will you?"

I've already taken it. It's sitting in my pocket, a ball of accusation. "Okay. Thanks."

"No sweat," he mutters.

I pat his back. It's not like Krow to care. Kin would say I'm rubbing off on him. And if that's true, then he wouldn't steal. I unroll the note in my pocket, still not entirely trusting him.

When we're in the station, I pull Kite closer and whisper in her ear. "Kelpie'll show you the ropes. I've got some business to attend to."

Before she can protest, I've disappeared into the crowd, tailing Krow as he walks with purpose to the eastside station.

Maybe I should've stayed with her. I wanted to. But the Kings are my family. Each and every one. I have to triage my attention. I need to make sure he's not doing something stupid.

Krow slinks through the crowd inconspicuously like the shadow over someone's shoulder. Being white, people don't notice him the way they do me. I cut my face with my cap, making an effort not to touch people. A dance I'm very used to. When we reach the upper level of the next station, he looks up at the clock and swears. I hide behind a large businessman, standing on my tiptoes to peek over his shoulder. The man rolls his shoulders and grunts, irritated, stepping forward.

I blink several times at what I see. Krow slinks toward the wall, finds his reflection in the brass panels, and removes his cap. He slicks his hair back with a comb, then licks his fingers to clean a smudge of dirt from his cheek. My eyebrows rise in surprise.

What the…?

He looks left and right like he's checking whether he's being followed and then exits the station. I duck down, following closely behind.

As I step in his sloping footsteps, I run through all the awful possibilities, starting with stealing, then gambling, then mob runner, drug dropper, back to stealing, and then the most horrifying of all, prostitution. My stomach turns and twists like a stretched jellybean. *The things I've seen kids do to survive…*

He crosses the street, shoulders low and hunched. Bright lights shine on the corner. D'Ogossini is written in large white letters over glass doors covered in paper ads.

Krow slips through the doors, his movements always smooth and steady, like a slow pour of coffee. I stall on the other side of the street. *It's stealing then.* Of all the options, it's probably the best one, but it's still really bad. It's a strict rule, and I've kicked out other kids for stealing. I brace myself for a confrontation and cross the street, zigzagging around high-heeled ladies with fur coat collars tickling their ears.

This is not a good place for me to be seen. Where Krow is a shadow, I'm more like a flashing neon sign on the upper side.

I reach the window of the grocery store and pause. Between posters advertising discount mincemeat and bottles of aspirin, I see Krow. He's smiling broadly, which is disturbing in of itself. Krow wearing an apron and tipping his chin as he hands a lady a paper bag bursting with green leaves and a cereal box.

My mouth falls open, and I touch the glass with my dirty fingers.

Krow got himself a job.

A cyclone of emotion swirls around me. I feel it try to press me down to the pavement and then lift me.

A man taps on the glass from inside in a warning way and I jolt backward, hurrying away from the store before Krow sees me.

The cyclone thins. Two emotions are teased out, battling with each other for dominance. Relief and jealousy. Relief that Krow did the right thing. That I didn't catch him picking pockets. Seeing him standing there, hair smoothed back, an uncommon smile on his face did strange things to me. He looked so ordinary. Just like any other bag boy. Average. Normal. Unlikely to catch attention. Likely to get a pat on the back. A kind greeting. Maybe even a tip.

The relief rustles through me, and I breathe it out. The other feeling, though—the jealously—sits heavy in my stomach. Stony and permanent.

He has what I want. He has what I can't have.

A job. A chance at a normal life.

Someone knocks my shoulder, and I make the mistake of looking up. When the man sees my face, his expression runs from shock to anger to pity. But mostly confusion. A kind of 'figuring out' that never goes anywhere. Mixed-race kids are like blue roses. Interesting. Nice to look at from a distance. But when people get close, they see unnaturalness. Something that's not meant to exist. It unnerves them.

I can't imagine I will ever get hired. And that stings like a hook to the heart.

I feel it hanging there, banging against my ribs as I walk away.

I pack it away with other scars and regrets.

Today is dumpster day. That's my job.

Chapter Nine

Kite

I think we look like a family of three. I think we need to look less so, and I break away from Kelpie and Frankie. My leg is improving, and I put more weight on it while keeping a watchful eye.

Kelpie drags us up from the subway, then heads straight for an alley caught between a delicatessen and sporting goods store. Crossed tennis rackets and sets of golf clubs in the store display window make me giggle at how far away our life has shifted from *that life.* Unwanted images make appearances in my mind, smothering that giggle. My mother and father dressed in white, wooden racquets hanging at their sides as they lean in to kiss one another. Frankie and I applauding on the sidelines. Bruises stretching between my shoulder blades as I tried to play. He always turned it to the side. Made sure it did maximum damage with minimal evidence. We were the picture of a perfect family. Shining white and pure. Hiding black and blue.

Kelpie shoots past people. He doesn't wait. Manners are a luxury street kids can't afford. When he tugs Frankie headlong into a large trash can, I'm too far behind to stop him.

He emerges, smile long and toothy as a crocodile, waving a handful of socks in his tight fist happily.

I screw up my nose, knowing what those are. They're the 'try on' socks.

Closing my eyes, I breathe in, though not too deeply. I don't want to quash his triumph. Frankie waves a deflated beach ball at me, making crunchy noises by jumping up and down on packaging. I sigh with relief at the bin they're in. It's just packaging and broken and used goods from the sports store. Stinky socks are not nearly as intimidating as the smell from the opposite bin.

Kelpie tips out of the bin, then pulls my sister's arms until she slides over the edge like a seal lion from a boardwalk. My sister. *My sister.* Picking through the contents of a dumpster.

If Father knew, he'd...

Armor crackles and builds over my skin. It starts at the base of my spine and claps up, tile by tile, scale by scale, over my ribs, up and down my arms. I am rigid and caught. Then she laughs. He laughs. They play in the alley, throwing smelly socks at each other. Wild and, most importantly, free.

Shivering at the briskness, I stare up at the sky, watching razorblade clouds dart over our heads.

Free.

Free.

I don't need to worry about what Father would do. *He is. He is. He is...*

Irrelevant.

Armor retreats. But I keep it in a safe place. Not ready to release it just yet. The metal scales gather in my skirts and I collect them, feeling their cold edges. They flutter with movement like feathers in a robin's breast, disturbed by the breeze.

Trickles of dirty water run under my feet. Blackened cobblestones dressed with slime make me pinch my toes in for balance. And I'm too distracted to stop Frankie from diving into the delicatessen dumpster. The moment her feet squelch into the bottom, the stink of cheese and rotten meat throws clouds no one would want to stand under or stare at into the sky.

Hitching up my skirt, I drag a crate over to climb more carefully into the dumpster. Frankie gurgles and gasps. She makes gagging noises and sick faces. But she is having the time of her life.

She waves her hand in front of her nose. "This stinks worse 'n' dat moldy blue cheese Deddy likes." She points at me, the devil in her grin. "Or Nor-ah's breath in da mornin'."

I cover my mouth. "Frankie!" Holding a sack in one hand, I turn to Kelpie, who gives me a serious expression. Sadly, he's the expert here, and I say as much, "Well, Kelpie, this is our first time. What are we looking for?"

Kelpie holds up a half-empty jar of pickles and shakes it. "Pickles n' preserves are good. Even if they've been opened. Dented cans are good too." He shakes his head. "But don't go taking anything with milk in it. That'll make you sick." He clutches his stomach. Eyes dimming for a moment. "Eating stuff that ain't pickled or cured can kill you. I know, okay?"

I nod my head. I believe him. And my heart breaks into sharp pieces that loll on the cobblestones at my feet. Death is everywhere for these kids. In the thrown-out food harboring bacteria, and the cold nights lashing out to freeze them. It is relentless.

I find a rolled-up piece of brown paper containing something squishy, grease stains coming through. Unwrapping it, I twist my face. "What about this?" It's some sort of salami or sausage.

He leans over and sniffs it. "S'okay."

I shrug, trusting his canine instincts, and place it in my bag.

We spend about half an hour rifling through the trash, but don't have much to show for it.

Frankie found a jar of cocktail weenies, and she's shaking it like a slippery maraca as we walk home. I feel the weight of provision pressing on my chest. It's not enough.

We need money. I know how to get a lot, but…

It's not going to be easy to convince Kettle.

Kelpie's blond head bobs between dark skirts and suits. He and Frankie have taken an instant liking to each other, and they talk about horrible, tragic things in their childish voices. I bite my lip and look to the sky, hoping those razorblade clouds will cut through some of the pain.

"Where's yer mommy?" Frankie asks, voice crackly. Her small mouth pinches, waiting for an answer.

Kelpie's small shoulders pull up like clothes pegged on a line. "Dunno. Maybe she's dead. Pops never did say what happened to her. All he said was she were no good." I touch my heart, rolling my button between my fingers like a single worry bead.

Frankie's eyes blink black and blue. She's the bruise we can't hide. "Like the milk."

Kelpie nods. "Yeah. Like the milk."

"Where's yer deddy then?" They talk too loudly, and I worry people are starting to listen.

Kelpie stops, turns to me, his round eyes painted with the stroke of violence. I know it well. "He was good for a while but then he went sour, just like the milk."

I lay a hand on his shoulder, some of the puff deflating from his chest. He is so little and his layers aren't as thick as mine. His armor is only just starting to grow. And when his eyes connect with mine, he becomes younger. "He went bad," I whisper. "But it wasn't your fault, Kelpie."

Kelpie nods, shutting a tiny, child-sized door over the memory, then puts his tiny hands in his tiny pockets. "Yeah, I know. He just went bad."

He starts to whistle and Frankie is easily distracted, looking longingly at his pursed lips. "Teach me, teach me."

We head toward the station, winter following us with cold bursts of ice on the wind. The cooler weather is coming. I shudder. The streets draped in snow will seem less magical and more dangerous, given our living situation.

I wrap my arms around them both, bringing the children to my hips. Big decisions will need to be made. Wishes for romance and fancy will be buried like so much dirt and trash.

The Kings reunite at the end of the day. Little heads appear in the door, followed by feet with too small and too big shoes. Everyone dumps their findings on the card table. Krow is last. While Kettle's back is to him, he scruffs his combed-back hair up and untucks his shirt. He's carrying a clean paper bag, which he empties onto the table. Dented boxes of crackers and some cans of beans draw awestruck gasps from the others.

Kettle looks up. "Nice haul, Krow. Where'd you find it?"

Krow's thin shoulders bunch and unwind, and he blows some hair from his eyes. "You know, around."

Kettle smiles tightly and cracks his neck. I can tell he's forcibly trying to make himself relax, but it's not working. He's a crushed coil desperate to spring. "Thanks."

They hand out the various foodstuffs, and the Kings retreat to their corners to eat dinner. The whole space fills with the smell of salt and vinegar.

Frankie is eager to try her cocktail weenies, and I begrudgingly grab a stale roll to accompany them.

She sits cross-legged on the edge of the bed, her tongue half-hanging out as I try to open the jar. Teeth clenched, I make a weird grunting noise just as Kettle appears holding a can of tinned asparagus and two forks. "Do you need some help?" he asks, holding out his hand for the jar.

I do. But…

I strain and twist and breathe a curse word under my breath while Kettle watches me in amusement. "I need to do it," I say, mostly to myself. I need to care for my sister. I need to be able to open a jar without someone else's help. Slackening my grip, my arm and the jar fall to my side.

Kettle smirks and taps the top. "See how the lid is drawn in? There's too much pressure because it's been sitting closed for so long." I grimace. I'm trying not to think too hard about how old the jar is. "You'll never open it that way. Wait…" He cups my face briefly and then jogs away, returning with a hammer and screwdriver.

As he hands me the tools, my first instinct is to give them right back and tell him to do it. Instead, I stop and listen, hoping to learn what is needed to survive out here. Because even if I don't intend for this to be permanent, it is all we have right now.

After I puncture the lid with a sharp bang, I hear the hiss as trapped air escapes. Then the lid unscrews easily. I let out a sigh of relief, placing a slimy sausage on the roll for Frankie with trepidation.

Measuring my expression with scale-like precision, he places a warm hand on my arm. Strokes it once. "It's safe."

He goes to remove it, and I put mine over the top. I want to force myself to loosen up, but I'm held together by hard, unbending things and years of propriety. "Have you ever fallen ill after eating something bad?"

He nods, mouth puckering at the memory. "A few times. But you soon get the hang of it."

He squeezes my arm and then his hand leaves me, a tattoo of his fingers pulsing nicely over my skin.

Kettle opens the can of asparagus, and we share the mushy green stuff. We try to convince Frankie to have some, but she is vehemently opposed to the idea. I push the stodgy vegetable around in my mouth. Make myself swallow. I don't really blame her.

Kettle gazes at me with blue eyes. Skies and waterfalls dance in those eyes. Splashes of color, tears, and tragedy.

His mouth twists into an undecided smile before falling to a frown.

"Are you okay, Kettle?" I ask.

He stares at the floor. "I'm fine." He jabs at the asparagus violently with a fork.

I tilt my head. His pages are written in a language I'm beginning to understand. "No, you're not; something's bothering you. I can tell."

He snorts. "You can tell, huh?"

"You can talk to me." I lean forward, wishing I could just reach out and bring his hand to my lips. And wishing he would do the same for me.

Frankie knocks me sharply with her elbow. "Can I go play with Kelpie? He's gonna show me some baseball cards." Her breath smells of hot dogs and pickle juice. I scowl.

"Sure." I wave her away, but by the time I've looked back, Kettle has moved to collect what's left of the food to put in the store box.

I stand to help him. The other Kings are packing up and bringing out old papers, magazines, and cards to play with. As I collect the opened cans, scraped clean of their contents, a small chubby hand reaches out and places a single can of peaches on the table.

I look down at the owner—a young teenage boy. His head falls, avoiding eye contact. "Hi," I say, offering a greeting. "Are you new?" Shaking his head, he pushes the peaches at me. His round face is painted with grime, but beneath it, proud copper skin glows and dark, almost black eyes shine with a kind intelligence.

Kettle chuckles. "That's just Kamo; he's not new. He's just quiet like a mouse, aren't you, big fella?" Kettle reaches out and almost musses the boy's hair, but seems to think better of it, and retreats. Kamo nods and steps backward.

I hold up the tin. "Thank you for the peaches, Kamo," I say, searching for him. My hand drops, and I tap my chin. "Where did he go?"

Kettle rattles the box of cans. "That's Kamo for you. He's good at disappearing."

I hear a small laugh and see dark eyes peering out from behind a pile of crates. I touch my heart, feeling spaces being made for these children. "Ah, Kamo as in camouflage?" Kettle nods. "Clever." I smile at him and wave. He blinks, melting into the background. "What a funny kid," I say with a small joy in a bubble-type laugh.

Kettle smiles proudly. "Yeah, he's a good one. Doesn't talk at all, but I get it." He scans the room and points at the curtain, striding over and pulling it back, saying, "Huh," when Kamo isn't there. Shrugging, he returns to me. "He likes to be left alone. Sometimes that can seem like a luxury in this place."

"And the talking?" I ask.

His eyes strike pain and lightning over water. "Well… when life seems completely out of your control, sometimes you take what little you can. You try to control just one thing. For Kamo, it's talking."

I nod, letting Kamo be alone. "For me, it was throwing Mother's things out the window."

Kettle stops. His mouth spreading into a thin line. Then he looks up, muttering, "I'll be forever grateful that's what you chose to do." My heart is wishing. Wishing. Wishing. It's reaching for him.

I whisper the words, "Me too," as he shuffles awkwardly and reaches for a cap that's no longer on his head. He chuckles quietly, nervously, and I grace him with a reprieve. "What do you do want to do with the trash?"

He holds up a bag. Krow throws something in, and Kettle's demeanor shifts. He's burrowing into his own thoughts. His own self-punishment by the looks of it. My heart nudges me forward. I want to ease the pain on his face, but I don't know how.

"Kettle..." I start, but his eyes ask me to wait. They ask me to give him a moment. "Let me do that. I'll take it to the bin for you." I take the bag from him and collect the rest of the trash, making sure I check every corner of the tunnel. I pick up small gum wrappers that have blown to the edges. After I use my hands to sweep balls of hair and fluff from between boxes and crates, I talk to every King to make sure I have everything.

Holding two bags, I approach Kettle, who's trying to help Kane sound out words from an old newspaper. "I'm going to take these out."

He stands. "Let me. I mean, I don't think you can..."

I humph, shaking the bags. "Kettle, I'm not completely useless. I'm sure I can find a trash can on my own."

He pauses, considers it and relents. "You're right. It's time you were treated like all the other Kings."

I nod definitively. "Yes, it is."

To further his point, he adds, "Lights out at ten. If you get back after that, be careful not to step on anyone's bed."

I march to the door. "I will."

To Frankie, I shout, "Brush your teeth." And then I'm out, wiggling my way down the narrow walkway and trying hard not to bang cans and bottles against the wall.

I can do this.

Chapter Ten

Kite

True to his word, when I return from my non-eventful trash drop, the lights are out. I pick my way carefully through the tunnel, my hands getting sandpapered by the rough stone wall. When I reach my room, I hear Frankie whispering to Kelpie. Sitting on the bed, I remove my shoes. Kelpie's head knocks against my hip. He's curled up like a dog at Frankie's feet.

I run a hand over his head. "Frankie," I whisper. "Can you…"

She cuts me off. "You should go an sleep in Kettle's bed like before," she says in a matter-of-fact tone. "He's got more room fer ya."

I growl low and lie down next to her, pushing her over so I can have a small corner of the pillow. "Move over."

She shuffles over a little, but I sense her irritation.

Closing my eyes, I pull my knees to my chest, letting the long length of the day drape over me like a silk scarf. There are so many things I need to work out and problems that need to be solved. Frankie needs to go back to school. Kelpie *should* be in school, too, but that's another more complicated problem. They all need something but my hands are empty. I have nothing to give. I open my palms to the ceiling. I should see about filling them, but my mind is full of just five words: *I'm not... I need... Sorry.*

I clap my hands over my ears.

I'm not... I need... Sorry.

I sit up.

I need to know the ends of these sentences. Standing, I leave my sister. Stepping more confidently toward Kettle's room, I part the curtain and kneel.

He breathes with the frequency of someone trying to force himself to sleep. "He got a job," he mutters.

I reach for him in the dark and find his hand. In the dark, we can do this. I squeeze. "Who got a job?"

Kettle sits up, pulls me to sit beside him. He is a layered stone, chipped and jeweled at its center. "Krow. Krow got a job. And I should be happy for him, shouldn't I? I mean, I am happy for him, but I also wish... I wish..."

His voice dissipates into sandy bricks and cold air. "You wish it were you," I finish for him, and his sigh is as deep as the subway. As dark as the unlit way.

He laughs sadly. "I wish it were me."

I lean my head on his shoulder gingerly. Scared of broaching the wall between us. We're a kid's craft project. Precarious and unstable. But oh so beautiful and full of promise. "But you don't think it could be you?"

His head lightly touches mine. Always careful, like I'm made of eggshells. "I *know* it can't be me."

I roll my head from under his, and our noses touch briefly. A kiss on the wings. "You're so hopeful in so many ways except this one. I *know* you will get a regular job one day. I *know* you can have what you want."

His hand tightens around mine. "And what do I want, Kite?" he says heatedly. The way he says my name is like it's in flight.

Heat crawls up my neck, and I pull back a breath. "A normal life. A home. A family."

He sighs again with pent-up anger and frustration still caught in his throat. "I have a family. And as for the rest, well, I think people like me don't always get what they want. In fact, they rarely do."

He collapses onto the bed, pulling me with him. We're building breakable things here. We're tying clouds together with nervous fingers. I lay my head on his chest, daring to place a leg over his. It feels more natural than the sun. "Maybe not," I whisper as his hand goes to my hair, gently teasing the knots out. "But you *deserve* those things more than anyone I know. And maybe sometimes, if we believe hard enough, we might just get what we deserve."

His chest rattles as he chuckles. "Sure. And I believe in fairies, too."

Our breathing sinks to a softer rhythm. Again, those words float up between us. *I'm not... I need... Sorry.*

I raise my head, trying to find his face in the dark. "Kettle?"

His sleepy voice mumbles, "Mm."

I nudge him. "Kettle..." He doesn't respond. And then I say his first name. The name he has only shared with a few people. "Hiro."

He disconnects from sleep, rolling to face me. "Hiro," he whispers wistfully. "I like the way that sounds coming from your lips. It feels true or like it could be... like I could be more than..."

My breath falters, and I try to remember what I was trying to ask him.

Deep breath in. Steel and swords. "What did you mean last night, when you said *I'm not... I need... Sorry.*"

He shifts beneath me, his hand resting on my shoulder. He breathes in slowly, deeply, and sighs. "I'm not good enough for you. I need you, but I know it's not fair or right to do so. And well, sorry is kind of self-explanatory, isn't it?"

"Oh." I push my lips together to stop the inappropriate giggle from fluttering out of my mouth, but it gets away from me. He tenses.

"That's funny to you?" he asks, hurt.

Wrapping an arm around his chest, I squeeze. "Oh, Hiro! Not one part of what you just said holds any truth at all."

Silence gathers like clouds to a mountaintop.

Not a single one.

Chapter Eleven

Hiro

I think about my mother. The name she gave me. It rests like a feather on my nose. Like her touch. Soft. Fingertips tapping with affection. Hiro. Hiro Jackson. Two words that shouldn't go together. That's me all over.

And when Kite says it, it sounds like a promise.

She elbows me gently. Her bag clattering with the presents the Kings have sent along for us to give to Kin. "What are you thinking about?"

That things change violently. It's never gentle and easy. Like ripping a book in half, it's ragged edges and sounds that make a person wince. I'm thinking about my brother; eighteen and finally free of the system. It makes me smile but at the same time Kin as an grown up is a jarring proposition. Mostly, I'm thinking I want him to come home.

Kite waits patiently for me to say something while I stare at her skirt. It's getting grubby around the base, and her stocking has a hole in it. As I reach for the hole, she glances around the empty bus, spots of pink appearing on her cheeks. It's just below her knee and I place a finger on her skin, tracing the edge of the tear. I hear her drag in a ragged breath.

"I can mend this for you," I whisper.

Small warm breaths escape her parted mouth. She places a hand on mine, leaving it on her knee. "Th... that would be... nice."

We stare out the window, watching the trees grow bare. Mountains of leaves piling in the gutters. Her leg has healed well, only the slightest limp when she's not concentrating. It's a good sign.

It has only been a few days since Frankie came back to her. But in those days, we've begun building this life. An unsteady life that makes me feel like I've been riding the tilt-o-whirl. Disoriented. Distracted. Not sure which way I'm supposed to be heading.

I gaze at the curve of her neck and her caramel-apple hair wound into a knot. Wherever I'm heading, I want her beside me. It's a dangerous, ridiculous thought I'm trying not to give into.

I'm not fairing so well in that department.

Kite plays with the button of her shirt, rolling it slowly. "What are *you* thinking about?" I ask as the bus bumps over a pothole. Part of me hopes that she's worrying about me. Mentally, I slap a palm over my face. This would be easier if she didn't blink honey eyes full of affection at me. If *she* had the sense to see how beneath her I really am.

"Frankie," she says, hand on the cold window. "Do you think she'll be okay? She's not used to fending for herself like the others."

The bus squeals to a stop, and I stand. "She's not alone. The Kings will look out for her. I made them swear they wouldn't leave the tunnel today. I trust them; don't you?"

She nods. "I do. It's just..."

I let her pass me, trying out this gentlemen thing, and we exit the bus. "It's just... that you only got her back a few days ago?"

Kite's chin drops to her chest. "I shouldn't have left her."

A breeze that's impersonating a winter wind sweeps between us, her skirts billowing, her hair flying out from its pins. "You promised Kin. And besides, this is the King's world. This is the way we live. The sooner Frankie gets used to it, the better." She's biting her lip. Frozen on the sidewalk. "I promise. She'll be fine. We're only going to be gone for a few hours."

Putting a hand to her back, I push her carefully toward Craftman House. There's a spring in my step. A lightness to my shadow. Seeing Kin again will be good for us both.

The street is bare, and it gives me a rare, unmonitored second. Pushing my cap back, I let the light fall on my face. Kite watches me with fascination. No one's watching or judging so I sweep her hand into mine. Watching the way our shadows loop together in one continuous shape like a single ink brush character.

Ducking through the wind chimes, we reach the front step and ring the bell. The door opens before the sound has finished. Miss Anna sways like a reed, her face grim. She tries to smile when she sees us, but her eyes are tired and worried. My body prepares for a blow.

"It's good you're here," she says, bowing to meet our eyes from her tall height.

My hand tightens around the bag of handmade gifts from the Kings. Paper-clip sculptures and a bag of sweets squash together in my grip. Kite's hand goes to my shoulder. "What is it, Miss Anna? Is everything okay with Mr.… Mr. Ikeda?" she asks with worry.

The screen door clangs behind us, and I tense. *Why must I always be robbed of joy?* I was happy for minutes. Minutes was all I was allowed to have. I laugh, and the two women turn to me curiously.

I hear a groan, and something clatters to the floor. Kin's deep voice bellows down the stairs. "Happy birthday to me. Happy birthday to me." His singing is off key and sarcastic.

We stare at Miss Anna, and she smiles sweetly. "It was bound to happen eventually."

"What was bound to happen?" I ask suspiciously, thinking they've worked out who he is and he's being shown the door.

She wraps long, slender arms around Kite and me, then leads us to the base of the stairs. "A setback."

"A setback. Is that it?" I put one foot on the stairs, the dark, stained banister swirls like a twisted piece of rope, while Kin's moaning floats to our ears.

Miss Anna shakes her head as Miss Lake comes plodding downward, the steps creaking under her weight. "It's not a small thing, young man. Realizing you're not improving as fast as you'd like. And maybe you'll never be who you once were."

My smiling face falls, getting replaced by a dark shadow. Miss Lake passes Kite climbing the winding staircase. "When you turn eighteen, the world should be your oyster," Miss Anna says, her face contorting with a memory of her own or of past patients. I find that statement to be completely untrue, but I let her go on. "Imagine how your friend feels, knowing he might have to live with his disadvantages forever."

Giving her a strange look, I wonder which particular disadvantage she's talking about: his injuries, his race, or the fact that he's homeless. "My brother is strong." I take the stairs quickly. Charging past framed yellowing photos of men in uniform to shake some sense into Kin. My brother is a survivor. A King.

Kite is waiting for me at the top outside of the room where Kin sings, the crack of a door casting light onto the landing. Her fingers are curled like she's holding onto invisible ladder rungs. It's a thing I've noticed she does, holding onto an imaginary something, when she feels like she's falling into nothing. It warns me not to go in there, but I must.

Deep breath, I push the door open, finding my friend lying in bed, green-faced and unhappy. His eyes widen when he sees me. "Little brother, you came!" His voice sounds strange. Almost drunk. The open bottle of pills by the bed explains some of the behavior.

"Happy birthday, Kin," I manage, though there seems to be nothing happy about him.

After I pull up two chairs, I let Kite sit first. Kin's eyes land on her blushing face, and he grins. "Future wife!"

She bows her head. "Happy birthday, Kin," she says shyly.

He shuffles into a sitting position, resting against the headboard, and looks between us both. "I've missed you, Kettle. Things are…" His head drops as he breathes in and out slowly. "Sometimes things are so hard here."

I lean forward, trying to find my friend in all this self-pity. "What's your deal? Why're you acting like such a wet rag?"

Kin smirks, parts of him coming back to life. "Wet rag? I'm hep. I'm always hep. It's just… This rehab thing is hard. I'm fighting against pain. Injuries. Some people's attitudes." His eyes slide to the window. "And well…" He sighs and straightens. "How are the rest of the Kings? Staying out of trouble?"

I know what he can't say; he misses his family. "Fat city! You know we do the best we can." Kite looks confused. "Oh, and we have a new member. Her name's Kricket; she's Kite's little sister."

Kin rolls the blanket down. Straightens his shirt. "Ah, my future sister-in-law." He winks at Kite and I should be happy that his mood has improved, but I want to smack that wink right off his face. He looks at me for a moment with mischief. I think he knows it, too.

He shifts awkwardly on the bed, his weak leg not cooperating. Kite puts her hand up to stop him. "You need to rest," she orders.

The sweat across his brow and the hardness of his mouth show his pain. It hurts me in so many ways I can't even count. He salutes her and leans back. "Yes, ma'am. I like a woman who can order her man around." Tensing, I roll my shoulders.

"Anyway, I have some gifts for you." I hold up the bag, and he winces as he tries to take it. I place it in his lap. "Can I help?"

He picks up the bottle and rattles it. "Hard to swallow these without something to wash it down with."

I grab his empty glass and stand, my gaze connecting with Kite's worried expression. It speaks of familiar heartbreak. "You'll be okay?" I ask her.

She nods. "Of course."

I rush to the kitchen, taking the steps fast.

Miss Lake is washing dishes and humming quietly to herself. Crooked shelves laden with dry stocks like flour and sugar in candy-colored containers lean dangerously over her head. "Can I get a drink of water for Mr. Ikeda?" I ask, holding the smudged glass up.

She turns suddenly, clasping her heart. "Oh my! You frightened me. Of course, of course, help yourself." She points to a refrigerator. I take a jug of cordial from a shelf, reveling in the sheer luxury of the appliance and the mist that floats around the food and drinks.

"It's hard for him here, you know?" she says as I place the jug back.

"Huh?"

Her kindness is overwhelming and foreign, and I honestly don't know how to take it. "He's so much younger than the rest of them. He would be better off with people his own age, don't you think?" She taps the table pointedly.

"Oh. Uh, my living arrangements are a little, well…" How to put *homeless* into terms she will understand and not be shocked by. "Um… impermanent."

Her eyes crinkle. "I see… Would you consider staying here for a time? Helping him come to terms with what his life will be like now? You'd be very welcome."

My eyes fall to the floor. The linoleum is dented and scratched but clean. "I can't." I wish I could, but I can't. I have so many lives that depend on me.

She makes a *hmm* sound, turning back to her dishes. "That's a shame."

Chapter Twelve

Kite

"You should ask him," Kin says as he puts the bottle of pills in his bedside drawer.

Paintings of cottage gardens hang off-kilter on the wall. I glance up from my hands. Kin's dark eyes are sincere, pained but determined. "Ask him what?" I say, though I know the answer.

Kin opens the bag. Pulls out the sweets. "I bet these are from Kane, right? He found a sweet shop that gives their funny-shaped stuff out to street kids on Wednesdays. Real nice people." He presses the blobs of candy through the plastic, the bag crinkling. "Ha! This one looks like Kamo…"

I tip my head. Wait for Kin to elaborate, but he doesn't. "He'll say no."

Kin laughs. "Yeah, probably. He has this idealistic notion of how things should be. The Kings is a prime example. A gang of street kids who work and never steal. Who's ever heard of such a far-out idea?" He chuckles. Admiration and affection light his eyes.

My face warms. "Hiro is special," I murmur.

His eyebrow arches. "*Hiro*. I haven't heard that name in a long time." Then he reaches for my hand, and I let him take it. "I'm pretty sure he thinks you're pretty damn special, too, Kite."

My eyes find the painting behind his head. An English thatched roof and roses climbing up the wall. It's idyllic and dreamy. Unreal. "What do you mean?"

Kin groans and squeezes my hand. "I think you know what I mean. Anyway, find your moment and ask him. I know my brother—he'll never say yes for the wrong reasons. But you're one very good reason."

Could I ask Kettle to marry me? Things are changing between us. Feelings are growing fast like that English climbing rose. Kin and I stare at each other. *It could be. It could be. It could be...* Perfect.

Something turns in Kin's expression. His eyes widen and his brows fall to the sides. There is desperation in his voice when he asks or almost begs, "Please, Kite. Please try." My hand hurts from how hard he's squeezing. "I don't want to stay here forever." He blinks. Eyes like mirrors. I know those eyes. There are secrets in there. They sit like three corner jacks. Sharp and embedded.

Hiro clears his throat, and we spring apart.

The mood in the room darkens a little as he crashes down in the chair.

Rolling his eyes, Kin teases. "You two looking so uncomfortable is about the best present you could've given me!"

Hiro lifts his fist to punch his brother but stops just short of connecting. "Shut up!"

Kin chuckles, and it's good to see some color in his cheeks even if it's coming at our expense. "No really, when are you two gonna make it official? Shacking up together without a wedding ring..." He holds up his ring finger. "It's scandalous."

Hiro grimaces. "You know, they said you were having a 'setback'." He huffs. "Your setbacks are like a sneeze. Where's all the moaning and groaning gone?"

Kin shrugs, palms to the ceiling. "What can I say? I'm just stronger than your average war hero." His act is convincing. Especially if, like Hiro, you're desperate to believe it.

Now Hiro rolls his eyes. "Seriously, though, it's good to see you smile." He claps a hand on Kin's shoulder and leans in, their foreheads almost touching. "Happy birthday, brother."

Kin's voice is smaller, a little less sure when he says in an almost-question, "And many more?"

Hiro crows, startling the other patients. "Definitely!"

We leave Craftman House with the promise that we'll be back soon.

Kin's ideas of marriage have watered seeds that were already planted. But I know right now, Hiro will say no. Things haven't changed that much in three days. Not enough anyway.

I remember when we first spoke of marriage, after I met Kin. Willow trees that shook secrets from my mouth. Forgiveness that led to trust and now to... *this*. I touch my heart. This unproclaimed feeling I can identify, but can't quite say. He'd said something like, *Don't look at me; I'm not marrying you either...*

Hiro is quiet on the ride home. Rattled by the state of his friend and by his inability to help him. The solution to our problems could be simple but then, if Hiro were the kind of man to marry me purely for money, I wouldn't want to marry him.

If the world could just operate on love alone, maybe we could make this work.

I wish love could be enough.

On the island of mermaids, fairies, and pirates, maybe it is.

A hand grips my arm and pulls me backward. "Nora!" a familiar voice shouts out, spinning me around. My eyes widen, moistening instantly at the sight of my father's accountant. I step back. Hiro melts into the crowd like a drop of water to the sea. Staying close but not wanting to be seen with me. I feel his eyes on my back, watchful. I know he won't leave me.

I tap my heart. "Mr. He… Hersch," I stammer, struggling to find words. Scared of questions.

He narrows his eyes, focusing on a point or person over my shoulder. "Are you well? Your father said you'd been very unwell. And how's little Frankie? I hope she's doing better…"

People bump into my shoulders, the press of the crowd trying to swallow me. I wish it *would* swallow me. Open its jaws like a crocodile and take me whole. I don't know what this man knows. I don't know what he suspects. I do know he's loyal to my father. He sits on the left-hand side of the ledger with all the others who watched and observed silently. Whose eyes skidded over my wounds like flat shoes over sleet in the street, and then simply turned away. I have faced more turned backs than I care to remember. There were very few strokes in the right-hand side.

Flustered, I quickly bow my head. "I'm sorry, Mr. Hersch, but I'm late for an appointment." He tries to grab me, and I can see this situation tumbling down to a place of broken bricks and bruises. My hands shake, my palms sweat. My chest tightens. The dark of night needs to come faster. The lighter shadows of day don't hide enough.

Suddenly, Mr. Hersch is bumped from the side. He stumbles into a shop window, colliding with a woman walking her dog. They tangle together, and Hiro's voice whispers in my ear, "Run."

My feet pick out spaces, my heart crams my chest full of fear. Fear of being followed, fear of being caught, fear of being thrown on the floor and kicked and kicked and kicked…

Hiro grips my arm, pulling me into the alley. We crouch, hiding behind a dumpster. I try to breathe, but it's like I'm standing on top of a mountain. The air is thin and cold, and it hurts.

"Kite." *Don't sigh my name. Speak it. I'm strong. I'm stronger than this.* Taking my wrists in his hands, he keeps my eyes on his. "Kite." *Yes.* "Breathe."

I take a big breath, and my anger swells. "I am so tired of feeling this way." This panic. This dragging my heels back into bad places.

"I know," he says, his head dipping. "But we don't have a choice."

I pull my hands from his. "You're wrong. There is at least one thing I can do."

Chapter Thirteen

Hiro

I heard them. And when she doesn't ask me to marry her, I feel a little disappointed. Which is stupid. I don't want to marry her. I can't… Not the way my life is right now. *No.* There's a proper way to do things. And this isn't it.

I lean against the wall, watching her sort through her things, placing them into two piles. "What are you doing?"

From her crouched position, she humphs and gives me a brief frown before returning to her sorting. She's like an obsessive squirrel. It's kind of cute, and it makes me smile. "I'm getting things together to sell."

Frankie's perched on the edge of the bed, watching her sister. Pointing at a long strand of pearls, she whines. "Not tat one, Nor-ah. Tats ma favorite," she says, snatching them from her big sister's fingers.

Kite sighs loudly and straightens, shuffling over to her sister on her knees. She cups the bouncing girl's face, speaks to her clearly. Not talking down to her. "Frankie, we need cash. If you want to live with me, I need enough money to petition for your custody."

Frankie tips her head, auburn hair flashing fire around her pale face. "What's custardy?"

Kite's face scrunches as she tries to come up with a reasonable explanation. I kneel next to her. "Right now, you father has legal custody of you. So, if something happened to you, like, say you got sick and had to go to hospital, well, they would call your father and he would make all your medical decisions."

Frankie nods solemnly. Her eyes webbed with an inherent fear. "But I'd want Nor-ah."

"Well, if Kite, I mean, Nora, had legal custody of you, then that's what would happen. She would be responsible for your welfare."

She breathes out, all rattlingly. "Okay. You can hev the pearls." She drops them in the pile.

Kite finds my eyes, determination painted across her crinkled forehead. "Do you think it's enough?"

I doubt it, but I don't dash her hopes just yet. "Only one way to find out."

As we ride the train, Kite runs through a myriad of different emotions, each one thrown out like a useless playing card. But she clutches one to her chest, the one that reads *worry*. She holds the pole like it's a tree branch, letting her weight drop her shoulders, her head kind of hanging. "She looks pale, don't you think?"

I chuckle, which makes her grimace. "Well, compared to me, yes, she looks pale."

Kite slaps my arm playfully, and a woman raises her eyebrows disapprovingly. I put distance between us. "I mean, she's used to being outside regularly. She needs fresh air. Sunlight,"

Kite whispers, her eyes sliding toward the lady, who has the decency to be embarrassed and stop staring.

"We just have to be real careful at the moment. If she's recognized…" I mutter, aware of listening ears.

She sets her chin. A sweet but fierce expression on her face. Her lips poke out, the color of a pink rose petal and just as delicate. I swallow. These thoughts are going to get me in trouble. "Mr. Inkham will know what to do." She crosses her arms over her chest, stumbling when the train comes to a stop.

I want to offer my arm. But we're not supposed to be together. Be *seen* together. We're two smashed paintings from different movements. Picasso and Monet. To their eyes, we don't fit. We belong in different wings of the museum.

When we exit the train, she hooks her arm through mine anyway. She doesn't seem to care that we draw attention everywhere we go. She thinks these two paintings may look funny together, but they're beautiful all the same. Sighing, I shake my head. Maybe one day, I'll come around to her way of thinking.

Sleazy Paul appears to subscribe to Kite's view of the world, and he gives me a congratulatory nod when we walk in. He also runs his eyes up and down Kite in a way that makes me want to reach over the counter and grab him by the scruff of his neck. But the idea of touching his hairy, smelly skin is enough to hold me back. That and the fact that Kite is looking at him down the length of her nose while simultaneously trying not to inhale.

He should straighten in his chair but, of course, he slouches. Swiveling a quarter turn away from us to prod chains lined up under the glass mindlessly. I clear my throat. "Paul, this is my friend, Kite. She has a few things to show you."

Kite clutches the bag, her fingers scratching at each other under the handle. I place my hand over hers to stop her, but she just does it more gently. Paul watches us, fascinated. "Kite," he says in that weird upper class-sounding voice I've never gotten used to. Kite doesn't cover her surprise very well either. "Kite is an unusual name."

She straightens and leans on the counter, her middle touching the glass. "It's a family name," she says straight-faced. And I wonder how truthful that really is. It fills me with pride and fear like a bird who's just learning to fly. Feathers and air. Falling and freedom.

Paul shrugs, swiping a fat paw over his thinning hair. "What have you got for me, young lady?" I hate the way his eyes swim. I step forward, then lean over the counter with her. Kite shoots me a look.

"Maybe you should wait outside, *Kettle*?" She says my King name like a warning. I narrow my eyes at her, and she stares me down. "I'm quite capable of handling this myself."

After she heaves the bag onto the counter, she undoes the clasp. "Paul, I think you'll find I have much that might interest you in here."

I step outside, the bell ringing. Again, that prideful feeling falls over my shoulders. She's taking steps toward her independence; I can't be unhappy about that. Besides, if he makes any untoward moves, I'll be in there like a shot.

Shoving my hands in my pockets, I turn to watch them through the window. Paul's eyebrows rise with surprise as Kite talks. He's thrown. That makes me chuckle. His pale, fat face, the color of lard, wobbles, and he looks irritated. Sharp winds poke cold fingers in my sides, and I shiver. The crackle of dried leaves brushing the sidewalk and the crunch of them under people's feet is a cold caveat. I hate winter.

Looking up from my feet, I see Kite placing her hands on her hips and shaking her head. She quickly piles everything back in the bag before starting toward the door. I don't rush to her side, waiting to see what happens. I've never seen Paul move faster than a snail over a lettuce leaf and I almost laugh out loud when he scrambles around his counter, his chair rolling across the floor and hitting his cash register with a metallic bang. He reaches out to grab Kite's arm. She freezes, and I tense. I see a tremble as memories pass through her body like ghosts on their way down to hell. But she bites her lip, clasps the bag tightly, and glares at where Paul's sausage-like fingers squeeze her skin.

"Mr. Paul, kindly remove your hand from my arm." Her voice is rickety with murder.

He releases her and steps back, and my eyes widen at his below-waist attire. He's wearing pajama pants and slippers, and I wonder if he's ever stepped out from behind the counter before.

A number is muttered that I can't hear through the glass, and Kite shakes her head. Poor Paul looks defeated. Poor Paul looks like he's been crushed. And it was my girl who crushed him.

Again, that icy wind shoves me in the side. My girl. *My* girl. I smile to myself, staring at the ground. *Kettle, you need to get a grip,* Kin would say. He'd also tell me to go for it. But that's his dream, not mine. Marry the rich girl, live in a fancy brownstone. I don't need any of that. *But...*

Sighing deeply, my eyes dart toward the sky. Simple. Dangerous.

That sums up my feelings for her. Simple and dangerous.

I'm startled from my thoughts by an elbow to the ribs. "Did you see that?" Kite's grin is adorable and deserved.

I nod, and she holds up her empty bag. "You destroyed that man." She suddenly looks concerned, and I laugh. "It's a good thing. Trust me."

Her smile gives me honey and gold. Shimmering stars that stab my heart. "I always do."

Chapter Fourteen

Kite

Mr. Inkham's office is neat and dark as hot chocolate, and rather modest. It's not in the part of town I would have expected given my mother was his client, but then maybe that was the point.

The gold lettering on the glass is worn, the I in Inkham appearing lowercase. The bell sounds a little ill when we open the door.

A secretary sits at a heavy brown desk. The smell of fresh coffee hits my nose and my eyes flutter closed, dreaming of a full cooked breakfast and Marie serving us pancakes and whipped cream. But there's always a punctured shadow over these desires, making them fade. Because being in that house was never worth the price.

The secretary stops tapping away at her typewriter, and glances up. "Can I help you?" she stares at Hiro, who shifts and shuffles backward, his head hitting a framed poster of the Canyonlands National Park. *Sunrise at famed mesa arch* is written in bold lettering across the top. It looks beautiful and wild and beyond me. I reach out my hand to touch it.

The secretary clears her throat, and I break my dreaminess. "I'm here to see Mr. Inkham," I say, trying to look poised. Trying to hide the grubby stains around the base of my skirt.

The secretary flips open a diary. "Name?"

I step closer to her desk. "Nora Deere."

The book claps shut, and she suddenly stands. "I'll tell Mr. Inkham you're here."

She hurries to the door, slipping through like a coin through a slot.

I turn to Hiro as if to say, *that was odd*. He nods in agreement, pointing to my hair. I pat it down. The frizz has escaped the ribbon.

The door opens, and the secretary takes her seat. Mr. Inkham stands in the entryway, smiling warily. He's wearing the same creased brown suit as the day he came to visit me at the house. "Miss Deere. It's good to see you again." He opens his arms to welcome me inside.

I open my arms to Hiro. "This is my friend, Hiro."

They shake hands awkwardly. Mr. Inkham no doubt sizing him up as a possible suitor. "Nice to meet you, er, Hiro… what is your last name?"

"Jackson," Hiro offers, and it sounds true.

"Jackson." His eyebrows rise further. "Right, well…" He smooths his shirt and says, "Please, please, come in."

We file in under watchful eyes. Mr. Inkham fusses about arranging two chairs in front of his desk. Finally, we sit. Wood creaking. Thoughts tumbling. Curiosity growing.

He clasps his hands on his desk over scattered papers. "Are you well?" he asks, his small face narrowing further as he runs his eyes over me, searching for injuries. I tuck my injured leg under my chair. Even though it feels better, it is scabby and scarred, and it is visible through my stockings.

"Very well, thank you," I answer, a slight wobble to my voice.

Mr. Inkham's eyes lift to the art on the wall. More travel posters. Campgrounds and canyons. Places where the earth opens to reveal its magic. "Miss Deere, you can tell me the truth. Anything you say will be held in the strictest of confidence. I'm bound by law."

I take a deep breath, Hiro a solid reassurance at my side. "I believe my sister and I are in eminent danger. We have decided we can no longer live under the same roof as my father."

"Where are you staying?" He leans over the desk. He reminds me of a toy soldier with his arms at right angles, face smooth and stalwart, and a deep sense of morality painted onto his expression.

Hiro speaks. "A safe place."

"A safe place," I repeat. "I want to talk to you about petitioning for full custody of Frankie. I mean, Frances." I pull out the money. "I have money."

He writes something on a piece of paper. "You don't need to pay me, Miss Deere." He eyes Hiro suspiciously. "Are you sure you are *well?* Don't you think it would be better for your *friend* to wait outside?"

Hiro begins to stand. "Certainly not. Hiro is here because I asked him to be." *I need him to be.*

"Very well, very well," he says, unconvinced as he taps his pen on the page.

Bracing myself, I can see the inclination to deny me in his eyes. There's a vacuum in there. Space and brittle stars, breaking apart. "What do I need to do to get Frankie?" I ask. "I mean legally."

He must know that we've run away and are in hiding. Although my father's need to protect his own reputation cannot be underestimated, he may have remained silent about our disappearance.

"Do you have a safe and permanent residence?" Questions planted on the knuckles of a fist. They hit me hard. They splinter what little hope I had threaded between my ribs. "A dependable income? Someone to care for Frances when you're not available?"

My confidence is disintegrating as my body turns pulpy and soft. Just like it always did after a beating. I don't need to answer. He can see it in my expression. "My apartment is small, but if you need a place to stay until you can make other arrangements..."

I shake my head. "It's too obvious. He'd find us. He'd hurt you."

I can't have that on my conscience.

Mr. Inkham looks genuinely upset and sorry for me. "I wish there was more I could do, but legally, unless you can prove you can care for your sister independently, the courts will not recognize you as her guardian."

I am crushed. I don't know what I thought would happen, but I'd hoped maybe there would be more he could do. A steady income. A residence. *How can I do either of these things without him finding me?* Sabotaging me. It seems insurmountable, as unclimbable as the Canyonland arch on Mr. Inkham's poster.

Feeling squashed by the weight of it, I stand shakily, extending a hand to Mr. Inkham. "Thank you for your time, Mr. Inkham."

He takes it delicately, barely touching me with two fingers. "I wish it were possible, but you simply cannot hide from him forever."

Hiro's voice is warm and sure. "We know, and we won't."

Chapter Fifteen

Hiro

We leave Mr. Inkham's office disappointed, but we're not even close to giving up. Kite clutches my arm as cold air shoots down the street like it's searching for winter. "Do you prefer people call you Hiro or Kettle? I should like to know how to introduce you," she asks, avoiding all the upsetting topics we probably should be talking about. But I get that she needs time to sift through her feelings.

I frown down at our arms. Brown and white. Both freckled, but mine are like ink spots and hers are caramel-colored sun kisses. "Kettle, I think." I shrug. But I really like it when she calls me Hiro. This is where I'd usually swallow my thoughts, allowing them to sink inside of me rather than sharing them. Leaning my head on hers, I decide to tell her, "But I really like it when you call me Hiro."

"I know." She squeezes my arm gently. "You already told me, but you were half asleep." Her squeeze is warm and always trying to bridge this gap I've installed between us. A solid shadow that presses its arms at our chests and pushes. She leans into the shadow, and I always lean away. Right now, I need to try *not* to lean away. She needs my support.

"In my thoughts, you are always Hiro."

And I'm really gone. Snowed, as Kin would say. Sinking below the waves of an unsure emotion. *In her thoughts.* The idea that she's made space for me in her mind lifts my feet a few atoms off the ground.

Her grip tightens into a coil around my forearm. Maybe the disappointment is hurting her more than she lets on. My cap is pulled low, so I barely register the shadows of people as they pass. Kite's fingernails burrow into my skin, and I stop as I feel her freeze beside me. The murky stain of a heavier shadow meets my feet. It wavers in with the clouds overhead.

Kite murmurs, "Hiro." Just a breath. A bruised breath. I feel her shrinking. Her confidence dying like an unfed fire.

I meet a dark and hateful gaze. Christopher Deere snarls, his lip curling under his dirty, blond moustache. His eyes just like Kite's, except dead. Wooden and malicious.

I stand tall, pulling her with me. I'll hold her up if she needs it, but I won't let her crumple before him. Turning to my side, I notice her fingers have relaxed and her eyes are clear. *Looks like I won't have to.*

He leans over us, voice low, eyes alert to possible eavesdropping. "What have you done with Frances?" he hisses.

Kite's voice shakes but is steady, like percussion. She's not backing away from this confrontation. Her mouth makes a determined line. "I'm not telling you."

His hand snaps and grabs like a trap, grasping her wrist and pulling it to his chest. She winces, and I move. "Hiro, no," she begs, her mouth pulling down. Fear beginning to drip from the corners of her eyes.

"Let her go," I say, ready for a fight. My fists are clenched. Kin's voice in the back of my head. *Thumbs out. On your toes.*

The wind flurries around us, rustling her skirts and covering our muttered threats. He laughs and pushes her hand back into her chest, hard and sharp. It makes a horrible thud, and she stumbles backward. Her eyes are wet. Her skin taut. She's terrified, but she holds her ground. I stand between them.

"I will find out where you're staying and when I do, I'll make sure he's charged with kidnapping." His eyes flick to me like I'm a cockroach and then back to Kite, whose chest is heaving fast. Color pooling in her cheeks and gone from the rest of her. "And you'll be lucky if you ever see the light of day again. I'll lock you and your sister up so tight you'll be desperate for fresh air. You'll be begging for the sting of my belt just so you can look out a window again."

Horror. Horror and violence.

His words are vile. Threatening. But he is powerless here in the street in front of witnesses. And we still have the photo.

They step back further from each other. Both drained from the exchange. "You wouldn't dare. What about the photo? Your reputation?" Kite says in a hurry of breath she can barely catch.

His eyes turn dark. There's a stretch of disappointment and failure to his voice. "I am no longer involved in the JA case."

Kite shakes her head, like she can't believe it. Like she's losing her will. "But… but your reputation," she repeats.

Christopher Deere flicks a switch inside. He lengthens. Strengthens. And seems to morph into a respectable man, brushing his coat with long fingers that have bruised and battered. Strangled and shook. "My reputation will survive. There's always two sides to a story. Besides," he says, overconfident. "*You* don't have the courage to fight *me*."

He turns and strides away. His shiny black shoes clipping the concrete like a battle drum.

Kite dips her head and whispers, "You're wrong," before her knees buckle and she collapses to the ground.

She stares at her hands. Her voice faraway. "He dropped out of the case," she says slowly. She counts invisible crimes on her fingers. "Or was forced to…"

I pull at her, but she's turned to stone. "It doesn't matter. Kite, we have to get out of here." My eyes widen as two cops, several blocks away, walk unhurriedly in our direction. I don't know if he's told them. But I can't risk it. "Get up. Get up."

Putting my hands under her arms, I lift her to her feet. Her eyes are so sad and cracked with remembered pain that it breaks my heart. "What are we going to do?" she says, voice as delicate and fragile as a feather. Her eyes are amber pools of dismay and disarray. "Oh my God, Hiro, what are we going to do?"

I don't have time to be gentle with her. "I dunno, Kite, but we'll figure it out, okay?" She stares blankly. "Just not here. We can't figure it out here."

She takes a step. Wobbling like a newborn deer. Voice breathless. Not quite her own. "Not here. No."

She takes another step, and it's stronger. I get it. He startled her. He threw her into the past. Sadly, we don't have a lot of time for her to get herself together, so I grab her hand and lead her away.

There's a diner ahead. Shiny silver with red wrap around neon lights that make it look like it's from another planet. Like it's actively traveling to a better place. The cops aren't rushing. Just doing their usual beat. My guess is Mr. Deere is not quite ready to risk exposing himself. He seemed like he was biding his time.

We duck into the diner and I push her carefully into the booth, shoving a menu at her and showing her how I hold it in front my face. She copies me, and we wait for the cops to pass.

A waitress humphs at us from the other side of the menus, and we both glance up. Her shock at a white girl and a Japanese boy together is not surprising. If she didn't react, I'd probably fall out of my booth. But at least she still serves us. "What can I get you, honey?" she asks Kite.

Kite just blinks dumbly at her.

"We'll have two sodas, thanks," I answer for her.

The waitress sighs, pencil abandoned at our poor order. But at least I didn't just ask for water. I wave a hand in front of Kite's face. "Kite. Nora... Wendy..."

"Huh?" Her brows knot in confusion. "Wendy?"

"Just thought I'd throw any old name out there to try to get your attention." I smirk, but she doesn't reciprocate.

Pursing her lips, she looks at me. "The photo isn't enough anymore. Hiro," she whispers, face falling into her hands. "We're so screwed."

I almost choke on a cough. I've never heard her talk that way. Curse. I take her hands in mine, the menu's falling to the table. "We have to believe it will be okay."

She laughs bitterly, lifting our hands up and then pushing them into the salmon-pink Formica table. "He'll never give up. You know that, right? It will never end."

"We won't either." I reach out and touch her cheek, feeling the beat of blood beneath her skin. The strength she's just learning has always been there. "You hear me, Kite? We will never stop fighting."

She clutches at my words with hungry fingers. "Never?"

I swallow, trying to be what I promise. Trying to believe. "Never."

And as we sit sipping our sodas, pretending we're just a normal couple taking a break from the cold, the first snowflakes begin to spiral and fall.

Chapter Sixteen

Kite

I watch him savor the soda, and I savor this rare time we have together. His dark brows rest softly over his eyes for a short, relaxed moment. I breathe in and sigh. Our lives are built out of tough and soft things. Everything is so hard for us. Everything is a struggle. But I believe him when he says *never*. I want to be with him in that never. I want him to believe me, too, and that's the difficult part.

I think of my father, touching my chest. There's a bruise spreading there. It hurts like it always does. A sick kind of comfort in the repetitive nature of my life. It's also a reminder not to get too comfortable.

Suddenly, Hiro reaches over the table, takes my drink, and presses it to my sternum gently. His eyes darken with worry. "Does it hurt?" I nod. He stays like that, holding the drink against my heart for what could be minutes, what I wish were hours. I barely breathe in that time as we just watch each other and share the hurt. I feel it leech from my bones slowly. Soothingly.

I take the glass from him slowly, brushing his fingers deliberately, and place it back on the table. I stir the drink with my straw, letting the ice cubes clink against each other. "Tell me something good," I say.

His skin is paler than it was. As the sun has moved further from the earth, his tan has faded. He stares at me with blue-ringed irises. Like the rings of Saturn. Beautiful, mysterious. Out of reach. His eyes crinkle when he thinks, and he rubs his thumb under his jaw. I throw a napkin at him. "Oh, it can't take that long to think of something!"

He smiles. Teeth white because I know he takes dental hygiene very seriously. "Something good…" he muses. His smiles are so dashing. So infrequent. They're like the touch of a bird's claw to a wire as it takes flight. A brief steadying motion that's invaluable.

I play with a coin, rolling it between my fingers. The way he looks at me sometimes, *it feels. It feels. It feels…* Like he's burning the air around me. Making clouds I can land on if I fall. I put the coin in the jukebox and pick a song.

"Once they brought us fudgsicles." His mouth softens around the memory. And his eyes wander outside. Snow is starting to pile up on the mailbox on the corner, icing it like a cake. His gaze returns to me, vulnerability sitting uneasily over his shoulders. His eyes drop. "It was so damn hot out there in the desert. Extreme. Hot as the surface of the sun during the day and freezing cold at night."

I rest my foot against his leg under the table. Carefully. Like I'm scared I'll frighten him away. The connection is deliciously new. "I love fudgsicles." I lick my lips.

He cheeks redden as he says, "Yeah, well, I'd never had one before, but on this day, one of the guards went out and got them. It must have been a real pain to do it. He had to buy a block of ice and keep them in an icebox until he got back. But I'll always remember the look on his face when he handed them out, like he was Santa. Like this was the most rewarding thing he'd ever done."

I smile, watching his expression warm around the memory. "So, they weren't all bad?"

Shaking his head, he takes another sip of his drink. "No. Not all of them."

"I'm glad there were nice moments. Even in the worst of circumstances, you found some good." I stare down at my drink, thinking of black puddles and the way darkness can swallow a person. And how he's always there, with a flashlight and a warm blanket. A hand to hold. It's what he does. "I think that's kind of what you do. You're hope. You find the good in people."

Hiro shakes his head again. "Not everyone has good to find."

"No," I reply. "Some people are just lost."

He sweeps the glasses to one side and takes my hand. My heart stumbles. Heat is growing between us as we open up to each other. Offering our wounds and scars, we begin to understand that's part of what makes us beautiful. He lifts my hand to his mouth and kisses it tenderly. It's a warm breeze coursing through my body. It's accelerated spring. "Your good was easy to find, Kite."

I want to lean across the table and kiss him. I want to tell him everything that's broken and splintered inside me. Not so he can fix it, but so he can know it. Know me completely. But then the waitress slams a bill down on the table, and taps the total with her chipped, red fingernail.

Hiro places my hand back on the table slowly, and his eyes rise to the judgment hovering over us. "I think you two kids should get going. Your parents must be wondering where you got to." She aims that last sentence at me.

I laugh. Sprinkling a tip on the table as we leave. "Oh, I'm sure he is!" I say to the confused woman, and even Hiro laughs at that one.

Chapter Seventeen

Hiro

I'm trying to find the *good* in this weather and failing. The waitress ruined something that was building between us. But that's probably for the best. This is what will happen—*everywhere we go*. She needs to understand that. I kick the mounded piles of snow, mixed with dirt and oil, across the sidewalk. Its purity lost. This early winter does the opposite to my mood that it does to Kite. She blinks with snowflake-shaped stars in her eyes. She turns in a circle with her palms upward, thinking of Christmas and hot cocoa, fur-lined coats and the park decorated like a fairy tale. But I understand why she's doing it. She needs to find some good right now. She needs to forget her father just punched her in the chest and threatened her. Even if it's just for a moment.

She hugs her coat close, smiling as she gazes up. "Isn't it beautiful?"

I grunt. The snow is thickening. I told everyone to stay in, but I'm eager to get home and do a headcount. Kids get lost in the snow. They get buried. "How far are we from the station?"

This neighborhood is unfamiliar to me. Kite's lawyer was in a part of town I don't know well, and I turn in a circle anxiously.

Kite puts her hands on my shoulders, and I tense. "Hiro, what's the matter?"

"It's just very cold," I answer, blowing air from my lips and watching it steam.

She blinks, not comprehending. There is still so much she doesn't appreciate about this life. "Button your coat then, silly."

Small fragments of anger peel away from my mind and land in my mouth. "You don't understand. You've never had to do this before."

"I understand plenty." Her mouth sets grimly, and she crosses her arms over her chest. "But tell me, oh wise man of the street. What am I missing?"

I take a step toward her, and she steps back. This dance reminds me that she doesn't know the street life as well as I do, but she knows a hard life. And when she steps back from me like that when I'm angry, it's because that hard life has set her bones in concrete to react like I'm a threat. Like I'll hurt her.

Sighing, I give her space. "The snow is just dangerous, okay? Kids can get lost in the snow. They…"

She stands still, flakes gathering on her shoulders and in her hair. Strange confetti for an unlikely bride. "They what?"

"They disappear."

I scan the tunnel counting the Kings. "Where's Krow?"

Kane shrugs, and Kelpie and Frankie wave. I stomp toward Kane, pulling the magazine from his grasp and holding it above his head. "Where's Krow?" I ask again.

Kane frowns and snatches at the magazine, missing. "How should I know? He left early this mornin'. Haven't seen him all day."

Something sharp and cold pounds at my chest. A deep dread.

Kite pats my arm. "He's probably on his way home from work. Don't worry."

I place a palm over my heart, feeling like something is off. Something's wrong. After I grab a scarf and some too-big gloves, I head for the door. Kite is wrapping herself back up and following me. I put a hand up. "No. You stay here, in case he does come back. You should keep an eye on the others."

She nods reluctantly.

I swing open the door, feeling that dread get thicker and thicker like smoke from a diesel engine. Taking fast strides down the dark passageway, I listen for noise. My hand on the knob, I get ready to slip out. I push.

I push, but the door won't budge. Someone is pressing on it from the outside. I hear Krow curse as he shoves the door, and I step back. Relief showers me like rain in the desert. "Where're you goin', Kettle?" he asks, dark brows pulled in.

Smiling, I shake my head. "Nowhere, man." I clap a hand on his shoulder, and we head back toward the tunnel.

Chapter Eighteen

Kite

Frankie wheezes, a rough sound to her breath like the old school radiator. Though if I hit her with a spanner, I'm sure that would make her worse, not better. Kelpie kicks my feet, grumbling in his sleep. Clutching her shivering shoulder, I whisper, "It's snowing outside."

Her body shudders. She may not see the snow, but she can feel it. I fold the blanket over so she gets double, and I get none. I'm worried she's going to get sick. I'm worried we won't be able to stay here much longer, and I don't know where else we can go.

A shuffle and a shift on the other side of the curtain. Hiro's voice is soft and nervous. "Are you coming to bed?" he asks.

I touch Frankie's face. It has warmed with the extra covering, and I exhale with marble-sized relief. A hand knocks my face as he searches for me in the dark. "Kite, come to bed, please."

I take his hand and he pulls me from the room to his side, making no sound. "Hiro, wait." I pull his hand backward, and he turns to face me. The dark whispers secrets in our ears. Telling us we're safe for now. We can leave the heat of our argument for day and kindle a different kind of heat in the night.

Ice bites into my feet, and I rise on my tiptoes to expose less of my skin to the ground. Hiro's hand is still in mine and I place it on my hip. My hands find his neck and close around it like the clasp of a locket. *I want. I want. I want...* Something bigger than me. Something closer, too. I want Hiro. Kettle. Both and all.

Slowly his hands overlap, bringing me closer. He breathes small, uneasy breaths. His arms are strong and safe. Young oak searching for the sky.

His cheek rests against mine, and I move so my nose grazes his face. He does the same, and our noses touch. Our lips just inches apart. "Kite," he whispers, though it sounds like music. "I..."

He tilts his head, and I think maybe the world tilts with him. It opens. The earth, the trees, all lean back and make space for us. For this.

His lips are like salt and jasmine. They're soft with rough parts like where the sea meets the hull of a boat. And it's so beautiful and feels so completely right that I start to cry, and my knees begin to buckle. I reach for him, letting him in, and he is careful with me. Respectful *of* me.

I never knew. I *never* knew. *I never knew...*

Anything.

My hand moves to his hair, it ruffles under my touch, springing back into place. His fingers spread on my back, but they don't wander. He is focused on this new and amazing discovery of our mouths. And I just can't remember why or even believe that we waited so long for this.

I break away, sensing his reluctance to let go. Feel the disappointment as his hands press into my skin desperately. But we need oxygen. Dancing over the dark ceiling, I imagine a swirl of stars, wings fluttering and comets colliding. Gold dust sweeping over the stones like a storm.

Taking a deep breath, I gather his face in mine, kissing him in an exploring kind of way, like I have all the time in the world. Still connected, he steps backward, leading me into his room. The curtain brushes over my shoulders, cocooning me like thick willow branches, ready to hide and protect me.

We sit on the bed, his hands still at my back. I want to throw my arms around him and push him onto the mattress, but...

There are things we do not do. There are ways in which they are done, an order in which to do them, and to Hiro, this is important.

I take his hands and clasp them in mine, my eyes blinking tears I'm glad he can't see. I'm scared. Not of him. Never of him. I'm scared of what he'll say. "Hiro," I whisper.

There's a small chuckle. The hitch of ribs as they move up and out of place. "I'm really starting to love it when you say my name."

I beam, and I'm sure my mouth is a floating crescent moon. "Hiro. Hiro. Hiro." He chuckles again, leaning in to kiss me as I speak his name aloud again, his lips landing on mine just as I whisper, "o".

Against my cheek, he murmurs, "Yes. Still love it."

"Hiro, I..." Words bang on my skull like three-foot neon signs, wanting to escape. They've been living in there for quite some time now, and they want to be seen. To be heard. "Hiro, I love you." He stops still. I'm swept up in first kisses and the deepest feelings. They lift me from the ground; they take me on a tour of the sky. I move off the bed, kneeling on the cold hard floor. "Hiro Jackson, will you marry me?"

His deep sigh is cavernous. "No." My wings snap in midair. I flutter, I fall, I fail.

His hand touches my face. Even though I should probably storm out, save my dignity before this gets worse, I stay. Leaning into his warm hand and listening to his explanation. "No." Two simple letters. A million reasons to run. But I'm glued to the floor. "But why? Don't you love me, too?"

I sniff, hating how pathetic I sound. Thing is that I know he loves me. There is no doubt in my mind.

"It doesn't matter if I love you or not; that's not the point. This isn't the way. We haven't even been on a single date, Kite. I'm just… I'm just…"

He breaks our hands apart, and I know without even seeing that he's raking a frustrated hand through his hair. That his eyes have blotted to dark clouds and his lips have thinned to a line.

My knees grind into the stone floor. "You're just what?"

"I'm just worried you're doing this for the wrong reasons. After what Mr. Inkham said, I know it's on your mind. I know you don't want to stay here forever, and that marriage would be a simple way to get the money you need. And I don't blame you, I don't, but I'm sorry, my answer has to be no."

My head sinks, and so does my heart. I get up to leave. He grabs my arm, running his fingers down the length of it and making me shiver. "Why does everything have to be so rushed? Can't you give me some time?"

Nodding, I fold into his arms. "But I do love you. That is the truth," I whisper, facing away from him. Letting my tears absorb into his pillow.

Into my hair, he murmurs, "I know."

I understand. It was rushed. It wasn't the right time, but I'm not sure that exists for us.

"You owe me a date then," I say.

Groaning, he hugs me tighter. "Okay, okay. One date." He thinks I don't hear him when he says minutes after, when our breath has settled and sleep is hovering like mist on the water, "Then you'll get it."

Get what?

Chapter Nineteen

Kite

Hiro shoots up out of bed like someone's poured a bucket of ice water over his head. He pulls the covers with him and my knees fly to my chest, feeling the instant cold of no blanket and no Hiro to warm me. "Kamo!" he whispers harshly.

My heart plummets faster than a fish searching for the bottom of the ocean. *How could we forget Kamo?* But then, isn't that what Hiro said? Everyone forgets Kamo. He's so quiet in his hidden corner of the world. He disappears, and no one notices him.

I swallow. I understand what Hiro was saying now about winter, about snow. I don't want to, but I do.

I am sandstone and mortar that is *crumbling, crumbling, crumbling.* We were so caught up in each other that we forgot Kamo.

Hiro strikes a match and by frantic candlelight, he dresses quickly, wrapping everything he owns around him. I do the same. He doesn't stop me. He doesn't tell me I can't come with him this time. I part the curtain of his room, and he grabs my arm. "Wait!" he whispers harshly.

I think he's going to make me stay, but I can't leave him to search for Kamo by himself. I open my mouth to protest, but he lifts a coat around my shoulders and places a wool hat on my head. Hiro's hand lingers at my throat as he straightens the collar, a touch burning like fire. His eyes are the dead sea. Dark, deep, and tomblike. He brushes my jaw with the rough pads of his fingers. "Thank you."

I watch the mouth I had just kissed hours ago turn to a grim line. Touching my fingers to his lips, I feel the warm breath pressing between them. "It will be okay." *Please let it be okay.*

His eyes close for one long second, living in this small, warm moment before we enter the cold, harsh outside. When he opens them, his eyes say, *you don't know that.* But he doesn't speak the words. He takes my hand, and we leave the safety of the tunnel. Splashing through icy water dripping from above.

I'm praying. Praying we find him, praying we don't. I just want Kamo to be alive. I want to find him hiding against the wall in the station, pressed into the background like so many peeling posters, his mischievous, contemplative eyes squinting at us in glee.

The station is empty save a few stumbling, mumbling drunks and older homeless people. They stay in their corners and drink, leaning against the colorful tiles. They ignore us.

He searches the restrooms, returning every time alone. No quiet, unassuming Kamo at his side, just Hiro's eyes getting rounder and harder, like a dying planet as hope stretches thinner.

Then he turns back toward home, and I'm surprised at how quickly he's given up. He runs like he's out of time, and I struggle to keep pace with him. A train pulls up to the station, and he jumps on. I follow.

Hiro's mood fills the rattling car. *Worry. Worry. Worry. Blame. Blame. Blame.*

I want to ease his pain, so I step closer. Not sitting, he grips the pole like he may rip it from its rivets. He's so tense it's like arranging a corpse with rigor mortis. I bite my lip, wishing that thought hadn't entered my head. "Hiro." I try to catch his eyes. "Try not to think the worst. You don't know what's happened to him. He may be perfectly fine." I pry his hand from the pole and place it around my waist, drawing him into me. He sighs deeply, burying his face in my hair. He is so much heart and hero. He is the lion *and* the knight. I press him close, feeling the fast rise of his chest as he breathes in sharp, unhappy breaths.

"I only know the worst," he mutters, sad words caressing my ear. I press my lips to his shoulder, kissing him over the top five layers of fabric. We are one beating, spluttering heart. Trying so hard to do the right thing. Trying so hard to rescue everyone. Always feeling like we're not enough. Wishing there was a place where we could be. Enough.

He holds me tight, and we breathe together on this empty subway car. One breath. Two breaths. Not wanting to let go, but knowing reality is about to make us.

The train squeals and stops, and the inertia pulls us apart. But I feel threaded to him even as we break away. We are more and more connected. Looped like chain mail and welded strong.

"Do you know where you're going?" I ask.

His expression is pained. He hides things beneath those smooth, dark cheeks. "Kamo has a few places he likes to go."

The doors to the outside rattle, swirls of white brushing the glass and gathering in piles at the foot of the entrance. Under the streetlights, they look like white moths, fluttering and dying. Never reaching the globe to rest.

Our eyes connect and I shake my head as he pushes the door open, mounds of fresh powdery snow spilling into the station. Hands to our faces we step into the blizzard. The immediacy of the bitter cold is hard as icicles to the chest. We lift our scarves over our faces, eyelashes painted white, and trudge down the street.

I shout through the howling wind, but it dies before it reaches him. This storm is formidable. We can't stay out here very long.

Hiro moves slowly through the snow, taking time to shelter in alcoves and under shop balconies. He points to a sign a few doors down. Two red and white poles of a barbershop look like giant candy canes in this winter horrorland. Hiro comes closer and lowers his scarf. "He likes to watch people go in looking one way and come out looking different." My mouth lifts for a spindly second at the unbearable sweetness of this silent child, but it freezes into a frown. Hiro points to a narrow alleyway, just wide enough for some trash cans and a side door, leading me down it.

It's a battle against the snow piling higher and higher, but at least there's light bouncing from the streetlights off the endless white. We kick and shove snow aside, looking up and down the alley. I breathe relief, but Hiro is unconvinced. He stomps through, feet sinking. I grab his shoulder, shake, and shout, "Let me go up there." I point to the end of the alley, where there are mounds that could be boxes covered in snow, resting against a chain-link fence. "I'm lighter than you. I can get there without sinking in so far."

He nods, hugging his arms to his sides. I shiver. My fingers are numb. My nose and ears sting. We will have to find shelter soon.

As carefully as I can, I pad toward the back. My feet sink down half a foot, but I can rest on the compacted snow. I scan for signs of life. There is nothing. My eyes rest on the wet and disintegrating tips of boxes. The edge of a metal trash can. Discarded hair from the barber shop.

Thick, black hair next to the trash can, not in it.

I draw in a gasp, cold air stabbing my lungs, and my hand flies to my mouth.

Let me become the sun. Let me burst with light and warmth and banish this snow from the alley.

Please.

Chapter Twenty

Hiro

Her hand flies to her chest, and my heart flies from my mine. She shakes as she leans down to sweep snow from something. I hope she's looking closer at a pile of trash. She's barely able to touch whatever it is. When she's crouching in snow up to her waist, I start pushing my way to her. I can't feel my feet and I wish the rest of me was so lucky.

She turns, sadness all over her graying face. She puts her hand up to stop me. But nothing can stop me.

Her tears are frozen to her cheeks. I wish they'd fall, not cling and bite her with more grief.

Kamo's round face is blue. Blue and sleeping. I kneel. It's difficult to breathe because of the cold and the grief. "Kamo…" I choke on his name. "Kamo."

I speak the names of the ones I've lost. The list is long, marking all of my years with death.

I sweep the snow from his face and shoulders. He is stone. He cannot be warmed by any fire. We're too late. Kite sniffs behind me. "Oh, Hiro. Is he…?"

I stand and step back. Swallowing acres of screams. It will do no good. "He's gone," I manage.

Kamo. One of the Lost Children. Now lost forever.

My teeth chatter. My jaw feels rigid. Kite's shaking uncontrollably, and I put my arm around her shoulders to warm her.

His face is wrong. Wrong color. Wrong expression. He looks peaceful. Did people see him and leave him here? I gulp back hot, furious tears as my throat tightens. He died alone in an alley. Like so many street kids. I stand and look to the sky, trying to find a star or something to pin my grief to. A light. A hope. But it's just an endless swirl of white. And now we must leave him here.

"We have to go," I say, turning Kite away from my friend's body and pushing her toward the street.

She clutches her hands together, every part of her rattling like bones in a bag. "Yes. Yes." Her mouth quivers. "We need to call someone."

I keep my mouth shut and rush us back to the station. One foot in front of the other because even in these terrible circumstances, there's no time to wallow or even come to terms. Survival comes first.

Kamo didn't survive. Maybe the world couldn't tolerate someone as sweet and unassuming as him. Maybe he'll go to a… I can't even finish the thought. I don't believe in better places. Heaven. Neverland. A place in the clouds. It's all bullshit.

There is concrete and cold and dirt.

There is death and disease every winter.

Squeezing my hands into fists, I shove the door open violently.

Kamo was the first casualty of the season. There have been many before and there will be others after. But I shouldn't have forgotten him. I could have prevented this night.

I let this happen.

Kite rushes to a payphone and picks up the receiver, finger poised to dial the emergency number. I press down on the button. "There's no point," I say flatly.

She stares at me, lips blue. Her face a tiger stripe of frozen and melting tears. "But… we can't just leave him there. He needs to be…" She stutters, from cold and shock, and I try to see it from her perspective. She's not used to the sight of death. Not the way I am.

I take the receiver from her gently, then hang up the phone. "They won't care, Kite," I explain. "Kamo is a street kid. He's already…" I can't finish my sentence. The word *dead* blares like an electric headache inside my brain. "Look, trust me. They won't come."

She's horrified. As her knees weaken, her body crumples to the floor. I sink with her, putting my grief aside for a moment. "But he deserves to be put to rest. He needs…" I fold her into my arms.

"When the snow melts, he will be," I say simply, feeling something move in my chest. A hard lump that grows like a tumor with every lost kid who stays lost. She sobs, then she pulls back. Her golden eyes find mine, an impossible amount of warmth pouring out.

Touching my face, she traces my eyebrows with the tips of her delicate fingers. "I'm sorry," she says, breathing calm into her voice. A solidness is now radiating from her like the brightest star. The star that outshone the moon. "I didn't know Kamo well, but you did, you must be…" She blinks, her face wet from melted snow, pools of water soaking into her clothes. "Oh, Hiro. Are *you* okay?"

My eyebrows rise. I don't get asked this question. Staring at the floor, I find the cracks in the tiles. My eyes follow the curl of the patterns—fern leaves and simplified daisies. "I'm fine," I mutter.

"You're not." Her words bloom like a cloud under my chin, pushing my face up. I feel my resolve cracking.

I rest my head on her shoulder. *God, it would be easier if I could cry.* But I'm an empty well, a bucket with a hole in it or something. There are no tears left. "No, you're right. I'm not okay."

As I rest on her shoulder, as I allow Kite to carry some of my weight, all I can think about is little Kamo. And how I'll be forever sorry that I couldn't do more for him. "He didn't deserve this. I should have done better. I'm sorry, Kamo. I'm so sorry."

Kite strokes my back and whispers, "This isn't your fault, Hiro."

And I try really hard to believe her.

Chapter Twenty-one

Kite

We leave Kamo as we found him with his face frozen in sleep and his heart an iceberg in his chest. Hiro tells me we have to leave him, but it feels so wrong. He tells me this is what they've always done. And I'm too scared to ask how many times this has happened before. But by the look on his face, it's a lot.

We drag ourselves home. *Home.* To a slightly less cold place. A place filled with hungry children. One less hungry child now. I gulp, and tears keep coming. When we open the door, Hiro breaks from me and storms to the back of the tunnel, flicking the lights on with a static crack. Tired faces creased by hessian and doll blankets blink and yawn as they rise from slumber. He stands in the middle of the room as they look to him expectantly. Hands on hips, he holds his weary body up. But he is weighed down by the responsibility of this loss.

"Kamo found his mom," he announces. The Kings all exchange glances, and sadness rings their eyes. It's obvious this is code for *Kamo has died*. But it's a disconnected sadness. Kind of like, *Oh, that's too bad*. They nod, tap their chests, and point to the sky, then some of them lay back down, pull their threadbare coverings over their heads, and close their eyes. "We'll go through his things in the morning."

He slams the light off, and I'm left standing near the doorway drowning in shadows, bewildered.

He finds me, and we walk back to his room.

"I don't understand."

"No, you don't." His voice is gruff, and there is so much grief built up inside there. Death is the mortar for this wall he surrounds himself with. He begins pulling my wet clothes from my body. His fingers clasping my collar tightly like it's a ledge he's scared he will fall from.

"I'm sorry," I say, not really knowing what else to say. My coat falls to the floor.

His words barely fit between his teeth. "You have nothing to be sorry for. This is the world we live in. It's all we have to work with. It's just the way it has to be."

I let him lay down and hold me with jerky movements as he begins to thaw. But I don't believe that we're stuck here and I know we can change things. One thing's for sure—these kids need a safer, warmer place to live.

Chapter Twenty-two

Hiro

I did it all wrong. And then, everything went wrong. She told me she loved me, and I didn't say it back even though I do. I love Kite. The moment we kissed, it was like the sun exploded through the bricks of the tunnel and sent them tumbling. Everything scattered and rearranged and settled into a better place. A *meant-to-be* place. But then I let my shit get in the way. And then Kamo… *God, poor little Kamo.*

I try so hard, but I will never get used to losing them. My heart breaks every single time. It's so battered and fractured I'm sure it could go in one of those medical marvel jars at the fair.

I swallow, making the pain a part of me so I can move on as best I can. Because the ones left alive still need me.

Folding Kamo's memory in half, I carefully pack it away.

I have two things to do today and both involve keeping promises.

One promise makes me so nervous I can't stop thinking about it. The other is never ending and never enough.

I've never missed Kin so much in my life. He would know what to do. He would have a plan. I've never dated before. When you're hopping turnstiles and dumpster diving for expired pickles, romance seems pretty unrealistic.

Pulling Krow aside, I ask him in a hushed voice, "How much do you think a movie ticket costs?"

"One ticket?" I shake my head, and he gives me this sly smile I don't really like. "Ah, two tickets. One for you and one for the dolly." He knocks his head toward Kite.

I manage a grunted yes, though I hate that he calls her a 'dolly'. I wonder what he's learning at this new job of his. It's on my long list to teach him a thing or two about how to be a gentleman. I can imagine Kin's rolling his eyes behind my back.

Kite is watching the other Kings, horrified, as they pick apart Kamo's belongings with her mouth agape and her eyes wide and blinking. At least they're divvying them out fairly. *This is such a bad idea.* So much of my life causes her to make that face. But we can't waste good blankets and bedding. Kelpie bounds toward me, then hands me Kamo's comic books. "You wanna put this one on the ledge?" he asks.

Krow pinches my arm, whispering, "I think it's about fifty cents a ticket."

With a solemn nod, I walk over to a section of the wall where we've chipped out a few bricks. Inside, we've put something from each kid who has 'found their mom'. I don't need to count them. I know the number. And it's too many.

I shake it off. It does no good to dwell.

The money from the sale of Kite's things would be more than enough, but it bothers me to take her money to pay for a date. I stare at my hands, feeling the need to go back to the docks.

Kite taps me on the shoulder nervously. "What are you thinking about?" she asks, her eyes tainted with one splinter of pain that I put there, and another one that's worked its way in—the result of living as a King.

"I was thinking…If I'm going to take you out on a date tonight, I need to go back to the docks to earn some cash."

I think she's going to argue with me. Tell me she has enough money to cover it, but she doesn't. And this is one of the reasons I love her. She knows it's important to me, so she lets me go.

"What can I do while you're gone?" she asks, swinging her hips coyly. I smile, each tooth humming. The memory of our kiss, and then kisses, rattles my nerves. The world always feels like it's spinning just a little too fast. And I'm never quite caught up.

"Krow?" I shout as I change into my work clothes. "Do you get an employee discount?"

He jumps, but has the decency to look sheepish. "Uh, yeah. Ten percent. Twenty-five on stock that's close to expiring."

I won't let her pay for the date, but she can certainly pay for groceries. "How about you do a quick inventory and then get what we need from the grocery store?"

She salutes me. It's adorable, and it's embarrassing that it makes me blush. I avoid eye contact with Krow because I know he's laughing at me.

Chapter Twenty-three

Kite

A date. *Tonight.* Hiro leaves, and it's like I'm caught in a tail wind. My heart tugging through the door but not able to follow. *The words, the words, the words.* I. Love. You. They catch in the door as he closes it behind him. The pain of not hearing it back has been pushed to the side. Kamo's death means I can't worry about such things.

Frankie coughs, and it echoes through the tunnel. Or maybe that's just how it sounds to me because it scares me. She can't be another unknown face in the alley. My heart turns cold. Kamo was not unknown to us, but that is how he shall be laid to rest. I worry about his small body after the snow melts and the sun warms the gaps between the buildings. I shudder. I can't think about it. I just can't.

We cannot stay here. But convincing Hiro of that will be a challenge. *A mountain to climb. A sea to drain.*

I touch my lips. The kiss lingers there. The press of his hands on my back as he drew me close leaves a brand. Someone tugs on my skirt, and I flush red. "Nor-ah, what ya dreamin' about?" Frankie stares at me, blue eyes showing signs of knowing, the skim of blue on the surface.

Taking a sharp breath, I rustle her hair. "Oh, nothing…"

She squirms out from under my hand and stands with her hands on her hips. "S'not nuthin'. But you never tell me nuthin'." Her face reddens, her breath rattling in fast. She steps forward, pushing my stomach pointedly. "You never ever tell me nuthin'!"

The Kings quieten around us. A bubble of nervous air billows out from where we stand. "Frankie, what's the matter?" I ask, taking her hands in mine before she shoves me again.

Her forehead, all splotchy and angry, creases. Freckles dotting her skin like a night compass. "You're always leavin'. You never tell me why, and you never say where you're going. You'll leave, and may-bee you won't come back!"

There are tears. Hard as diamonds for how much they sting me. I kneel to face her. "Oh Frankie, I'm so sorry. I know you've been through a lot. I'm worried if I take you outside, you'll be recognized." I run my thumb over her fair freckles. "I'm just trying to protect you."

She draws in a wheezy breath. Mouth thin and dry. "From Deddy."

I nod. Swiping my miserable face. "Yes. From Daddy."

She sniffs, wipes her nose with the back of her hand and then on her dress, which is starting to look quite filthy. "I do know things. I know what he's done. And this is ma problem, too, ya know."

My chin falls. "I know, darling, I know." *Of course I know.* I guess in protecting her, I left her out of the decision-making process. And even though she's only eight, she deserves a say in what happens in her life.

Kelpie creeps up behind Frankie, putting an arm over her shoulder. His blond curls falling in his eyes. "You okay, Krick-et?"

She huffs, her angular shoulders up around her ears. "I'm fine. Me and Nor-ah just had somethin' to discuss."

Her serious voice makes me smile. I cup her cheek. Her skin is so soft, not patched together with bruises and breaks. It needs to stay that way. She leans into me. "What is it you would like to know? I will tell you everything."

She frowns, shaking her head. "I don't wanna know every-thin'. I am only eight. May-bee just somethin'." She presses her finger and thumb together. "Just a little somethin'"

I press my palm to my heart. "Anything."

Satisfied, she asks, "Are you an Kettle, um, are you a..." She claps her hands together and looks up at the ceiling, search-ing for the right words. Not finding any, she settles on, "What are you an Kettle?"

I know my cheeks are pink. My eyes moisten. My heart pounds at the rate of her frantic bobbing. "I'm not really sure."

She puts up her finger. "I tink I know."

"You do?" I lean in, placing too much stock in her thoughts on the matter.

"You're like with tha diamond ring... What's the word? Be-troffed."

I giggle, wishing she was right. "You mean betrothed?"

She folds her arms over her chest. "Dat's what I said. Be-troffed."

I shake my head sadly. "We are not betrothed, Frankie." Pulling her into my lap, I whisper so the boys can't hear me. "I wish we were, but we're not."

Unwilling to concede, she just frowns and sets her chin de-terminedly. "Well, you're about to be. Or close to bein'"

I hope she's right. But I'm not sure. He said no. And he seemed pretty set about it.

"Well, I guess you could say we're dating..." Does it count if the date hasn't even happened yet? Nervousness starts to pound *up, up, up* my throat. "Is there anything else you want to ask me?" I say, trying to sweep the conversation to the left.

She tips her head up, her neck twisting to find my eyes. "Hmm…" She taps her chin. Then her voice changes, grows younger and softer. "Are we ever gonna go home?"

"I really don't know. It's very complicated. If Daddy is there, we can't go back. We can't trust him. Do you understand?"

She nods. "But we can go home if Daddy's not there?"

How do I tell her that will never happen?

"We might just have to find a new home…" I say loudly without meaning to. My chin resting over her shoulder.

Kelpie's eyes round, and he looks upset. "You're gonna leave us?" he asks.

My eyes sweep the room. The boys are doing their chores and having small conversations. The miraculous way they've learned to survive all around me. They've each earned a place in my heart, and it hurts to think of leaving them behind. Hiro's conflict opens like a broken window in a dark, dark room.

Leaving this life would be impossible. It has to come with us, and that's where the biggest problem lies.

Kelpie still stares at me, waiting for an answer. I muss his curls. "I could never leave you, Kelpie!" Not sure if I'm lying or not. If I am, it's a lie I desperately want to believe.

I pull on my coat, patting my pocket full of cash.

First things first. I need to go to the grocery store with Krow.

Krow is not one for conversation. He slumps into his pockets, head down, eyes on his feet. He seems nervous and completely put out by my presence at the same time. "So how long have you known Kettle?" I ask as the subway car sways around a corner and all the passengers lean to the right.

Frankie clings to my leg, looking ridiculous with a frilly dress and a baseball cap on. I need to keep her face hidden. I haven't seen anything in the papers, but I can't risk her being seen. My own head is wrapped in a scarf. Krow shrugs and mutters, "A while."

I roll my eyes. This is harder than pulling teeth. "Do you like working at D'Ogossini's?"

"S'all right." He barely opens his mouth when he speaks. Like words are precious mouthfuls of food.

I give up.

I follow him out of the subway, Frankie tripping over her skirts as we climb into the bitter cold. Krow kicks a lump of snow aggressively just like Hiro did. I didn't understand it then, but I do now. Winter is the enemy to these kids. He huddles down in his jacket, gesturing for us to cross the road.

Snow makes it harder to hide, to blend in. We all stand out like black shoes on a white tile floor. We look suspicious; I just know it. I watch women filing into the store. Mostly maids and nannies. They walk and look a certain way, always in a hurry. Their plain faces, hair pulled tightly back and minimal make up, blend together. I stop at the front to fix my hair and tighten the scarf. Bending down to Frankie, I whisper, "Call me Miss Kite in there, okay?"

She nods. "Miss Kite, okay Nor-ah." I sigh. This might be difficult.

I squeeze her hand. "Just pretend I'm Marie or Miss Candace. Don't treat me like your sister."

She grins. "I love pretendin' games!" She salutes me, and Krow groans loudly.

He opens the door, surprising me by letting me go in first. I smile graciously and lead Frankie in, my eyes on the checkered floor.

"Davey!" a man exclaims, walking over to clap Krow on the back. *Davey?* I arch an eyebrow. Frankie giggles.

Krow straightens and smiles, smoothing his hair back self-consciously. "Uh, hi Mr. Jones." It flops back over his eye.

Mr. Jones smiles broadly, pushing his glasses back up his nose. "You're not supposed to be working today, are you?" He wipes his hands on his apron, then gazes down at Frankie. "And who's this little one?" He takes a step toward her and she steps back, pressing into my skirt. It's heartbreaking to see how she reacts to men in the world. Like every last one is dangerous. Though sadly, it's probably the smartest way to behave.

Krow shakes his head. "No, sir. Just wonderin' if I can use my employee discount today. Our mom's been awful busy, and she asked me to pick up some things…"

He waves at Krow, still trying to catch Frankie's eyes from beneath the cap. "Yes, of course, of course." His eyebrows rise as some memory wakes in him. He points at her. "You look familiar…" he says, and I wonder if I missed something in the papers. If he recognizes her because my father has reported her missing.

I feel Krow's hand reassuringly at my back and I know he's getting ready to run, to fight our way out if need be. This touch makes me want to curl around it. It's so precious, so fierce, I almost feel like I'll choke on a cry right here in front of Mr. Jones. Because I know without a doubt that even though he is careful with his words, and he looks at me like I'm foreign and hard to understand, Krow is family. He views me as such. He would help me. He would lose his job for me. He is a King. And so are Frankie and I.

It adds steel to my frame and strength to my fading in and out heart.

Frankie turns her face to my skirt, burying herself and poking me with the brim of her cap. Mr. Jones chuckles. "A little shy, huh? I was just going to say you look just like my niece, Lucy. She has that same fire-red hair."

Krow and I collectively sigh with relief. "Sorry, sir. She's just a little tired and cold. She not usually this shy." I stroke Frankie's hair gently and slip the cap from her head.

Mr. Jones gives me a kind nod and turns, talking loudly, "I know just the thing to cure tiredness *and* coldness!" He reaches into a large jar and produces a lollipop, then he taps it gently on the back of Frankie's head. She spins around, eyes sugar hungry, and licks her lips. "Tanks!" she says, snatching the candy from the man's hairy hand.

Krow grabs a cart. "We better get started. Right, sis?" I nod, and we head down an aisle.

The moment we're out of sight, Krow returns to his normal self—silent and cautious. He walks beside me, guarding, while Frankie bites down noisily on her lollipop, making my teeth hurt with all the crunching.

We carefully pick through the shelves, trying to stretch our money as far as it will go. Choosing close to expired food, canned goods, and things that don't need refrigeration. Things that can keep for a long time. We also buy soap. Toothpaste. Batteries for Frankie's hearing aid. I surreptitiously slip a box of sanitary pads in the trolley. If Krow sees, he doesn't draw attention to it.

Frankie asks for everything we can't buy—cereal, chocolate bars—and I find myself mindlessly saying no to her every five seconds like a harried housewife. I'm so focused on my task that I don't notice Marie until Frankie has her arms wrapped around the round woman's waist. I swallow horror and fear, trying to pretend that everything's okay. But I give Krow a quick look to split. He understands and takes the cart, wheeling it away from us.

"Miss Nora! Miss Frankie!" Marie exclaims, and I'm reminded of how much I loathe her panicky voice. Because it's the voice of someone who *knows* everything but has never *said* anything. She shuffles closer, acting like eyes are on her.

"Where have you been?" she whispers. "Your father is suffering awful much in your absence."

I clench my fists, counting slowly in my head. "I'm sorry to hear that," I say, forcing my tone to be even. Unfeeling. But I know it's not working. I sound like I'm about to slit her throat. Anger is getting the better of me. But *she knows. She knows. She knows.*

How can she stand here and pretend *he* deserves our pity? It is beyond my understanding. I know I can't stay here. I can't talk to her. "Miss Nora? Are you quite all right?" It's such a stupid question.

Yanking Frankie from her grasp, I connect with Marie's eyes. Her raisin-sized eyes that have witnessed so much violence. I know now that silence can be deadly and her silence could have killed me. I shove Frankie behind me, then whisper terse, punched-out words, "You did not see us. You hear me, Marie? Do this one thing for me. Then, maybe one day, I can forgive every time you turned your back when he struck me. Every time you washed my bloodstained clothes without batting an eyelid." My voice is strong. Detached.

She steps back, blinks, and I almost think I see shimmers of regret there. Some tiny splash of responsibility for her part in this. She shakes her head sorrowfully, grasps her cart, and spins away from us. Quickly, I stoop to Frankie. "Where's Marie goin?" she asks around the lollipop stick she's chewing. Her tongue has turned bright red. Her eyes are bright with sugar and food coloring.

"Marie needed to leave. I had to make sure she didn't tell Daddy she saw us. Do you understand?"

She nods.

My heart is heavy and hurt. I try to breathe deeply and calm myself, but it's so damn hard. Krow returns to us once Marie has left the store. His dark eyes are colored with compassion, turning an iridescent raven blue. He simply says, "It's not easy when they come lookin'. It's even harder when you know they're only lookin' to hurt you." Shivers run down my spine. I place my hand on his arm and squeeze gently. Wiping my eyes before the tears have a chance to run rivers down my face.

After we finish our shopping, we take it to the counter.

Krow pulls out a long, thick ribbon that was tucked behind a tin of beans. It's pale blue satin, and it has tiny stars of a slightly darker blue embroidered on it. He places it on the counter. He goes to say something, but he can't quite get it out. Once we've paid, he shoves it at me.

I take it, roll it carefully, and place it in my pocket. "Thank you, Krow."

As we walk away from the store, he manages to mumble, "Well, you should have something nice for yer date. You can put it in yer hair or somethin'"

It's so sweet I can barely breathe.

Frankie tries to steal it from my pocket.

Chapter Twenty-four

Hiro

I wash away the salt and grime of work. Watching dirt pool between my bare feet and then suck down the drain. The docks were gray and sullen today. The ice on the containers made it hard to think about anything other than not falling. But now all I can think is—what have I got myself into?

I scrub the used bar of soap through my hair. It feels wiry and plastic like doll's hair. If only I could scrub away the rest of my cares like the dirt. I'm nervous. I'm worried it won't go well, that I'll disappoint her. I'm also worried about the complete opposite. That it will go well and make me want something I shouldn't really have.

Kite said I find the good. I find hope. I can do that for other people. I'm just not very good at finding it for myself.

I turn off the squeaky taps and stand still, letting the drips run down my skin. Swoop down the bridge of my nose and drop like new tears to join the ocean. Either way I look at it, I'm screwed.

The other men at the Y stare at me when I exit the shower room. I curse and move to the mirror, trying to flatten my hair. When it doesn't really cooperate, I shrug. She's seen me after dock work and sleeping in the alley. Anything after that will be an improvement.

I leave the Y trying to leave my expectations there, too. I made a promise and I just need to keep it.

Walking the street with my head down, my eyes swing up to shop windows every now and then. White models clad in fur and holding skis. A foreign world. A foreign life.

I wonder if Kite's ever been skiing. I snort. Probably.

But I need to check my prejudice. Stopping, I stare at the models. Vacant eyes. Easily shattered bodies. I remind myself that whatever benefit her rich parents provided her came at a heavy, heavy cost.

I think about buying her flowers. But they would die without light. And they're a waste of money. Shoving my hands in my pockets, I head down to the subway.

This whole date thing is a waste of money.

I open the door. Full of preconceptions. Nervous energy and doubt.

But then...

She comes to me with stars in her hair. Bruised and beautiful. And I forget all my sullenness. My doubts. I forget everything except how many steps it will take for her to reach me. Kite smiles shyly, and Frankie pushes her forward. "Ta da!" she exclaims loudly.

Keg chuckles but Krow smacks his head, and the rest of them turn away, giving us precious privacy in this open space. This is something normal carved out of something very not-normal. I feel like they wish me well even if they don't really understand it.

I step forward. "You look beautiful," I mutter. Again, there's some chuckling from the boys and another smack as Krow shushes them. She has color on her lips but no other makeup. Her bruises are fading to yellowish around her jaw. "But then, you always do. Look beautiful, that is."

Sniggers.

She dips her head. Her hair neatly curled under. She's wearing the outfit she had on when I pulled her from the window. It feels like so long ago. But it's not. We're still pretty new to each other. Still finding and losing our feet. "Thank you, Hiro. You look very nice, too."

I stare down at my clean shirt and crinkled trousers. I look like a street kid impersonating a regular kid. I stifle my snort because her eyes are so earnest and truthful. She sees me differently. Under a light that most people don't even know exists. Some shade of color invisible to most. I offer my arm, and she takes it.

"Get some rest, Frankie. Krow and Kelpie are here if you need anything." She bends down and kisses her sister's forehead. Gets butted in the process. "Are you sure you're okay with me leaving?" She rubs the spot where Frankie has hit her.

"Yes. I'll be fine. You go hev fun, Nor-ah!" She scuttles behind her sister, pushes her in the back. Kite stumbles, and I catch her before she hits the ground.

"So, what's the plan?" she asks as we take the strangest trip from the front door to transport that anyone has ever taken on their first date. Splashing through muddy water, skirts and pant legs held up so we don't get them dirty. Other kids take a garden path or porch steps to a car, but there's nothing *usual* about this situation.

"I thought we'd see a movie and then dinner, if that's all right with you?" I ask, sounding formal. Trying to do the things I think I'm supposed to do.

"Sounds lovely." We wait for the platform to empty, ears pressed to the door. "This is strange," she whispers.

I let out a small puff of bellows, a tight laugh. "It sure is."

Then she says something that glues more affection for her to the inside of my chest. "I like that it's strange."

We step out onto the platform. I think she should let go of my arm, but she refuses. We're in between the subway rushes, so at least there are not many people around but we still get stared at. I try to be like Kite and not let it get to me.

Keeping my head in the clouds is difficult because I can't see the firmness of alley stones beneath my feet.

We step onto the train and she sits down, patting the seat beside her. I shake my head. She looks disappointed. I've already made a mistake, and we're not even there yet.

"Where are we going?" she asks, legs jittering a little.

I picked a place that might afford us some level of cover. "Chinatown."

She claps her hands loudly. "Oh, I've never been!" Putting up a hand to calm her, I can't help grinning at her excitement.

"Well, I have a feeling you'll like it." A man grimaces at us and I ignore him. I lean down, catching myself in the gold light of her eyes. "Just be patient with me. This is my first time." She smiles, teeth clanging. I catch her hope, slinging it around my wrist to check from time to time.

"Only if you'll allow me the same patience." I raise my eyebrows in surprise. *She's eighteen. She's a society girl. How can she have never dated before?* Picking up on my surprise, she says quietly, "You think my father let me date?"

The mood dries to cracks in the desert floor. I place my finger under her chin. She doesn't resist me, and her sad eyes connect with mine. "Okay. Since we're both new at this, let's set some rules. Number one, no talking about *him*."

She nods solemnly in agreement. "Number two..." She takes my hand in hers. "No avoiding physical contact."

I frown at that, but nod.

"Number three?" I ask, her hand feeling too right in mine. And too delicate.

She taps her chin. "Hm. Number three... What was it Frankie said?" Pushing out her lips, she vibrates like her little sister. Using a husky voice, she says, "Hev fun!"

I chuckle. "Sounds like a good plan."

She squeezes my hand, sending waves of summer through me. "It certainly does."

We get out at the right station and walk into the frozen city. It's not dark yet, and the neon lights of Chinatown are unlit and sugarcoated with mounds of snow. Kite holds my hand tightly as we walk, like she's scared I'll float away. I squeeze back. I'm trying my best to live in this moment. And trying not to fail her.

"So, there were never any boys?" I ask, wishing I could take the words back. I stare at the gritty white ground, embarrassed.

Giggling, she covers her mouth with her hand. "There were boys. I did go to a co-ed."

Yeah, I shouldn't have asked.

"Just no dates..." I guess.

She shakes her head, then leans it on my shoulder. "No dates."

I want to ask other questions. Because right now, my head is filled with a lineup of prep-school boys, all richer and better than me. They have prospects spilling from their tailored blazer pockets. When I think of them being close to her, my heartrate spikes. "No dates," I repeat. At least I get that. I get to be the first.

She says it very quietly. Apprehensively. "There's never been anyone worth writing home about until you, Hiro."

My chest fills with sweet, warm air, and I think maybe I will float away. I lean into her. Let the smell of her weakening perfume brush my cheek. *I'm worth writing home about.* We reach the entrance to the theater and study the posters and times. Our choices are Walt Disney's *Peter Pan* and *War of the Worlds*. "You can pick," I say, knowing what she'll choose.

"I don't really feel like death and destruction today." She points at the poster, running her finger over the words. "*At this very moment, spaceships from the beyond may be on their way to destroy our planet!*" She reads the rather long tagline in a dark and sinister voice and laughs.

I read the tagline for Peter Pan using the same kind of end-of-the-world serious voice, "*It will live in your heart forever!*" I hold my arm straight out in front of me like a zombie, walking jerkily toward her while pulling a scary face. She clutches her heart and descends into hysterical fits of laughter. It fulfils me in a way I've not felt before. Like making her laugh suddenly became my number-one priority.

Breathless, she leans against the poster and smiles, sending shots of starlight and moonbeams flurrying around me. "How did you manage to make such a sweet story like Peter Pan sound like a horror story?"

I shrug. "Pure talent." She knocks my shoulder lightly.

We make it to the ticket box, and the man inside doesn't give us a funny look at all. This is shocking to me, and I stumble as I say, "Two for Peter Pan, please." Sliding the money under the glass. Nodding, he breaks off the tickets. He looks like a dancing monkey in his red and gold vest. When he smiles, he shows that his teeth are in worse condition than a dancing monkey and I try not to stare. "Have a nice evening." He tips his hat.

I snatch the tickets like they're made of gold, and we enter the velvety theater. Two happy young people. Out for a 'nice evening'.

If this is all I get, it would almost be enough.

Chapter Twenty-five

Kite

Hiro buys me candy and popcorn. Handing it over while trying to smother his do-not-waste-this expression. We shuffle into the theater with other patrons. Most look more like him and less like me in this part of town. I think it helps him relax, shoulders dropping an inch. His face seems less stretched and tense and his eyes are not always looking for trouble.

I feel like I'm not quite touching the ground—like Wendy as she is splashed with fairy dust and lifts from the floor. It's all too much, and I'm scared I will want more.

We nestle into the seats, and curtains roll back slowly. The music begins to play, and we both suck in an awestruck breath. A painted London scene is revealed slowly. Velvet cushions at our backs and nothing stopping us from being a couple on a first date. It feels like the curtains open just for us, showing us a life possible. A way to take flight.

It is wonderful.

A dream. A dream. A dream.

And it becomes even more wonderful when Hiro tentatively stretches his arm behind me to rest it over my shoulders.

Oh, let me live in this moment forever.

I breathe in happy little sighs, alternately gobbling popcorn and candy until I feel like I could burst from salt and sweet. And I stare at him instead of the movie, watching his reaction to the lost boys and Wendy, John, and Michael Darling as they try to adapt to life in Neverland. His handsome face is calm, lit by bluish light.

Here in the dark, we are easy.

We are as light as feathers. We can best Hook, defeat the crocodile, and sail home on a magic pirate ship.

He breathes the same kind of tranquility as me, breaking off a piece to share.

I lay my ear on his chest, listening to the determined beat of his heart.

I know it can't always be like this, but the memory of this experience will live in my heart forever just as the poster promised. It will sustain me. Laughing, I touch my sternum.

Hiro leans down, his lips brushing my ear. I startle at the touch, shiver, see stars. "You okay?"

"Peachy," I whisper as he strokes my hair gently. Treats me like I'm not only precious but deeply desired.

"Me too." His voice like hot, poured coffee.

"Gosh! Don't you think Frankie is just like Tinkerbell?" I ask as we leave the dark cinema, blinking and filled with happy thoughts.

Hiro chuckles. "You know what? She really is."

I stomp my foot like Tink does after Peter Pan ignores her. It's just like Frankie when she feels like she's not being listened to. "And the temper…"

Hiro reaches for my hand. It's a small but significant gesture because it seems to come without thought. Without doubt. "Yes, the temper is pretty damn close."

"One of the lost boys reminded me of Kamo," I say more softly. A sad smile painting my face like the lick of brush. Maybe it was wrong to say it, but these things can't be buried. I can't go back to that kind of life.

Hiro smiles with sadness, too. "I know the one you mean. The one dressed like a skunk, right?" I forget. Hiro's not like that. He may be guarded but he has always been honest with me.

I squeeze his hand. "That's the one."

He swipes at his face, fog slipping from his mouth, and says, "I miss that kid."

I kiss his cheek. "I know you do."

He pats his pockets, seems to put aside the grief. The sadness pops up like a pretty weed, grabbing attention for a moment before it withers away. Only to return next spring. "Are you hungry?"

I nod eagerly, though I'm packed with popcorn and chocolate. "Did you have a place in mind?" People stream around us and out into the open air. It's nighttime now, and they all seem to be following the lantern light to delicious smells and language that sounds like hushed music. I jump up and down excitedly.

"I know a place," he says rather secretively.

I cover my mouth dramatically. "Ooh, intriguing!" He winks. And I try to keep up with him while simultaneously starting to melt.

He seems to know where he's going. My eyes lift to read the signs. A big one reading Golden Dragon Restaurant and Bar grabs my attention, and I pause to stare. The snake-like dragon winds through the letters, breathing fire with a long tongue. Mine is almost hanging out from all the stimulation, and Hiro puts a hand to my back, ushering me into a smaller place with no neon lights. There's just a simple hand-painted sign that reads *Chop Suey* in uneven black lettering.

It smells mouthwateringly unfamiliar and I float in on flavored steam, while Hiro sniggers behind me.

I wait at the door for the maître d, hands clasped in front of me. "You just sit here. It's not silver service or anything," Hiro says, walking past me.

We find a table and sit, creaking on plastic chairs. Mirrors reflect roasted ducks hanging from hooks through their necks in the window. Wielding giant cleavers, the chef skillfully chop the birds into small pieces. A man behind us lifts his eyes briefly, but his regard is merely curious. We don't garner the kind of attention we have in other places. If they have a problem, they're keeping it to themselves. The man draws in a snort that sounds full of mucous, and I try not to scrunch my nose in disgust.

I finally look at Hiro. He appears anxious. Hands knotted on the table, leaning in, and searching my eyes for approval. "Is this okay?"

I smile broadly and gesture wildly with my hands, drawing attention from the other patrons. "This is more than okay. It's magical!"

His eyebrows rise, and he shakes his head. "You're something else, Kite."

I take it as a compliment.

We are thrown some menus. I let Hiro order for us because I've never eaten Chinese food before, and I have no idea what any of it is. He orders egg rolls and pork chop suey and two cokes.

The server places chopsticks in front of Hiro and a fork in front of me.

It's the first separation, and I try not to make anything of it. Hiro's eyes darken one shade, and I look up at the small woman with a smile. "Can I try the chopsticks?"

She bows fast, then comes back with chopsticks.

There's no lifting the small slip of darkness in his eyes, but it doesn't bother me. I know this is the world we live in. We are an odd pair but that doesn't mean we shouldn't be together. We stand out, a bold pattern amongst a pile of beiges and neutrals. I think it makes us beautiful and unique. I know he thinks these things, too, but with the added painting of a target on our backs.

We are opposition and attraction. Seeming to collect electricity and create light shows across the sky.

I try to copy the way he holds the chopsticks. Smiling gently, he shakes his head, and I think I've managed to break him from his thoughts at least for a while. "No. No. You're doing it all wrong." He arranges my fingers, his touch charged. "See?"

He picks up a piece of meat with ease. Drops it into his mouth. I pick up a piece… and drop it on the table. We both giggle. "I think I'll just take the fork for now. Otherwise, we'll be here all night."

He swallows. "I'm not sure that's such a bad thing…" I bite my lip, thinking maybe I'll combust to ashes right here in Chinatown. "I'll teach you later. It took me while to get the hang of it, too. But I had a very patient teacher."

This promise of a future time gives me hope. "Someone taught you?" I ask.

"Yes. I was brought up in an American orphanage. I only learned how to use chopsticks in the camps. Kin's mother taught me." His face takes on a strange peace. A kind memory crossing his thoughts.

"She sounds like she was a really nice lady," I say, forking the delicious food and crunching on the egg roll, which explodes with flavor in my mouth.

He watches me with desert dust flying over his eyes. "She was. She was the first person to give me some sense of who I was and where I came from. Before her, everything was a locked-up secret. She gave me a tiny piece of Japan. I'll always be grateful to her for that." He swirls the food on his plate.

I place a hand over his. "If you ever wanted to learn more about your background, you could…"

I expect a dismissal. But he contemplates it for a moment. "Maybe one day…" His eyes wander over the character scrolls hanging from the walls. "What about you? Where's your family from?"

Leaning back, I blink. "I thought I knew, but it appears my mother had secrets she never shared with me. I know my father comes from a working-class English background. But the rest is a bit of a mystery."

"Do you want to know more?" he asks, and I purse my lips.

Maybe I did once, but it feels rather unimportant to me now. I'm building a new family and my past seems like history – something from an old dusty book. It doesn't hold much interest to me. "I know what I need to know to move forward. It's different for me since I know who my parents are/were and why they did what they did. For my sanity I think I need to leave the past where it is. Whereas, you've got a lot of holes to fill."

"That sounds a little weird."

I laugh. "Yes. I suppose it does."

We unfold each other like the napkins on the table as we learn new things about the other person. We are building a latticework of shared experience. The compassion and love growing between us is a little unsteady but it strengthens with every story we tell.

I'm getting to know Hiro the young man. Not the leader of the Kings, who is heavy with responsibility and hiding from the world. This side is young and funny and fresh to new things. Open to them. It's just another part of him that I embrace.

I've got an armful of reasons to love him now. It fulfils me and scares me at the same time because it will be even harder when he refuses me again.

Chapter Twenty-six

Hiro

I think I knew it would go well. Part of me dreaded it also. It strengthens the bandages that tie us together, and makes me want things. Like soft lips and warm breath on my face. Her hand always clasped in mine.

I shake my head.

If only the rest of the world would follow. Turn with us not away from us.

Chapter Twenty-seven

Kite

Is violence my signature? Is it in my blood? A calling, a clue. A welcome mat for men to brush their steel-capped boots on?

The lights of Chinatown are leery and bright but they act as a shelter. People take in the view instead of picking out differences. Faces are painted in red or gold reflections. Hiro sweeps my hand into his, pressing it to his heart. I feel the thrum and beat pulsing like love notes up my arm. I saw one other couple like us, and it gave me hope. His comfort in this place gives me hope, too. In the half light, he doesn't hide his eyes and face as he strolls more confidently. He soaks in the world rather than letting it push him to the shadows.

I turn to face him. Standing under a dragon. People walk around us. Not into us. "I've had a wonderful time tonight, Hiro. Thank you."

His eyebrows rise as he gazes at my flushed face and the closing distance between us. "You know what? So did I."

"You seem surprised." I frown and he traces the lines on my forehead with his finger, which is as rough as mermaid scales.

His touch moves down the side of my face, over my cheek, and to my neck. "I am surprised. I just thought this might be harder. That people would be more…" His hand rests on my pulse, which is fluttering like a lady's fan.

"More judgmental?" I offer.

"Yeah," he whispers, leaning down and brushing my ear with his lips. It's soft skin on soft skin. It's making me want.

I make a strange gasping sound and shiver. Snow melts into my stockings. He pulls back and says, "We should get home, before we…" I know he's about to say freeze to death, but he stops himself. The fresh memory of Kamo is as powdery and dangerous as the snow gathering on the streets.

I nod and he takes my hand as we cross the street, leaving the lights of Chinatown behind.

We hurry along as the temperature drops. Shoulder to shoulder, heads down, we move as quickly as we can under lamplight and neon signs.

At this late hour, people look like creeping ghouls across the white of the snow. I glance up from my frozen shoes to see a hull composed of bodies coasting toward us, laughing raucously and bumping each other in play. The men are drunk and happy.

Hiro tenses beside me. Removing his hand from mine, he remains close.

As they approach, we move to the wall of a building to let them pass. They don't seem to notice us until one of them sways and collides with Hiro, who helps stabilize the stranger with a brief touch. Their eyes connect. The strange light doing macabre things to the man's face. He smiles, slurring a little as he thanks us. But as he gets a closer look, he begins to squint and frown.

It's a strange strike-of-lightning moment. After a twist of the face, there's a moment of recognition and a flash of hate. The man straightens suddenly. Violently. Hiro steps backward, pulling me with him. Backs against the wall.

The man snarls. Hands scrunching into gloved fists. But then the group calls to him, and he releases his stare. He gallops lopsidedly to join his friends like he is standing on the deck of a boat. They move around the corner, their voices hushing. All the breath I was holding escapes in one large sigh.

Hiro faces me, running his hands over my shoulders and brushing the snowflakes from my coat. "Are you okay?" he asks, words coming out harsh. I shudder forcefully, the cold really starting to bite into my bones. That, paired with the sense of dread, has my whole body trembling. He grabs the edges of my coat and tugs them together, pulling it tight over my chest. "You're really feeling the cold." Eyes like navy nights caress me. "We should get out of here."

Starting to remove his coat, his concern for me is so sweet. Even when he frowns, he looks handsome. I reach out and take his coat collar, intending to pull it closed and stop him from taking it off. But instead, I hastily pull him to me. His mouth collides with mine just for a short magical second. It's enough to warm me all the way down to my toes, which feel like they've slipped into cloud slippers.

I close my eyes dreamily. *He is...*

He is ripped from my arms, and he lands hard in a pillow of dirty snow. It flies at my face, stinging like sand and grit. "What do think you're up to, you dirty yellow bastard?" He spits on the ground. "You think you can take our women? You need to stick to your own kind."

I cover my mouth as the shadow of a man shoves Hiro to the ground. He makes a horrible noise as words are knocked from his lungs. But he quickly recovers and kicks the drunken shadow in the chest, sending him flying into the stairs behind us. The man growls and groans but doesn't get up.

The other men come running and I do the only thing I can think of: I scream.

I scream as loud as I can. The few people on the street look our way, beginning to turn toward us. I swing my bag around, the volume of my voice increasing as I call for help. The men stop a few yards in front of us, and I put my hand up. "Don't you come any closer," I warn.

I kneel beside Hiro, who's cradling his jaw and wearing this awful, heart destroying and defeated expression. I help him up. He slings his arm over my shoulder and we run across the street, just as a cop car rolls past us.

The men hoist their friend up and scatter, muttering words I don't want to hear. Words I don't want Hiro to hear.

But it's too late. I know just as his bruises are growing, so are all the doubts he had about us.

The ride home is silent. Just the rattle of the cars to keep us company.

And I just *pray and pray and pray* that this one idiot hasn't torn it all down. These men full of hatred are like the sea dragging its fingers into a sandcastle. Stealing pieces, pulling out the foundations. Always seeking to destroy good things.

Hiro is in his own world that he won't show me. I sense skyscrapers of anger and doubt being constructed in that head of his.

We enter the tunnel to the sounds of sleeping Kings. There are so many words that need to be said, but we can't say them yet. Hiro holds my hand loosely, and we pick our way over the sleeping children. Leading me to the back of the tunnel. "Come with me," he whispers, taking me down to the railways tracks and tugging me backward as far as they go. Then he releases my hand, and I feel like he's trying to cut something between us. But it's resistant to the blade. It can't be severed that easily.

I step toward him, my hand out. We are folded under the shadow of the platform. Krow lit a candle for us, but it's right at the entrance. "Are you hurt?" I ask in a small voice.

Shaking his head, he laughs strangely. "I'm fine." He's not fine. He's furious.

"You're not fine." My chin sinks to my chest. "Please, Hiro, don't let this ruin our date. It was good. *So* good. Apart from those drunk idiots, it was wonderful."

He huffs and paces. Stepping over the tracks and onto the ground repeatedly. I watch his feet pace in agitation. "Don't you see? It's always going to be like that. Wherever we go. It's always *been* like that for me. And now I'm dragging you into it, too." His arms flap at his sides.

I clench my teeth. Tears threatening. "You didn't drag me anywhere. I willingly walked into your life. I love your life."

Again, he laughs; it's bitter and gravely. Hard to swallow. "You're too dreamy for your own good. You're not being realistic." He throws his hands in the air as if summoning clouds. "Hell, neither was I. I think I just got so caught up in my feelings that I forgot the truth."

"And what is the truth?" I say, feeling my own anger growing. *Why does everything have to be practical and realistic?*

"That this world won't make space for you and me, Kite." His voice splashes like the last of the water. His huff is replaced with exhaustion.

I'm not that easily dissuaded. "Then we make our own space. We carve it out. We blow it up. We don't let the world tell us what we can and can't have."

I hear his whispered frustrations and see his hands thrown up in anger, but I don't feel threatened. I feel completely safe. This is why he is worth fighting for. This and so many other reasons.

"You say you love my life. But that feeling will fade when people are always staring at you. When they make you feel like you're less than human. It will eat at you. It will change you."

I can't keep up with his movement and I sit on the tracks, my skirts fanning out around me like the spokes of the sun. "I love your life because I love you, Hiro. I love you and everything that comes with you. The Kings, the tunnel, the work. The fact that you're a half-Japanese orphan. Everything. You won't give this a chance." I gesture between us. "You need to give me a chance." I speak to the tracks. They lead to a dead end, but there's always something on the other side. Always.

He freezes, standing over me, chest heaving. He offers his hands and pulls me up. "Oh Kite, I love you, too, but..."

I don't let him finish. I don't want to hear all the reasons why he shouldn't love me, and I shouldn't love him. Bringing my mouth to his, I kiss him passionately. Clumsily. With so much heat and need that we stumble until his back hits the lip of the platform above us.

His kiss is filled with hunger but also sadness. A pressure of pain that he can't let go. I want to take it for him. I want to lay it down on the tracks and let it be obliterated.

I want. I want. I want...

Him.

Breathless, we break apart reluctantly. More words hang on the other side of this kiss. But he loves me. He said it. And the first words that come out of my mouth are, "Marry me."

"No."

"But you love me."

"Yes"

"Then marry me," I demand.

"No, Kite." A burning sigh. "Have you even thought about what marriage would be like for us?" he asks. He waits only a beat for an answer and then answers himself. "I have."

I'm still pressed against his chest. I'm not moving. He's not pushing me away. Not my body anyway. "You have?"

His nose touches mine. I want to cry for the agony of this moment. For how brief our pleasure is compared to the pain that follows. "Of course I have. What about children? Have you thought about what their lives would be like?" This only makes me smile. Which was probably not the aim.

I picture children, dark skin with honey eyes. Or pale with dark blue eyes. Or some other stunning mix of the two of us. "Our children would be beautiful."

He frowns, his arms wrapped around my waist. "They would also be a curiosity."

"They would be unique. They would have challenges but they would be so loved. That's the difference. You'd be there to help them. And so would I."

"But life would be harder for them." There's a sliver of the unconvinced in his voice. Like maybe he hears me.

Gazing at his face, I can't help but see the many years of abuse and being looked down upon have scratched deep scars into his heart. I understand that. But we can't be afraid to walk a different path. We have to keep moving forward. "Life is hard. But if we let the world dictate how we live it, we might as well give up. Change is good. It's necessary. Otherwise, we just stop."

His mind opens and closes. Hears me, but then lets years of experience cover his ears. "I don't want to be the first one. The damn flagship for interracial marriage."

I take a deep breath in. "If everyone thought this way, nothing would ever change. Love changes the world. Courage makes its stick. If the options are to be with you and have a tougher life or to not be with you and have a slightly easier one, than I choose you. I don't want a life without you. Do you want a life without me?

He shakes his head. "No." Raking that hand through his hair.

His heart beats against mine. "Then it shouldn't matter how hard our life will be. It will be worth it."

"I just can't marry you, Kite. It's not fair." I see want in his eyes. I hear sacrifice in his voice.

I kiss him again. Softer. Letting our lips linger together as I talk. "Hiro, marry me," I whisper against his mouth. "I won't ask you again."

My heart's already broken. And I know what his answer will be, but I am brave. I am here with him, and he makes me feel like I'm the planet that could occlude the sun, trapping the light, so only I can decide where it will shine.

"No. I'm sorry, Kite. I can't marry you."

Chapter Twenty-eight

Hiro

Marry me, she said. And I said no. *Again.* When almost every single part of me except this one sliver of my heart wanted to say yes. I've dashed my hopes and thrown them like a sack of kittens off a bridge. She won't ask me again. *It's how it should be, right?* People like me aren't supposed to get what they want.

Even though her heart holds me together and her view of the future is intoxicating, it doesn't fill real. It's like a painting in an art gallery that I can only view from afar while wondering what the artist was truly thinking. Kite is the artist, and I wish I could think the way she does.

A splash of her color crosses my vision. Playing children look up as I walk through the door. They run to me screaming, 'Daddy,' as I hang my hat. It's a fantasy and so unreal. The world she talks about would have to start with people like us, and I'm not sure I'm ready for the pioneer life.

We've fought so hard just to get to this place.

And I'm tired of fighting.

I think if she'd gone back to her room, it would have destroyed me. But her heart is bigger than most, which means it can take more hurt than most, too. She lies with her back to me, knees up and restless. Tonight, she sleeps like she's a breath away from attack which is what it must have been like for her every night in that brownstone. She's not always like this with me, but I guess she has a reason to be tense tonight. I ruined our date. Maybe I ruined everything.

I smile thinking about my hands on hers, trying to show her how to use chopsticks. She is so willing to try to be with me, and I just slammed the door in her face.

Kettle, what's wrong with you, man? Kin would say.

I sit up. Agitated. *The world is what's wrong with me.*

And what the hell does the world have to do with you and Kite?

I don't know.

My head hits the pallets stacked behind me, and another memory crosses my mind. Kin telling me we can't do this forever. Me never wanting to acknowledge that truth.

I'm stuck. I don't want to lose her, but I'm scared of all the things that could go wrong if I marry her. That fear might be the thing that finally pushes her away.

I stare up, picturing the grand arch of the ceiling. This tunnel saved us. The idea of leaving it feels like abandoning the only thing keeping me steady. It has always been the one constant I could count on. In here, I am a King and I am free.

But I'm also hiding.

Slapping a hand over my face, I drag it down, trying to stop the whirlwind of thoughts. I need to sleep.

A cough comes from across the room. Kite stirs, and I pat her shoulder. "I'll go."

Mumbling, she pulls the blanket over her head. "Kay."

I lay my coat over her shivering body, then stroke her hair. It hurts to touch her. *Does it hurt her to be touched?*

I find my way in the dark, stumbling across that space between the two rooms. A small, sharp thing collides with my legs and sniffs. "I cain't sleep," Frankie says a little too loudly.

"Sh!" I whisper as her pokey little hands find my waist and wrap around it.

She wheezes a little. "I need ma inhaler," she says into my stomach.

Patting her head, I tell her to wait while I fetch a candle.

I light it and we search for the inhaler, careful not to wake Kelpie, who's curled up at the foot of the bed. She points it out and we retreat to the back of the tunnel, away from everyone.

"Can you help me?" she asks, blue eyes searching mine.

I nod and smile, setting the candle down. "Sure thing, kid." She shows me what to do as she takes deep hollow-sounding breaths. Slowly, her wheezing begins to ease.

She crosses her legs and sits facing me, scrutinizing my face in a curious way. Tilting and tracing my features. "I love ma sister," she whispers hoarsely.

The love blooms like a powerful bubble from her chest. "I know you do." I stare at the ground, picking at loose mortar with my fingernail. "I love her, too."

Giggling, she crosses her arms. "I know you do, too." Then, more seriously, she says, "So why're you fightin'? You shouldn't be fightin'."

My eyes drop again. Her stare is like a tractor beam. I don't know how to mask the truth when she looks at me like that. "You heard us?"

She nods up, down, up, down. Her knees jut out like the angles of a set square. "Everyone heard you." She pokes my leg sharply.

"I'm sorry."

Suddenly, she springs up excitedly and taps my head like I'm the young child. "Wait here!" Before I can stop her, she's disappeared into the dark. I wait, hoping she's not woken Kite or the others.

She returns, flapping a piece of paper in front of me. She sits down with a thud before dropping it in my lap. It's a picture of me, Kite, and the others, all holding hands like we're a family. Over our heads is a roof. We're all smiling and standing inside a real house.

I sigh, the image breaking into smaller, more easily absorbed pieces that try to work their way into my heart. "Thank you, Kricket." She beams when I call her that.

I trace our round, out-of-proportion heads. The big, gooey smiles on our faces. "You can be heppy," she says super seriously. "If you married ma sister, you could be heppy."

"Maybe," I murmur.

"Write down your wish, Hiro," she says, her smile spreads thin like a dying sunset. Colors clinging to the clouds.

She helps me write the characters in tiny print. The words Home *and* Family.

She pats my head. "That's a very good wish."

She writes Love *and* Health *on her paper, and it makes my chest ache. She will only get one of those wishes.*

We fold them into tiny stars, then put them in a jar with the rest. I saw the words the other prisoners had written. Freedom. Peace. Safety.

Simply wishes for people who have had everything taken away from them.

"Will it come true?" I ask.

Smoothing her dress, she stares down at her ink-smudged fingers. "The wish is the first step. We make it come true by our will."

I hold up Kricket's drawing. "Can I teach you something?"

She smiles and nods. "Teach me what?" Her head tipping from side to side. Never still. Always alert.

I begin folding her picture. At first, she gasps and tries to stop me. "I'm not going to damage it, I promise."

This little girl trusts me, which is amazing in the first place considering what she's been through. That she wants me to be part of her family is even more incredible. My affection for her grows as I see how sweet and loving she can be, just like her sister, though more angular and mischievous.

I place a paper star on her knee. "For you, little Kricket."

She stares down at it as it toddles on her jiggling knee, and then back up at me. "What is it?"

"It's a wish."

She toys with it, treating it like it's fragile and may disintegrate at her touch. "A wish?"

I nod. "A wish I'm trying to find the will to make true."

She pokes at the corners.

I understand that love is like this. Folding yourself over and into another. Creasing and compromising until you've made something beautiful.

Closing her hand over the star, she yawns, scrunching up and laying her head in my lap. Soon her eyes have closed, and her breath has returned to its rattling but sound state.

Scooping her up, I take her back to bed.

She keeps a tight hold on the star.

Keep it safe for me, kid.

Chapter Twenty-nine

Hiro

The morning starts with an awkwardness and… an aching. I see it in her eyes the moment they open, and she flushes beneath my gaze. Color like a red mist, and then her face tightens and the blush disappears. Knees going to her chest.

I touch her cheek, pushing her hair behind her ear. "I'm going to see Kin today. Would you like to come?"

She stands very suddenly, grabbing something from her bag and tucking it into her pocket. "I, um, I… will you excuse me?" She hurries to where the makeshift bathroom is.

Sitting with my elbows on my knees, I wait for her return, starting to regret everything I said to her last night. I let the outside world get to me. Again. I should be stronger than this.

The boys are shuffling out for the day. I make sure they're all wearing gloves and scarves and coats, warning them not to stay out past daylight. They mutter and grunt and make promises I hope they'll keep. Kamo's death sits on their shoulders, cautioning them to cover up, stay warm and above all else, come home before dark.

When Kite finally comes back from the bathroom, it's just Kricket and me left in the tunnel. I stand as she approaches. She walks straight past me and folds up on the bed, looking a little pale. A little uncomfortable. "Are you okay?" I ask.

Kricket jumps on the bed beside her, and Kite shoots her a disparaging look. "Please Frankie, not now. I'm not feeling well."

I kneel. She keeps her forearm pressed over her middle, and she's breathing funny. "Are you ill?" I ask, putting a hand to her forehead.

She shakes her head. "What's wrawng, Nor-ah?" Kricket grabs her sister's hip and shakes it like she's trying to wake a giant, earning a gentle slap.

Kite's eyes connect with mine and she whispers, redness rising in her cheeks. "I, um… I have my…" She pats her stomach.

"Your stomach hurts. Maybe we should take you to a doctor." Rolling her eyes, she grimaces.

"Hiro. I just got my monthly visitor." She speaks to me like I'm dumb, and it takes me far too long to understand what she's saying. When I do, I blanch. Embarrassed that she had to spell it out for me.

"Monthly visitor?" Kricket shouts. "Who's visiting?"

Kite groans again. "No one, Frankie. That's not what I meant…" Her voice trails.

I grit my teeth and come closer, battling against my own discomfort. "Do you need anything?"

She shakes her head, pressing it into her pillow. She's clearly in a lot of pain, and Frankie climbing all over her isn't helping. "Frankie, please stop." She waves her hand listlessly.

My brows knot. I have little to no experience with this, but I don't like that she's in so much pain. "Are you sure you're okay?" I ask. "Is this normal? You seem like you're in a lot of, um, distress."

She glances up, mouth pursed. Still beautiful even when her face is scrunched, and her skin is sweat sheened. She is mortified and exhausted and being pummeled by her clueless little sister. "I'm fine. You go see Kin. I'll just rest here for a while. The pain doesn't usually last very long."

I can tell Frankie's working her last nerve, and I scoop the little insect off the bed. "How about I take you with me, little Kricket? Give your big sister some peace and quiet."

Kite looks at me with pure gratitude.

I dress Kricket, help her attach her hearing aid, and we leave, though I don't feel confident about the decision. I worry about the way we left things last night and how unwell she seems. But she pretty much demands we leave her alone. I walk out with a stone in the shape of a wedding ring in my stomach.

Chapter Thirty

Kite

This is normal. This is normal. This is normal.

The pain comes in rippling waves as my stomach knots like a fist. The intense sensation blares angrily at me like the pulsing aftermath of a beating, making me feel nauseous.

I roll to my side, breathing in too fast, not breathing out at the same pace. My face creased. My toes pointed.

Blood seeps through my dress. I jump up. Feel dizzy, but I will not soil the bed. I grab clothes to go to the bathroom to change again.

The blood flow is heavy. And though my monthly is never really 'monthly' and has always been unpredictable, it's never been like this. I try to remember when it last came, and can't. It could be over two months.

I lie back down, try to lay flat like a board instead of curling into a ball.

It will pass. It will pass. It will pass. It always passes.

I lie in pain for what seems like hours. Cramping. My lips dry. My face permanently crinkled. My heart clenches at the events of last night. It wants to wrap around the good parts and set aside the bad. But the pain is reaching out and slapping me, taking my attention. It can't take away one thing, though. He said he loved me. I hold those words like a key in my fist, not letting them go.

Another wave rolls through me, unsympathetically washing away any sense of happiness. I find Hiro's watch. It's been four hours. It never lasts this long.

This is not normal.

The idea of Hiro and Frankie finding me like this is unacceptable. I roll from the bed. Change my underclothes again, then dress for outside.

Something's wrong.

I am grim, and I am gathered. I can take care of this myself.

And I know where to go.

Dr. Keneally, our family physician, is not exactly someone I wholly trust, but I don't feel I have much of an option right now.

I claw my way onto the subway and lower myself onto a seat, gripping the metal pole as another wave of pain hits me like a shuddering earthquake. Like I'm coming apart violently. Not stitch by stitch, more like a violent tear. Crossing my legs, I grimace.

An old man leans down and speaks to me, his voice garbled by my lack of concentration on anything other than holding my body together. I think he asks me if I'm *quite all right*. I try to feign a smile, attempting to move as little as possible. He backs away carefully, hands fanning the earth, like I'm a wild animal giving birth, and sits down opposite me. Too watchful.

I bow my head and pull my hair to form a curtain around my face, hiding as best I can. But the connection between my head and my body is breaking. I am running on panic and pain. I fear what's happening to me, and I clutch my stomach under my coat.

Walking briskly away from the subway station, my legs somehow perform this amazing feat. I hope I don't get lost since it's been a long time since I've visited our family doctor. Not since before Mother died. I place my hand on the edge of a garbage can to steady myself. It rattles and burns my palms with cold. Embarrassment drives me forward. The idea of blood coming through my skirt in the street is too horrifying to contemplate.

Clenching my jaw, I press on. Using every stationary object in front of me like a climber's notch. Throwing fingers out like grappling hooks. *Anything, Anything. Anything.* To get me closer.

When the black-and-white sign for Doctor Keneally's practice swings in the wind in front of my eyes, I want to lay down on the welcome mat and die. It sings to me in squeaky tones. *You made it.* My eyes threaten to spill. I want someone else to take care of me. *Please, just for a few minutes. Can someone hold my wings? Fold them over and pat them free of dirt. Store them in the coat closet and lead me to a bed.* But of course, that's not going to happen. I shoulder the door open. The receptionist looks up at me in shock, and I manage, "My name is Nora Deere. Help me. Please," before falling to my knees and vomiting on carpet the color of cool, wet moss.

Chapter Thirty-one

Hiro

Kricket doesn't leave me much room for thought. Like a parent pulling their child back from an icy pond, every time my mind dips into the events of the last twenty-four hours, she pokes me or leans over to look out the window, yanking me back into the present. She stands up suddenly at every stop, eager to disembark. I pull her arm gently back to sitting, worried about how strange we are as traveling companions. How everyone must be looking at us. And then I curse under my breath, realizing this is the kind of thinking that got me here in the first place. It doesn't bother Kricket. It never bothered Kite. *So why does it sit like a cold shadow over my back?*

I hunch, feeling it wrap around me cruel and icy. It comes from years of not belonging to anyone. I have lost too many who accepted me into their lives. I can't quite believe this one will stick. If I start to, it will disappear...

Kricket bounces in her seat. "Kettle, when're we gonna get there?" she asks, eyes bright as crystal. Nose and cheeks red from the cold. She leans into me, and I have to force myself to stay still and not lean away. *Just stop. Even if people are staring, you can't let them get to you.*

Her hair is like flames caught at sunrise. I rest my chin on her head. "Not long now."

"And we're going to visit Kin?" she asks huskily, checking the details. I nod. "And he's your brother, kinda?" I nod again. "Do you think Nor-ah's okay?"

An arrow to the heart that I don't know how to defend.

"She said she was okay." I press my lips together, worried. She told me to leave. Maybe I shouldn't have listened. But we're hours from home now.

She rolls her eyes exaggeratedly. "She always says she's *okay*. You're the same, you and Nor-ah. Always sayin' you're okay, when there's really somethin' goin' on you don't wanna tell me."

Pouting, her hands lock together in her lap. "I've told you everything, Kricket."

She frowns, mulls my words over, and nods. "Mebbe." Then she kicks her legs and presses them against the back of the seat in front, causing the person sitting in it to pitch forward.

They turn around and glare, and I put my hand up. "Sorry. It's been a long drive. She's a bit restless." I force a grin. The woman huffs and turns around. Her intricately wound hair looks like a gray and white double helix. I imagine it took some work. Putting my hands over Kricket's legs, I try to still her. "Is there something in particular you want to know?" I ask, trying to distract her.

"I wanna know why grown-ups make everythin' so hard?" She crosses her arms, staring out the window at the endless white with the occasional crystalized tree branch.

I laugh out loud for two reasons. One, because I never really considered myself a grown-up. And two, because if I could answer that question, I'd probably be able to solve not only my own problems but also the world's.

I knock her shoulder. "Let me tell you about the movie your sister and I went to last night." I start describing Peter Pan, and her body seems to lull. She is engrossed in my story until we pull up to the stop near Craftman House.

The screen door opens before we reach the end of the garden path. Miss Anna moves as delicately as a ribbon on the wind. "It's good to see you! Your brother is outside, stubborn man." She claps. Bending down from her lengthy height to lock eyes with Kricket and smile with sugary teeth. "And who's this little cherub?" She places a long claw-like finger under Kricket's chin and peers into the child's sparkling eyes, which narrow at the intense scrutiny.

The little girl steps backward into me, pressing against my stomach. Her vertebrae sticking into me like pebbles lined up on a rock wall. Putting my hands on her shoulders, I squeeze gently. The kid puts too much faith and trust in me. I feel like I've barely earned it. "This is Kricket." Kricket gives me a strange look. "Or Frankie..."

Miss Anna unfolds fast like a mouse trap and puts her hands on her hips. "Well, which is it, child?" She's playing, but I'm not sure Kricket understands the difference.

Hands behind her back, she whispers, "Kricket, I guess."

"You okay, kid?" I ask, whispering in her ear.

"She looks like ma mommy." She bows her head solemnly, and I pat her back.

"Miss Anna and Miss Lake are real nice ladies," I reassure her. "They've taken good care of Kin."

She nods, but still seems off.

The smell of cigarettes wafts through the house and mixes with savory scents like gravy and roast meat. We walk down the hallway as Miss Anna explains the type of crickets or cicadas they get in summertime at Craftman. Kricket nods along quietly. It's the most subdued she's ever been, and I start to worry she's also feeling unwell. I put a hand to her forehead, but she wiggles away from my touch. It makes me think of Kite, scrunched in a ball on my bed, clutching her stomach.

Before we head to the backyard, I squat down and find Kricket's eyes. "Was that normal for Nora?" My eyes drop to the ground, which is wet from muddy boots and trekked in snow. "I mean with her…" My voice drops even lower. "Monthly."

Kricket shrugs, tapping the side of her face. Her hearing aid squeals when someone turns up the radio in the other room. "Whaddya mean?"

Miss Anna sails past us. She's helping a couple of the men cook a meal. I hear Miss Lake talking loudly in the other room. Melted sleet is soaking into my good trousers. "I mean is it normal for her to be in that much pain?"

At this, Kricket seems to shrink. Curling in on herself like a tapped pill bug as it armors itself by rolling into a tight ball. Her eyes are wet, and she lets her hair fall in front of her face. It's getting dirtier and stringier. It makes her look more like a King, and it's also a very Kite-like thing to do. "It's normal. Nora was always sufferin' from pain." It's like a blast of fire to my face. A dirty slap. It cuts me in a new way over the scab of old pain. Because of course she was. Her father beat her. There would be no way for Kricket to discern between monthly pain and pain from being battered and broken. I swallow hard, feeling a familiar darkness of pure hatred sink inside me. But the thought of Kite, her toughness and her hope in the face of evil, pulls me back from the edge of anger.

I feel her pain. I just need to take on her strength as well.

Kricket stares at me with wide eyes. Waiting. I scruff her hair as I would one of the Kings, and she smiles sweetly. "Your sister is pretty incredible."

She then grins with all her teeth and some extra shine of white that comes from inside. "Dat's why you should marry her!"

A voice I would rather not hear right in this moment combines with the rusty creak of the back door. Kin shakes snowflakes from his hair as he winks at Kricket. "Who's getting married?"

I wish there was a crack in the floorboards. Since I'm pretty lean, I'm sure I could slip right through with a bit of wriggling. Anything to avoid the coming conversation.

Chapter Thirty-two

Kite

Arms arrange me on a narrow white bed in another room. And I'm filled with relief as I am fussed over and cared for. A nurse strokes my head and says, "The doctor will be in to see you shortly, Miss Deere." She hands me a couple of pills, which I swallow without hesitation. Anything to ease this pain. She looks at me with sympathy and knowing. As any woman would.

I say softly through cracked lips. "Something's not right."

She smiles, dark eyes with an unfolded fan of wrinkles to frame them. Her gray hair neatly curled under a white bonnet. "Well, dear, it's your body. You know it best. If something's not right, then something's not right. We'll get to the bottom of it."

I could almost cry for thankfulness, for the softness in her voice and her surety. The doctor comes in, head down, staring at notes on a clipboard like they hold the cure. His moustache reminds me of a cheap plastic comb. When he glances up, he frowns at me. "Nora. We haven't seen you in quite some time."

I try not to growl as I remember how he set my broken arm and treated my deeper cuts. All without question. That's how they get away with it. Don't ask. Don't tell. "No, Doctor. Not for a while." I prop myself up on my elbows to find his eyes. "Not since I turned eighteen and am a legal adult," I say pointedly, reminding him of his obligation to keep my visit private.

If he's surprised, he doesn't show it. He just nods and rakes his eyes over my awkward, rolled-up position. "So, are you having reproductive problems?" I give him a quizzical look, and he points at my stomach. The pills are starting to kick in and I begin to relax, a fuzzy warmth crawling over my body like the sun over a wilting field. "Am I right to assume this is something to do with your menstruation?"

I turn scarlet and nod. The nurse pipes in, "She said it's not normal for her to be in this much pain, Doctor."

He gives her a sideways *be quiet* look, then pats my hand. "All right then, Nora, tell me what doesn't feel normal and *I*, your doctor, will tell you if it's anything to be concerned about."

I try to leave my embarrassment at the door, barely keeping myself from wincing when I'm examined. And I try very hard not to panic when he suddenly straightens and leaves the room.

He returns with a large device on a wheeled cart. His face has changed from disinterest to interest.

I don't want to ask. I don't want to ask. I don't want to ask.

No one talks to me. They run an instrument over my stomach, staring intently at grainy images on the screen. They press and prod and make strange noises that sound like disbelief.

I have to ask.

"Doctor, what do you think is wrong?" I ask, staring up at the perforated ceiling tiles. My hands clasped neatly over my chest.

He clears his throat and startles, almost like he forgot there was a person attached to the symptoms.

The nurse's face has gone from kind sympathy to pity. "Does she need an x-ray?" she asks, her eyes on the screen, which just looks like a mass of spider webs and black spots. I think of the old woman who swallowed a spider, letting out a nervous giggle.

She swallowed the spider to catch the fly. I don't know why she swallowed the fly. I guess she'll...

He breathes in deeply, and I wait.

He breathes out loudly through his nose like a displeased bull, and I wait.

What is it? The silence is unbearable. The things I'm concocting in my head are probably far worse than anything he could say. He pats my leg. "No, that won't be necessary, Nurse. Nora, how about you get dressed? Take your time. Sylvia will bring you to my office to discuss the results of the ultrasound when you're ready."

The pain has eased. The bleeding has settled, too. Maybe it was just a painful and heavy monthly. Maybe I'm overreacting. The nurse, Sylvia, helps me up. "Are your periods usually regular?" she asks. "Once every twenty-eight days or so?"

My voice is the patter of rain hitting a hot sidewalk. Promise that evaporates. "No. Not always. Sometimes I can go months without anything. And it's not usually as painful as this. Is that bad?" I lean forward. My eyes moistening. I'm not an idiot. I can tell there's something wrong.

She shakes her head a little too vehemently. "No. No. It's not bad. Do you usually have pain in your abdomen between periods?"

I have had pain almost every day of my life for as long as I can remember. My head sways sorrowfully from side to side, no.

The nurse seems confused. Like she's searching the rubble for a survivor. A clue. "Have you been in a car accident recently?"

The question seems simultaneously ridiculous and terrifying. "No. I have not. Why would you ask me that?"

She stops then, hands me my clothing and a stack of sanitary products. "I think it best you speak to Doctor Keneally. He will be able to explain things further. Has your pain settled?"

"Yes," I manage through trembling lips.

"That's good then." But her expression says nothing good.

She leaves me alone in this cold room. White and silver and sterile.

I suddenly wish Hiro were here with me but he's not. I am alone and I must face this. Alone.

I pull my coat tight, walking through one door and into another. A curtain opening on the next act of my story.

The man in a white coat sits behind his desk, looking all kinds of sorry. He is now the messenger.

I want to run.

I have to stay.

"Miss Deere…" he begins.

Don't say it. Don't say it. Don't say it.

They are sharp in my mind. Bright faces, dark skin, and blue eyes. A boy and a girl. They play on the fancy rug in our sitting room, paper strewn around in a pattern. Like autumn leaves beneath a maple tree. Crayons held in chubby hands. They look at me with love. They call me momma. I sweep them into my arms and their warmth is intoxicating. They are made from pure love. They break barriers just by being. They are clear, and they are beautiful. They are part me and part Hiro. They are a dream. They are everything.

And now, they are nothing.

Chapter Thirty-three

Hiro

Kin is like rain to a battling flower. Petals turning in and sheltering from a harsh climate. And the moment Kricket and he connect, I know there'll be no breaking their bond. He winks at her and offers a hand, which she takes. "Is this the young lady you're going to marry?" he asks, teasing and holding her arm up until she's on her tiptoes. He raises an eyebrow. "She's terribly short."

Kricket giggles and swings her skirts, clasping them in her other hand. When Kin releases her, she pokes him in the chest. He wobbles on his haunches. "Yer Kin."

I appraise my brother. He looks well. Flush to his skin. Pants wet to the knees. Same determined and devilish expression on his face. He pokes her right back. "Hey, I remember you. You're the suspender snapper!" He works his hands up the wall until he can stand. I offer an arm, but he refuses. "I've been looking for you for a while now! I owe you a snap." He growls, but it's a toothless bear, more huggable than scary.

Kricket pokes out her tongue and he laughs, deep and short like timpani. I think maybe I've escaped the interrogation. As I start toward the lounge, my neck is caught by my collar as Kin yanks me backward with impressive strength.

"Whoa, little brother! I asked you a question." His tone is teasing, but his eyes hold a dark flash of seriousness.

Somehow, Kricket has managed to shuffle over without me noticing and they stand next to each other, giving me disappointed glares. They've formed a hunting party, and I'm the quarry. "Yeah-eah," Kricket sings. "He ask-ed you a question."

Kin slings his arm over Kricket's shoulders, clucks his tongue, and addresses her, "What are we going to do with him?"

Shaking her autumn-leaf hair, she replies, "I dunno, Kin. I really dunno." Enjoying this comradery. The two ganging up on me and peck, peck, pecking like pigeons on a crust of bread.

This took a very sudden turn. I gulp.

Kin limps forward, leading us to a sitting room with armchairs and sofas from every era since furniture existed. He collapses on a lounge with Kricket and points at the grand armchair beside it, swirling and high-backed like a throne. Though I feel anything but royalty right now. "Sit. I think it's time we had *the talk*." He says it with mirth, but there are messages and warning behind it.

"The talk?" I repeat, more nervous than I should be.

Kin nods and Kricket copies him, bobbing her head like she's sitting in the jury of my love life. "Yes. *The talk*. The talk about how you don't think you deserve to be happy. How you love that girl, and it's time you damn well did something about it!"

Oh, that talk.

I place my hands on my knees and brace myself as two of the dearest people to my heart, other than Kite, rip me to shreds.

Kin reaches over, nearly falls from his seat, and slaps my thigh hard. "What the h-e-l-l are you doing, man?"

Kricket leans over and smacks my leg, too, then crosses her arms. "Yeah, what the hell, man?" We both raise an eyebrow, and she scowls. "Jest coz I've got hearin' problems doesn't mean I cain't spell." She rolls her eyes.

Kin laughs, clapping his hands together. "Oh, I like her. I like her very much!"

She blushes rose pink, crossing her feet at the ankles. She's trying to look demure, but the intense glare is ruining the effect.

They both stare silently as I gather myself. As I try to brush my thoughts into a single pile I can sort through.

Kin blows out a frustrated sigh. "What's stopping you? Is it that you think she'll say no?"

I smile, remembering her kneeling, looking up at me with earnest eyes the color of burnt butter. Her words. *I love you, Hiro.* "Considering she's already asked me to marry her twice, I doubt it."

Kin growls low and irritated. "Twice?" Then he holds up two fingers. "Twice!" His head falls in his hands as he mumbles, "Oh, this is worse than I thought." I know he's struggling to understand because even if he didn't love her, he would have said yes. It's a ticket out, and he's wondering how on earth I could be so stupid. "Let me guess, you said no because it's not *the way.*" There's no use arguing with him since he knows me too well. "And then you said no again because you're worried about how it looks coz she's rich and you're, well…" He points at me, finger hanging in the air for too long. A kite that's losing the wind.

"A King," I say with some of the usual pride sucked out of it.

Kin shakes his head. "No, Kettle. You need to face the music. You're a street kid. You're a half-Japanese, half-white street kid with a dangerous, s-h-i-t job and a mob of other street kids you've pledged to look after." He runs a hand through his lengthening hair. "You do everything for everyone, yet never get anything out of it."

I look up at the ceiling, peeling wallpaper curls around a chandelier that's missing half its crystals. It hangs at a loose angle. It makes me want to stand on a table to even up the remaining crystals so it sits square. "You hit the nail on the head there, brother."

He makes such a loud, frustrated groan that some of the other men jump and turn our way. Dragging a hand down his face, he pulls his skin so his eye sockets show red. "You're just not getting it, are you?"

"That I'm not good enough? Yeah, I hear you loud and clear, Kin." I stand to leave, and Kin bangs his cane loudly on the floor. I pause. Anger radiates from his body.

"I wish I could punch some sense into you." His hands make fists. "But you'd probably take it on the chin and then tell me you forgive me, right? Everyone's got it worse than you, right?" His teeth clench together on the 't'.

I nod, confused. "Right."

Kricket glances between the two of us, concerned. Her little legs jiggling against the sofa base, scuffing already scuffed tea roses and winding thorns. "No! Not right! You have done so much for all of us. I wouldn't have survived without you. The Kings would probably all be dead or worse. We owe you everything. We are grateful, and we know we can never really pay you back."

Hands up, I gesture to the ceiling. "I never expected you to pay me back."

"Ugh! I know. But now we expect something from you. You owe *us* something."

I sit back down in the chair. It's too much. The way he talks like I'm some big hero. Like everyone's waiting for me to do something. I don't like the attention. I don't want it. "What's that?" I ask shakily. "What do I owe you?"

Kin leans over and I think he's going to slap me again, but he just grabs my arm and squeezes. "This is your reward, Kettle. And you owe it to us to take your goddamned reward. This amazing thing has happened to you. You fell in love, and your love is returned. You can't let her background hold you back. Part of you thinks it's a negative thing that's she's rich and white, but you're the only one who thinks so. Yes, you owe it to all of us, to every kid you saved and every one you've lost, to take the good thing in front of you and hold onto it. Screw what other people think. You have so many of us standing behind you, ready to back you up. A whole damn kingdom, in fact. And now, we're just waiting for you to catch up, and we'll be ready." His voice strains because he's trying so hard to get through to me.

"Take my reward," I repeat.

He nods. "I have to believe, after everything you have been through, that this is exactly what you deserve. A woman who loves you, a home, and a life free from fear and poverty."

I want to believe him so badly. I want to let his words sprout wings and carry me forward. Kricket stands and bounds toward me, wrapping her arms around my neck. "Your brother is funny," she whispers.

"Yes, he is. But do you think he's right?" I whisper, feeling my heart turn in my chest. I can turn toward happiness instead of away from it. It's opening to the possibility that maybe I can have what I want. That maybe it will be a fight, but it will be a fight worth having if Kite is by my side.

She nods. "I tink he's right."

Kin chuckles. "See, the kid gets it!" Kricket settles in my lap, and I find my brother's eyes. He's smiling, but his eyes speak of truth. "Do you get it, little brother?"

I half smile. "I think I'm starting to."

Kin's grin is contagious. Soon, we're all smiling wide. "And hey, if the side effect of all this altruistic behavior gets me out of here and into a lovely brownstone, then that's just the icing on the cake!"

Then I reach out and smack him. Which earns me a sharp scolding from Miss Lake about her feelings on people who think it's okay to abuse invalids.

Kin pulls faces at me the entire time from behind her back. "C'mon, bowling ball, I did hit him first."

"So, what are you going to do?" Kin asks, eyebrows jiggling. He is the embodiment of coercion. But somehow, he managed to blow a hole through the steel doors inside my chest. He's right. I can do this. I deserve this. I wipe my hands on my pants.

"I guess I'm going to ask Kite to marry me?" I say with very little conviction, and Kin notices.

"C'mon. You're Kettle. You're a King. You've flown over the ocean. You lived through a war. You've broken out of a prison and never been captured. Compared to that, this should be a cake walk." He slaps me on the back, and pats Kricket's head. "You'll help him, won't you, kid? When it comes to romance, I think I got the lion's share of skill." He runs a hand over his jaw. "Got the lion's share in the looks department, too. But hey, he's gotta work with what God gave him." These quips are flying over her head and getting caught in her hair. Things I'll have to explain to her later. She tips her head, hanging on every ridiculous word. "My point is, my poor brother here might need some tips on how to woo your sister."

I roll my eyes. We're not actually related. We didn't come from the same gene pool, so what he said makes no sense, but I do wish I had some of his confidence. It's so much harder being the one asking. I have new and deep-felt admiration for what Kite did. It also makes me feel extremely guilty. "Shut up!"

Again, he addresses Kricket, her little eyes and ears are absorbing everything he says like its melting chocolate. I grumble. He will be such a bad influence on her when we're all together again. The thought lifts me a half an inch from the floor. "You'll make sure he follows through, won't you?"

She nods slowly. "I'll make sure he does what he's s'posed to."

I laugh. This has all gone very strangely, but it feels good. It feels like maybe, just maybe, something wonderful is about to happen to me. Like wind in desperate sails. Long overdue.

Chapter Thirty-four

Kite

I sit in the doctor's office still clutching my stomach, though the pain has all but gone. Medical terms are bouncing around my brain but finding no place to rest. Adhesions from multiple traumas. Explanations of my unpredictable menstrual cycles. Surgery is an option, but not likely to entirely correct the problem. Too severe. Too much damage. I laugh.

"Miss Deere…" Doctor Keneally gives me a curious look. He thinks I'm hysterical. Reacting to the news in an inappropriate way. "I know this information must sound shocking to you…"

I laugh again. It hurts like a blade is being propelled up my throat with the air. "No, not really, Doctor. Does it sound shocking to you?" I ask bluntly, eyes challenging.

He leans back in his chair and strokes his bristly moustache. I want to reach over and slap him. But that's not me. I am better than that. I don't hit people. And now… I don't cover it up either.

"What do you mean?" he asks warily, his reputation coming undone like the loosening knot of his tie.

"Well, surgery and the subsequent recovery may be a little challenging for me since I currently live on the streets. And, well, we both know this news cannot come as a surprise, especially to you. The man who has overseen my medical care since my birth."

He coughs and walks briskly to the door, preparing to shut it. I put a hand up and say in a low voice that's devoid of hope. Devoid of anything really. Because it's all gone. Everything is gone like a dream I wasn't supposed to have. *He* took it. He took everything away. "We don't want anyone to hear, now do we, Doctor?"

"Nora," he says quietly. "I know you must be terribly upset to learn this news. Perhaps I can call your father, and you can talk about it as a family."

This game we play. Round and round. Turn away. Look past. *Deny. Deny. Deny.*

Never again.

I snort, disgusted. "You mention one word of this to my father and I will make sure everyone knows how you treated me, my mother, and my sister, knowing full well we were being beaten. You knew, and you never did a thing to stop it." I throw my head in the air and half laugh, half sneer. "*Repeated trauma.* You meant to say repeated punches to the stomach, right? You meant to say, your father, Christopher Deere, has punched and kicked you so many times that your body is damaged beyond repair. You meant to say, your womb is too broken to harbor a life. You ought to say, *I'm sorry I let it happen.*" My voice runs ragged and breathless as the last pieces of my future shatter. My finger hovers in the air. "You let this happen. You share the blame for this." I motion to my stomach. "You and so many others who just looked the other way. God! When it first started, I was only a child. I was an innocent child."

And now, there will be no more.

His face drains of color and I leave him in his chair, hoping the blood will continue to run from his body until he disappears. He has already begun to disappear from my mind. There is no room for him now. I only have one room for grief. And an entire house for what I will grieve in the future.

I walk or tumble. I feel like my feet are trudging through blackness. I follow the sidewalks up and down the streets like they might lead me somewhere other than to the corner of a building or to the edge of the park. I walk in circles and blocks, and just can't stop. The second I stop, I think.

I don't want to think.

Thinking leads to breaking, sinking to my knees and screaming like I've swallowed a black hole.

I clench my fists. The snow has melted, and it's just cold and wet and miserable.

I hug my coat around my body, sniffing. Not sure if I'm still crying or it's just the rain.

Everything feels too hard: the ground beneath my feet, the way my stomach tightens and contracts, which it does for nothing.

Nothing. Nothing. Nothing.

The light dims, and the cold starts to dig into my bones. I can't stay out here much longer, and I edge my way closer to home. Home. At least I can be a King, and stay where none of this matters. At least I can keep Frankie safe. My head falls as the heartbreak begins to push up from the depths of my chest. Squeezing my heart harder. *Hurting. Hurting. Hurting.*

At least Hiro said no.

Chapter Thirty-six

Kite

When I open the door to the King's tunnel, my senses are flooded with warm candlelight. The room appears empty, and I search for the others, landing on beds and cases and finding only a trail of paper stars like breadcrumbs in a fairy tale leading to the back of the large cavern.

I wipe my eyes and smooth down my hair, hoping I don't look as empty as I feel. Leaning down, I scoop up a handful of the tiny, folded shapes, poking them with my finger. Most are made from newspaper. Delicate and beautiful. I follow the path to the rear of the tunnel. Hiro's curtain is closed, and voices come from Frankie's room. Candlelight brings the night sky into the room—golden twinkles against sandy stone.

Frankie's head appears from behind the curtain, and she grins impishly. As I step toward her, she frowns, flicking her hands and nudging me toward the path of stars. Confused, I do as she tells me. When I turn back, she's disappeared.

This is all very strange. But I feel safe. I also feel devastated.

I point my toes and move to where candles have been placed in every crevice of the collapsed end. A dead end that's been filled with life. Hiro's shadow stands strong and sure against the stones. My heart leaps to life, and my head fills with sorrow.

I must press it *down. Down. Down.*

Everything is yes. When it must be no.

He comes to me across a bridge of stars. His blue eyes catch the light like the sea reflecting the harbor lights. He looks nervous and handsome beyond words, and I'm going to ruin it.

I am the hurricane to his heart, ripping the structure out from beneath his feet and wrenching the walls away to leave him exposed.

Tipping his head, he smiles warily. Reading my face. What he sees is a jumbled mess.

His voice is shaky and unbearably sweet when he lays his love over me like a blanket, and I can't take it. "Look at you, you're soaking wet. Though you still look beautiful. You always look beautiful." He takes my soaked coat and rubs my arms, and I stare at him wordlessly. There isn't anything good to say. He takes his jacket off, then drapes it over my shoulders. "Kite. Um, Nora…" he starts.

"Kite, please," I whisper. "Always Kite."

He nods, a small spark in his eyes. "Kite. I'm so sorry about before. I, um, I just…"

Drips of water run down my neck and nose. My body begins to shake, and he takes my hands. They're ice. I'm icing over. Becoming a stone. A worthless, barren stone.

"Kite. I love you." Hiro bends on one knee. His words ring truer than a bell. But they sound out *defeat* in my ears. He holds out a simple metal band with a star on it. No diamond. No gold. I stare at it. It's perfect.

I want it. I want it. I want it.

My hand aches for it.

I can't take it. I can't take it. I can't take it.

I shake my head, slowly at first, and then faster. "Hiro," I start.

His eyes plead with mine. "Please, let me say this. I wish I hadn't said no to you. I wish I could take it back but you know it wasn't because I didn't love you." His eyes drop. "I hurt you, and I was wrong to think we couldn't make this work. That we didn't deserve to be happy. Kite…" He says my name like the last sweet note of a song. "I know you still love me."

I'm breaking apart. I can feel cracks forming in my skin like fault lines. There is no mending this.

I nod. "I do, but…"

Hiro holds up the ring to my shaking hand, saying the words I want. The words I need. The words that will kill me. "Kite, I thought you were the corner of the sky I could never reach. But somehow, you lifted me up there. You made me feel like I could fly. Like together we could and can do anything. I'm eighteen in a few weeks, and I want to know." His nervous smile is shattering. "Will you marry me?"

His hand is on mine. The ring touches the tip of my finger. Offers a dream I can't take. I yank my hand away.

The Kings emerge from their hiding places. Faces going from hopeful and happy to fearful and forlorn. Instantly, the golden light turns sour and yellowing as everyone watches me come completely undone.

"No," I whisper, backing away, crushing paper stars under my feet.

I thought I was out of tears, but fresh full-of-regret-and-pain ones come crashing down. I am the sea. Unforgiving and threatening. And I will drown us all.

I turn from his stricken face and run from the tunnel while my sister shouts my name.

The sound of the ring hitting the floor is like a hammer striking an anvil. Loud and final.

I don't know where to go. I just know I'm too broken even for Hiro. This is one thing he cannot fix, and if I said yes, he would eventually regret asking me. I am sure of it.

The hurricane doesn't get good things. It blusters and buries until there is nothing left. And then it simply disappears.

Chapter Thirty-seven

Kite

Blinded by tears, I push past the crowd and onto the subway. I huddle between two people who shuffle away from my sniveling, shaking body. I was offered everything I wanted, and I said no. The look on his face will never leave me. It will be the wallpaper of my mind. The glass behind my head thumps as the car pulls away. I turn to see Hiro standing on the platform, mouthing the words, "Wait, Kite." Even in his humiliation, he is concerned for me, he came for me, and it hurts harder and deeper. Scraping out space between organs. Setting a crooked break inside me that will never heal properly. Because I can't wait. Waiting won't change anything.

I stumble onto the street, cold and alone. I'm still wearing Hiro's coat and I pull it around me, wishing it were his arms. Burying my nose in the collar, I inhale. It smells so much like him. Soap. Salt. A boy who always wanted to be better, when he was already the best one.

My lips tremble. My body propels forward. My heart hangs so heavy in my chest it may well snap its bindings and land on my stomach. I thump my chest, wishing it would just leave me. I don't deserve it anyway. I'm as pathetic and useless as my father always said I was.

People stand aside as I wobble and kick my way down the street. Streaked with tears that dig deep into my skin. The world doesn't only look gray—it *feels* gray. Like color can't live here any longer. Love has died, and a colorless drear has taken its place.

It begins to rain again, and black water splashes my clothes. I look down at my legs, a red drip running down my pale stocking. I sigh hard. There is no end to my indignity.

Head down, I shuffle into the first empty alleyway I see. I'm going to have to change my undergarments in the street. I find a dumpster to hide behind, then kick off one shoe. It lands upside down in the drain. I start peeling my stockings from my legs.

The dumpster lid being opened and slammed shut makes me freeze. I've only managed to get one leg out, one foot still in my shoe. I press my back against the wall as sharp footsteps wind around the large metal bin. Black leather shoes. A rhythm of walking I've come to know like my own heartbeat.

I hold my breath. I hug my chest. *I pray. I pray. I pray.*

But no one hears me. No one will save me.

"What the hell are you doing?" My father's voice anchors into the cobblestones with anger and disgust, breaking them up, and I curl around the tone. *I am disgusting. I am...* His eyes slide from my bare leg and stained stockings to my red face. I look past him, afraid to meet his eyes. The new apartment building is taking shape. Remnants of the fire are all but gone save some black stains on parts of the salvaged wall. They leech into the bricks. *Forever shadows.* I'm in the alley behind my house. I shake my head slowly, wondering how I could have found my way here without realizing.

His hand shoots out and grabs my collar. "Whose clothes are you wearing?" His fingers clench around the rough fabric. "Is this that Japanese kid's coat?" His eyes rake over me like I'm already dead.

I bite my lip. "Yes, this is Hiro's coat," I mumble.

He points at my bare leg, my disarray and disaster. "Were you using the alley as a bathroom? What has happened to you? You've become nothing but a vagrant. No manners. No dignity. I can't believe you're my daughter. That you are my blood."

I straighten. Still holding one stocking leg in my hand. "I'm sure this will make you even more *uncomfortable*, but I just got my monthly and I was trying to change my clothes." I hold up the bloodstained leg, and his face flares. It's rage. Disbelief. Embarrassment.

He grips my collar furiously, then pulls it upward so I must stand on tiptoes to stop from choking. "How dare you speak to me this way."

I can't help it. I should. But I can't. I laugh. It's not a funny laugh. Nor a bitter one. It's a laugh born from all that is ridiculous in my life. That I found myself here. That my situation embarrasses him. That he thinks he even has the right to be offended by my presence in his alleyway.

It is a mistake. I should roll over and agree, not spark out like a camera flash. Not give him any more fuel, because I can tell by the way he looks left and right, checking for witnesses, that I'm in trouble. I bow my head. "I'm sorry, Father. I'm not feeling very well... I..."

He shoves me hard against the wall, and my breath is knocked from my lungs. I am the cocoon after the butterfly has escaped. An empty shell. "Where's Frances?" he demands. "You know I gave up the case of a lifetime so I could be a better father. So I could raise her at home with me."

You gave up the case of a lifetime because I had dirt on you. Because I photographed you beating one of your clients. I don't say it. It won't do any good. He believes in some alternate reality. His forearm is a bar across my chest. *Pushing, pushing, pushing*. My spine is crushed against the stones behind me. I feel my skin ripping and my bones grinding.

"I will never let you near her," I manage with the slim amount of oxygen that's getting through my narrowed windpipe.

He releases me and I fall to the ground, knees knocking against hard, cold cobblestones. I look up to see him wipe his forehead and remove his jacket. He neatly folds it before placing it on top of the bin. It is the meticulous preparation before the violence, and I know it well.

I push myself up; I need to run.

The pound of his boot into my stomach is familiar and almost… normal. "I don't know why you make me do this." I collapse as my head hits the ground, ripping the skin off my hands. But I push up again, crawling toward the street. There are black stars in my eyes, as my vision falters.

"Please…" I cough.

"Take that off! You look like a whore." Grabbing the back of Hiro's coat, he yanks it off. I shiver from cold and fear, one bare leg and not enough clothing. Streetlamps start to come on. Beacons of light just out of reach. Desperately, I stretch a hand, but am dragged back into the dark.

He flings me against the dumpster. It makes a loud metallic boom, but this doesn't seem to bother him. He pulls me to my feet. "Get up," he spits. "Get up! You think you can get away with this? You think I don't know what you're trying to do?"

My hands come together. "I'm not trying to do anything."

His fist finds my face, and my words are gone. My mouth fills with blood, and my vision goes fuzzy. I clutch the bin behind me, hands slipping on the metal surface. There is nothing to hold onto. He hits me again. I slide down until I'm sitting on the ground, and he kicks me.

The lights are so close; they float like fireflies.

He comes at me again, and I cross my arms in front of my face. "Stop! Please!" my swollen lips stammer into my skin.

He grabs my arm, twisting it hard until it snaps. I scream.

That's when he leans down, holding my head with both hands, and slams it against the dumpster. "Shut up! Just shut up. Shut up! Shut up!"

The side door opens, and I hear a soft voice. A frightened, faraway voice. Small light from a candle illuminates a slice of the alley, and I stare down at the ground with detachment. I frown. *There's so much blood. That can't be my blood.*

"Miss Nora!"

My father's just a lost shadow in the dark. "Get out of here, Marie!" he snarls as he sends my head into the dumpster again. My head will be blue. I'm becoming part of the painted metal with every thump. I will have *Smith and Co. Garbage Disposal* tattooed across my back.

I find my voice. "Marie. Help me," I gurgle. My vision is closing like a cartoon hole. Narrowing. Light escaping. Darkness prevailing. Another bang. I seem flatter. Like paper. I can hardly feel it now.

I'm slipping. Slipping. Slipping.

The circle of light comes closer. A small sun. The smallest. "You'll kill her!" Marie's high-pitched voice is pure panic.

He releases me, and I hear thuds and soft ruffling. Growling and panting.

I can't feel my legs. They're wooden. I guess wooden is better than pain. I close my eyes. A door closes. Marie has left me. I'm not surprised.

My body relaxes, and I fall. Dirty water in my ear. Coldness covering me like winter. I think he's gone. Or if he's still hitting me, I can't feel it. That's good. That's something.

I always believed there would be a limit. A limit to my suffering, to my pain. Maybe that limit was here in the alley with my death.

Chapter Thirty-eight

Hiro

She rolls away from the platform with my heart in her trembling fingers. She said no. *No.* Though the look on her face was so conflicted, I know there must be more to the story. I stand still on the platform, waiting for the next train.

Krow takes my arm. "In my experience, sometimes a girl just needs time to think it over."

I shouldn't be so hopeful, but I look to Krow's beak-like face and say, "You think?" Even though, his 'experience' would be pretty damn limited.

He shrugs. "Sure."

"Shouldn't I follow her?" I ask, my feet want to run. To search.

He shakes his head. "Give her some space. I bet once she's had a couple of hours to mull it over, she'll come home."

I know I hurt her before. Maybe she's just letting me stew for a while. I guess I kind of deserve it. I slam my hands in my pockets. My legs glued to the ground. "Women are strange creatures," I mutter to the floor. Strange, beautiful, unpredictable.

Krow slaps my back. "You said it!"

The Kings are frantically collecting armfuls of paper stars. Collecting them in their shirts and throwing them in the trash. It makes me smile. They're good kids. Keg nudges me. "Wanna play poker?" He rattles the box of buttons and paper clips. They slide around in the oversized container. My heart feels like that right now. Like's it's shrunk two sizes too small and is rattling around in my rib cage.

I nod. "Sure." I take a seat at the table, and Kricket comes to my side.

"Nor-ah was jest surprised. She don't like being surprised." Krow clears his throat and sits on a corner, asking to be dealt in. Cards skid across the vinyl surface, and we catch them before they slide off the edge.

"How about we teach Kricket here how to play poker like a King?" He pats the crate next to him and she eagerly jumps over to it, distracted for the moment.

My Kings crowd around in support. They don't bring up earlier neither do they commiserate or humiliate. They know to leave well enough alone.

Besides, what would they say?

I'll give her some time. Just not too much.

Chapter Thirty-nine

Kite

A flicker over my eyelids. Red, white, and blue. Red the color of blood. White the color of starlight. Blue the color of a bruise.

The barest touch to my temple, two fingers, a little shaky. Very soft. "Sh," she hums. "Sh, dear, sh."

"Mother." My lips form an impossible word when I hear the care in the voice. The guilt.

I try to move. "Sh, stay still, dear. Stay still."

My eyes open to broken angles and crooked limbs. *My hand.* I squint as I stare at the broken skin on my knuckles, the blood and the white flakes melting to pink water. Ice kisses on tiny freckles that are ripped and not where they should be.

Boots crunching on new snow. I shiver. I want to pull my knees to my chest. *I want to use the gaps between the stones like handholds and climb out of this picture frame.*

I was, I was, I was... Dead.

A deep voice, brassy like a gong, sounds above me. "She's in bad shape." I imagine I am the shape of a broken kite, all sharp angles and splintered wood. A board is pushed underneath me with force and care.

"Will she be all right?" Focus. Unfocus. An apron heaving. Blood like a butcher's streak splashed across it.

"I hope so, ma'am. Do you want to ride with her?"

Small again. Meeker. "No, I can't." Regret running in rings.

The hand falls from my temple. There are so many voices. All men. All serious and somber, except for one. One is fighting and spitting and is as unhinged as castle gates blown open. I'm lifted from the ground. "You're making a mistake," he shouts. "Marie. Marie. Come here and tell the policeman the truth. Tell them we found her like this. You tell them now!" His voice is pungent with desperation.

Sit up. I push up on one elbow. My other arm smarts like exposed wiring runs from my hand to my shoulder. *I have to see this.*

Forcing my eyes open, I watch as my father is handcuffed. He struggles, sweat covering his face, blood covering his hands and shirt. This image can't be real. I still feel a little like I'm floating between this life and the next. *Is that my blood on him?* It seems like a lot.

Marie's round shape comes into focus. She solidifies like she's a rumbling mountain that's coming to rest. The policeman towers over her, but she stands sturdy and sure as she points at my father. His eyes look like dead coals as another policeman presses down on his head and shoves him into the back of the car. She nods sharply. The policeman writes something down in a ringed notebook, punctuating his text with tip of his pen as Marie speaks. Her face is different. Instead of soft, malleable skin and terrified mouse-like eyes, I see something harder and tougher there. I also see a modicum of reprieve. Like she's let something go.

I'm caught in a whirl. A tempest of pain and dizziness that's playing catch up around my body. "Marie," I say. "You did it. You spoke up." She became the shield, facing the danger instead of hiding from it.

"I couldn't let him kill you, Miss Nora." Her eyes fall to her lap, to her fiddling fingers.

I try to reach for her, wanting to pat her hand and tell her it's okay. I understand the power Christopher Deere held over the women around him. I hated it, but I understood its monstrous form.

Crackles in my throat. Air slipping. Thinning. He's gone, yet I'm being crushed.

Marie's expression is horror. *Stretching. Stretching. Stretching.*

It stretches until I see nothing but white.

Not starlight. A burning empty nothing.

Chapter Forty

Hiro

I curve around the cold space where Kite should be lying next to me. A ball of energy and hope. Someone who has managed to tape herself back together using nothing but found things. Just like me.

Sitting up, I glance at my watch. It's after midnight. She should be back by now.

Sliding the curtain aside, I step into the space between the rooms. So many things have happened in this small passage. Compromises. Feet swishing across dust and dirt in a dance. A kiss that shook the subway foundations. It has always been the bridge. It is the place to gather courage and be brave. I stand there, wondering what happens next. How do we move forward? Can we cross the bridge now? Or did I burn it?

Kricket coughs and I walk to the divide, pushing the curtain aside loudly, thinking Kite's probably here, with her sister. She didn't want to come to me after all that has passed between us. It's understandable.

I scan the bed. Kricket is sitting up, her small hands wrung and fretful. "Where's ma sister, Kettle? She should be here." I take her inhaler and hold it to her mouth. She breathes in, and I feel like I'm breathing out flecks of glass.

Yes, she should be. No matter what is between us, she's still a King and she should be here. A lurking fear pulls itself further from the lake.

I shouldn't have let her go. I should have looked for her.

Reaching out, I pat Kricket's hair and get her to lie back down. I add an extra blanket to her bed. "She'll be home soon, kid. Just try to get some sleep." I listen to her breathing. Make sure it's even and calm.

I hope I haven't pushed her so far that she won't come back. Running a hand through my hair, I grip the ends in my fingers and frown. *I thought this was what she wanted.* It doesn't make any sense.

I console myself with the fact that she won't leave her sister behind. When she comes back for her, I can explain. At least the weather has been milder. She may get wet, but she's not going to freeze to death tonight.

I should never have listened to Kin. He made me think I could have this. I was fine before he started putting stupid ideas in my head.

I'm lying to myself, and it doesn't make me feel any better. When she said no, I felt like someone had pulled the floor away. Like I was one second away from falling into nothingness. A horrible, bottomless place where no one would hear me scream.

The other truth is I expected it.

And there's nothing more disappointing than getting exactly what you expect.

I stalk back to my room, then throw myself on the bed. It puffs with dust and disillusionment.

If she's not back by morning, I will bring her home myself.

Chapter Forty-one

Kite

I have a blackboard in my mind, covered in white strokes that count the times I've been here before. So many hours and days spent staring at plain walls, lying on sterile sheets. I sweep across the chalk with my hand, leaving a streak like feathered clouds.

A man's shadow in the corner of the room approaches.

Yes, I've been here before.

It's always. Always. Always. The same.

I tense, bracing myself for either a threat or a threat veiled as an apology. His menacing body comes closer, looking fuzzy as a storm cloud that's breaking apart. *I could run.* I could almost laugh if that wouldn't cause my bones to dismantle. My body is a handful of broken parts. My skin is thin and splitting. I can't even sit up.

He's got me right where he wants me.

"Miss Deere," an unfamiliar voice whispers with deep, deep pity. "I am so very sorry."

I try really hard to focus. "You're sorry?" Sorry can be a nonsense word.

The man puts his fingers to the pulse at my wrist. "I am. Truly." *Concentrate.* But concentration leads to being awake, which leads to pain.

But pain at least means I'm alive. I'm alive, and I didn't tell him where Frankie was. "What happened?" I ask, waiting for him to feed me my story. Expecting him to tell me that I fell or tripped. My head banged on the counter, and my memories are confused.

"You don't remember?" he asks, eyebrow rising. His face sharpens at the question. He looks about the same age as my father, broad but with brown eyes that have seen all kinds of awful things, but he is not Christopher Deere.

A burning hope shoots into the sky like a small firework.

"Can you help me sit up, please?" He adjusts my bed. "I remember."

I remember bad news blackening everything around me. I remember Hiro's heart. A devastating question. And then, *him.* The dark end of everything.

The doctor sits on the edge of the bed. "So, you remember that your father beat you to within an inch of your life?"

My heart rate escalates, and my breath quickens. I feel heavy and dry like I've been force fed a sack of rice. Trying to shift, I am pressed down in the bed, every part of my body is a hotplate of hurt. "Who are you?" I demand. "Did he send you here to make sure I get my story straight? I'm not lying anymore. You tell him I'm not going to let him do this to me again. Ever."

Standing, the doctor pushes a button by the bed. A plastic click, click, click. My head swirls with a gooey feeling, and I put my hand up. "Please. Tell him I won't come near the house again. It was a mistake. I won't bother him. If he would just leave me and my sister alone."

The doctor's face tears open to reveal such sympathy I don't know where to put it. "Nora, I read your file." His expression turns to regret and a pinch of irritation. "I know you've endured more than anyone should ever have to, and that no one has helped you in the past. But you can trust me when I say your father will never be able to hurt you ever again."

Never is a nonsense word. It's a promise no one can keep. "What are you saying?" This is a dream. A strange, beautiful, and painful dream.

The gooeyness eases, clarity just on the other side. "I'm saying, your father has been arrested. Your housemaid called the police during the... incident, and he was caught violently assaulting you. My understanding is that she has agreed to testify to not only this, but also a long pattern of abuse stretching over ten years."

My lip quivers as my heart beats in strange staccato. "It can't be true. No. You're lying." *I don't believe it.* Anything this man tells me will float through my mind and out. *It can't be true.* I shake my head as tears drop mercilessly down my cheeks and onto my chest. "It can't be. It can't be." My hand turns to a fist, and I thump the mattress weakly. I look to him, eyes wide. Imploring him to stop toying with me. To stop torturing me. "Please," I whisper. "Don't lie to me."

A nurse comes in, and her eyes look the same as his. Her satisfied expression looks familiar. She comes to my side and says, "You may not remember me, but I was here the day your sister was brought into the ER with a head injury and bleeding from the ears."

I gulp, nodding. This is too much.

"You always stuck in my mind, dear. So young to be so tough. So guarded. We're not lying to you. It's over. Your father is going to jail." She puts a hand on mine, and I freeze. I feel like the thin layer of ice that skaters could fall through. "He can't hurt you anymore."

"He can't hurt me anymore," I repeat woodenly.

"You're safe," she says.

"I'm… safe."

The words have too much meaning, they stick on the inside of my throat, and I can barely get them out.

The doctor clears his throat. "You are safe from further harm, but you've also sustained many injuries you'll need to overcome." Again, he clicks a button by my head and I drift away. "You need to rest."

I can rest. Finally. I can rest.

Chapter Forty-two

Hiro

My head is splitting, like an axe through my skull. A night I will never forget working its way deep and painfully into my brain.

The boys are dispersing for the day and Kricket bounds onto my bed, rattling me awake. "We should find No-rah. I bet she's changed her mind. I bet she's gonna say yes."

Kelpie hangs back, leaning against my shelves. He looks disappointed. I know they all are. I think that's why they all seem anxious to leave. "See ya tonight, Kettle," he says forcefully casual. I nod.

The ring we found in a drugstore that seemed perfect at the time sits heavily on my wooden chest. Burning a hole through the timber. *I was such an idiot.* The remaining crushed paper stars on the ground are a path leading to nothing. All the air squashed out of them. The cuts on the tips of my fingers from all the folding are a better feeling than what's going on inside me.

Kricket grabs my shoulders with a pincer grip, shaking me hard. I grimace.

"Okay, okay, I'm getting up. Geez." I brush her hands from my body, but the angular little bug keeps flapping in my face.

"Kettle, Kettle, Kettle." She doesn't get it. Kite said no. I don't think I can ask her again. I don't think she wants me to. *God, the look on her face.*

I sigh. I know there's a reason for the answer but I'm scared to ask. The most likely answer is that she finally realized she's too good for me and that the challenges we'd face aren't worth the aggravation. I groan and flop back into bed, which sends another scurry of elbows and pointy knees at my poor defenseless body.

It's why I'm dragging my feet. Getting up means getting out and facing the truth. And I'm not sure I'm ready for it.

Kricket grabs the covers, then yanks them from my legs. My eyes narrow, and I snap at her before I can stop myself, "Goddamn it, kid, will you just leave me the hell alone!"

I want to pull the string of anger back, but it's too late. Little Kricket's eyes water. She folds up and scuttles away like a frightened beetle. The flash of her hair as it disappears behind the curtain is a flag of regret. *Great. Now I've upset her, too.*

Taking a deep breath, I swallow my heartache. A twin emotion stands beside me. A memory that's not my own, but I feel it all the same. This must have been what it was like for Kite every time I said no. I swallow the pain, putting on a brave face to hide the devastation for her sister's sake.

Except my pain is just my pride. My pain is giving up on something I took too long to want. It's my fault it happened this way. I did this.

After I quickly dress, I splash some water on my face. I bury my hurt underneath boxes and blankets before walking over to talk to Kricket.

She's curled at the end of the bed, rummaging through a suitcase. Chin on knees. She throws things on the bed as she goes. She doesn't look up when I enter.

"Ya didn't need ta yell tat me," she says. She finds her hearing aid and slides it into her ear, struggling with the mess of wires, pulling them apart like warm taffy.

I bow my head. "I know. I'm sorry. It's just been a long couple of days."

She flashes her blue eyes at me. Dark. Like an untroubled storm happily traveling along, throwing spikes of lightning at passersby. "Every day is the same. Cain't be longer or shorter." She holds up her fingers, flashing ten twice and then four. "Twentee-four hours."

I chuckle. *This kid.* I help her unwind and fasten the aid to her hip. "You're absolutely right."

She pulls something out of the bottom of the case, staring at it, tipping at an angle. It's a photo. I know what it is before she turns it to me. "This is you."

I nod. "Yes. That is me."

She points at her father. "This is Deddy. Deddy hurts people. Deddy's done hurt to No-rah. A lot of hurt." She blows her hair from her face. Just like every King here, she has a case full of bad memories. Old injuries. Ghosts that chase her.

He did a lot of hurt. Taking the photo from her, I examine it. It was supposed to be our ticket to leaving him behind. She never thought he would just abandon the case. She always gave him too much credit. Her big heart led to big hurt. Where's the reward in that?

I place the photo face down in the case, then stack other things on top. It doesn't matter now. "I think your father has a sickness. He can't stop hurting people, even people he's supposed to care about."

She nods solemnly. "No-rah has one, too."

I tilt my head. "She does?"

Kricket looks at me like I'm an idiot. "Yeah. She cain't stop pro-tacting people." She holds her arms up in a cross over her face. It's a horrible and awakening image.

Kids have this funny way of cutting through all the bullshit, shining light through the cracks of life. "Gosh, you're so right, Kricket." I offer my hand and pull her up. "But she needs to understand she doesn't need to do that anymore."

I pull on one of Kin's old coats. After Kite flew away with mine, it was the last thing I saw as she huddled down inside it like it was armor as she escaped on the subway.

I feel tightened and strengthened by this realization. If she's trying to protect me from her father, then there's a chance I can change her mind. Together, we're stronger. My face slips for a moment, but I force it back up. *I thought she knew that already.*

With Kricket's small pale hand in mine, we wait by the door. There's a man smoking and leaning against it, and the little girl's breathing is getting louder and wheezier as the smoke wafts through the gapped boards.

People board and disembark around him. I wait for him to move, but he seems content to just smoke and people watch. I roll my eyes.

The platform is empty except for this one round man.

I do something I've never done before.

Shoving on the door, I send the man stumbling forward, his cigarette bouncing onto the tracks. He pines after it like it's a hundred-dollar bill, then stares wide-eyed at Kricket and me emerging from the wall. I shake my head, and Kricket coughs.

She glares at him as we board the next train. "Ya shouldn't smoke!"

His red face wobbles with shock as he fumbles with his lighter.

I laugh.

Chapter Forty-three

Kite

There's a square of light in the wall and I think it must be a window. I lift my hand to touch it. *Drifting. Drifting. Drifting.* There are things I should be doing, but I can't remember.

A shadow pulls across the window, and I tense. Beeping increases. More shadows, more hands on my body. Adjusting, checking.

They keep telling me I'm safe.

They keep telling me he can't hurt me anymore.

I grasp the words, but they slip through my fingers.

"Nora…" A man's voice penetrates the fuzz of drugs. "We're going to start weaning you off the pain relief. There's someone here who needs to talk to you. He says it's urgent."

I nod. I'm floating on a sea of jello. I'm floating *down, down, down* until suddenly the sky cracks and I'm falling through. Pain erupts over every inch of my body. My eyes focus, hard and chiseled.

The man comes into focus. "Miss Deere."

I nod, reaching for a glass of water. The grasping of it feels like a victory.

"I need to ask you some questions." Pen poised over paper.

A statement. Details are given. I am thanked and assured. "The case is open and shut," he says. Open and shut. It sounds more violent than intended. Like a door slammed. A book snapped closed.

The nurse comes in to adjust my pillow. Her eyes are dark and purplish underneath. "You should go home," I say. "You look tired."

She smiles proudly. "You did very well, my dear."

The square of light turns dark, and I am alone again.

I reach for Hiro. I catch the cuff of his trousers as he jumps from the windowsill, but I can't hold on.

Chapter Forty-four

Hiro

Fear that started as a trickle has now turned to a flood. Kricket and I search the usual places. I check alleyways, behind dumpsters, and we enter every store we think she might go into. Nothing.

We even creep up to her old brownstone, though I can't imagine why she would be here. The smell of fresh paint moves through the alley. The new apartment building looking nearly finished. A flash of Kin scolding me for saving that woman from the fire plays like a strange movie over the charred bricks. When I peer through the front window, it appears empty. Lifeless. I press my face to the glass, and Kricket pulls on my arm anxiously. She doesn't want to be caught here.

I don't blame her.

My anxiety is starting to stretch to the sky, dragging holes through the gray blue. *Where are you?*

The cold is closing in. The one day of reprieve has disappeared and, in its place, is a biting, snapping wind, sharp as crocodile teeth. Dangerous. Picking up a newspaper, I scan the weather section while the vendor gives me dagger eyes. They're predicting another snowstorm. Kricket's breathing sounds like a loose fan belt, and I hug her close to keep her warm. I need to get her home before she develops pneumonia. We head down to the subway as the sun starts to disappear. The days are getting shorter. I bite my lip, praying Kite is in the tunnel.

Picturing the reunion, I have so many things to say. The first being that no matter what she says, no matter what she decides, I still love her.

Kricket stumbles, her movements becoming uncoordinated with tiredness. I scoop her up, holding her against my chest as we board the train. The subway rumbles and bumps. "Be home," I whisper under my breath. "Please, be home."

With hope and a sleeping child in my arms, I knock on the King's door with my elbow. It opens to a familiar face.

Krow's expression is dire as he mutters, "She's not here."

I stalk in. Kricket shakes a little and I lay her down on the bed, covering her with extra blankets. Kelpie sneaks over to snuggle at her feet.

I know something's wrong. But I also know Kite's first priority would always be her sister. So, I do what I must to make sure Kricket is safe, warm, and well. Even as every fiber of me stretches to the outside, searching for the other half of my heart.

"What the hell are you doing? Are you crazy?" Krow's voice is angry, splashed with a small speckle of sympathy. Staring at the glass doors, the outside world is barely visible, swirling with white. The doors shudder violently with the wind, warning me not to go through like sentinels with crossed spears. The handle burns my palms for how cold it is. This is worse than the storm that killed Kamo.

"She's out there. I have to find her." I can't think straight, when she could be caught in this storm, fighting against the freeze.

Krow throws a hand on my shoulder to yank me backward. "You can't go out there. You'll die like Kamo. Like Kipper. Like K…"

"But how can I stay and do nothing when she could be…?" I feel choked and desperate. The air thins while my panic rises. "What the hell happened?" I ask no one. "How did it all go so wrong?"

Krow stands between me and the door, rigid and uncomfortable, but completely determined. "I ain't gonna hug you or nothin', but I will stop you from going out there and getting yourself killed."

Taking a deep breath, I stare at the painted ceiling. So much effort was put into this underground space but no one looks at it anymore. "I need to find her. I don't know what I'll do if she's…" I start.

Krow turns me rather forcefully, then propels me back down the stairs. "You'll have to wait til' the storm is over."

"I can't…" I could fight him. Two thirds of me wants to shove him aside and run. But he's right, if I go out, I wouldn't last very long at all .

He keeps pushing me back to the tunnel. Back to a home that doesn't feel like a home anymore. Not without Kite. "You don't have a choice," he says sharply to the back of my head.

No. It seems like I never really do.

Chapter Forty-five

Kite

Snow batters the window. It's almost impossible to tell if it's night or day with the clouds so low they're sitting comfortably on the sidewalk. As my head clears, memories of what I said to Hiro come back to me. He must be so angry and hurt. And Frankie…

Tightening my fists, I try to sit up. I need to get back to her. She might think I've abandoned her. I would never…

My head aches as thoughts ping around in my skull. I swing my legs around to try to get off the bed but several wires and tubes are still attached to me, and machines come crashing down with spectacular noise. A nurse rushes in to force me easily back into bed. "What are you doing, miss?"

"I need to leave," I say, searching the room. "Where's my coat?"

A man enters the room with sad eyes and a pitying glance. He takes a sharp breath in at the sight of me as he dusts the snow from his jacket. "Nora," he says in a sigh. "I'm so sorry."

Sorry. Everyone is sorry.

My voice shakes. "I want my coat."

Mr. Inkham turns to the nurse. "Nurse, where is Miss Deere's coat?"

The nurse opens a closet in the corner of the room and pulls out Hiro's coat, handing it to the lawyer. "It was the only clothing she had that wasn't stained with blood." He holds it up and I reach for it, too many tears in my eyes. They can't decide which one will fall first. I snatch it to my chest. Breathing in the smell of the only man I truly feel safe with. *Why hasn't he found me?*

Trying to put my arms through, I get tangled and frustrated. "Nora, you can't leave yet. The doctor says you're too unwell to travel."

I huff. *I don't care. I don't care. I don't care.* "Mr. Inkham, why are you here?"

"Because I have wonderful news," he announces, flipping his briefcase onto the hospital tray table. I arch an eyebrow, and he blushes. "Er, I mean I have *important* news... for you." Holding out my hand, I indicate for him to go on. "Your father's incarceration changes the structure of your mother's will, the living allowance, and the timeline for your inheritance."

Hope is dangerous and these words fill me with doubt. "In what way?" When I shift my head, pain spikes through my neck and spine.

"The living allowance, the house, it all goes to you and your sister Frances." When he says this with optimism and animation. I wish I could share it, but it's too much to believe. I can't trust it.

"You mean in trust until my father is released." My voice is flat. Unmarked.

Mr. Inkham shakes his head as he approaches me. His eyes wash over my bruised and broken body, pausing at my split and bulging lip. He doesn't even know how torn apart I am on the inside. The barrenness that spreads like a dust storm from my womb to my heart. He chances a touch of my hand and I don't have the energy to remove it. "No. It will be permanent. Your father's arrest meant all rights transfer to you temporarily, but once he is found guilty and is sentenced, the transfer will be permanent."

There's the catch. It was waiting just above our heads, ready to snag me. "So, it is temporary." This isn't a triumphant victory because there's always a catch.

Mr. Inkham's eyes break in the corners like they're brittle and painted, and I see what he sees. A defeated, helpless, hopeless girl. But I've learned through the crack of a baton to the sting of a palm to my face that things don't work out for people like me. "Nora, he is guilty. He won't get out of prison for a very long time. The police witnessed your… assault."

Everyone has a hard time saying that word. There's always a break in the sentence like they need a moment to catch their breath. People don't want to believe these things happen and it's why they easily turn away from the signs.

"Your housemaid's testimony is solid, and it points to a long history of abuse. I know you have no reason to believe me, but I'm telling you the truth. I would never give you false hope. This is happening."

In the back of mind, excitement starts to bubble like pursing mouths ready to blow a trumpet. But I'm unsure. Unsure. Unsure.

Believe him. Let the music roar. Let it rattle your lungs and blast the windows.

"I can go home?" I whisper. Not sure if I can clean away the nightmares that live in every corner of that place.

His expression is like coming to rest. A calming heart. "If you want to, yes, you can go home."

If I want to.

Those words are powerful but they lose just a little of their potency without two people here to hear them with me.

Chapter Forty-six

Hiro

The cold temperatures mix with cabin fever, getting the best of everyone. The smell of this many kids trapped inside isn't too good, either.

I hear a scuffle in the corner and the card table shoots up in the air, landing on its side, cards scatter everywhere. "You cheated," Keg shouts, pointing at a new kid we haven't even named yet. Keg looms over the scrap of a boy, whose brown curls are tied back in a ponytail. The scrap grins, showing rotten teeth and freckles the size of food stamps. I storm over and grab Keg's collar. He's getting big, and it's a struggle to hold him back.

Krow comes to my aid, standing between the two of them. He slaps the new kid's head and curses. "For Pete's sake, you're only playing for buttons. What the hell does it matter?" he snaps angrily.

Keg straightens, the violence rippling out of his body, and I let him go. "It's da principal."

This makes the new kid snicker, which is a mistake. Keg lunges at him, trying to scratch the giant freckles from the kid's face. He lands a swipe but doesn't do too much damage. I try to concentrate on what's in front of me, not on the ghost that waits for me outside. *Kite*. But it's pointless. Her absence is killing me second by second.

"What's your name kid?" I ask, offering a hand. He takes it gingerly. The general and warranted distrust of a street kid shining through.

"Um…" He's reluctant. They always are.

Rubbing my chin, I squint at him. "Doesn't matter anyway. If you're staying with us, you can pick a new name."

Keg snorts. "How about Krook!"

I shoot Keg a look, then bend down. The kid can't be more than about twelve. But he's cocky. Keg's about three times bigger, but the new kid was ready to face him. "You look like a…" The way he smiles like he's got a trick or two up his sleeve. "How about Krafty?"

The kid's chest swells with pride and so does mine for a short, closed-up moment. Like a magician's box has been opened and closed before I could see what was inside. I've always loved this part, but it loses something. "Krafty suits me to a tee," he says in an older, deeper voice than I would've expected.

I gaze around the room, feeling squeezed by our cramped quarters. More come in from the cold this time of year, and the stink of too many boys in too-close quarters sits like smog above us. "I'm going to check the papers. See how long they think this blizzard's going to last for." Kelpie and Kricket are playing in the back. I point my finger over the whole room. "You all look like you need some fresh air." I wave my hand in front of my nose. "You all smell like it, too!" They give blunt laughs.

I jerk my head in Kricket's direction, and Krow nods. He'll look after her until I get back.

And if the snow has eased, I can get back to searching for Kite.

The guy at this newsstand is one of the few men who treats me like everyone else. As in, he treats everyone with the same growling irritation. I put my hand on the neatly folded stack of newspapers, and he grunts at me. "Oi, you touch, you buy!" Swiping the paper up, I flick him a coin. He grunts, tucks the coin into a zipped bag, and goes back to his magazine.

The snowstorm is the top story. Worst storm to hit city in over a decade. I roll my eyes. Everything's always the worst *something* in a decade. Scrolling down, it says the storm front will hopefully pass over by tomorrow.

My eyes roll over black letters. Adds for department store sales, something about Walt Disney, and then…

My hands scrunch until it looks like I'm holding two paper fans. The small headline on the skinny side, where they put local crimes and murders, reads:

Lawyer Arrested for Attempted Murder of Daughter. No bail. Several people, including police, witnessed the violent beating of a young woman by the accused, Christopher Deere, in the alley behind his residence. Court date yet to be set. Rumors he will defend himself. Condition of victim, unknown.

How can the worst thing to ever happen take up so little space? One small column, one inch of text.

I tear the paper apart. Ripping it down the middle like I can change the words and rearrange them into something less horrifying. It drops from my hands, and people immediately walk over it, covering it with wet, muddy boot prints to send it coasting across the tiled floor in shredded pieces.

Attempted. Attempted. That means she's still alive. I hold onto those words like a buoy in a storm but the word *murder* sinks into me like a blade. *How could this happen?*

How could I let this happen?

I don't even brace myself. I can't feel the cold. I have no coat, just a holey woolen sweater and my own dread to keep me warm.

I run, slipping on ice, knocking into people, and swearing. I don't care.

I need to see her now. And nothing's going to stop me. Not even the sky.

Chapter Forty-seven

Hiro

I burst through the hospital doors like a monster. I'm King Kong searching for Ann. I'm frozen through, blue-lipped, teeth chattering. But my heart is on fire. It searches for its home. I breathe in large gulps of warm air. *I'm. I'm. I'm...*

I shrink. *How do I tell her how sorry I am? How do I explain why it's taken me so long to find her?* My last thought almost brings me to my knees. *What if she's so badly broken that I can't reach her?*

I wobble, reminding myself to be brave. That I can do this. I walk up to the reception and ask for Nora Deere. The woman looks down her nose at me, and I stare squarely into her eyes. "And who are you?"

Without faltering, I say, "I'm her fiancé. Hiro. Hiro Jackson."

Putting a finger up to my face, she picks up the phone. "One moment, please."

My eyes do what they always do-search for exits, for security guards, for cops. But it's a tired version because I'm so sick of running. The woman swings away from me in her swivel chair, covering her mouth as she speaks. Her nasty eyes appraise me and find me all too Asian and all too lacking, but she eventually nods in a concessional type of way and finally finds my eyes. "All right, Mr. *Jackson*..." She says my name like it's a lie. It kind of is since I have no real connection to that side of my family. "Miss Deere, *your fiancée*, confirmed your relationship." The woman talks like certain words taste bitter on her tongue. I ignore her sourness. "She's on the fourth floor. Just go to the nurse's station, and they'll show you to her room."

Being awake is one mark in the positive side of the ledger. I'm glad she's alert enough to confirm my lie. I breathe in and hold it. *Four floors to prepare myself. Four floors to come up with something other than I'm sorry.*

Gulping, I step into the elevator, holding the door open for a pregnant woman and her husband. They smile and push the number for their floor. I stare at my feet, always in the habit of hiding my face.

Looking up when the bell dings, I see how the woman holds her belly lovingly, rocking on her heels. Her husband keeps an arm protectively around her shoulder. They don't look much older than me. Just a young couple doing one of those normal *life* things I've never really thought about.

The doors close, and I'm faced with my own warped reflection in the lift doors. He looks scared out of his skin, like he hasn't slept in days, and exactly how one'd expect a man in love to look if he'd just found out his fiancée was almost murdered.

Laughing in a gulping, garbled way, I warn myself not to get my hopes up. Just because she backed up my deceit doesn't mean anything. She's probably just doing what Frankie said she always does: 'Pro-tacting' me.

The doors slide open, and I feel like I got there too fast. I'm standing at the nurse's station and they're nodding to me solemnly. Their sad eyes make me start to really panic and picture terrible things. The nurse says, "Follow me, sir."

Sir. Act like a *sir.* A man who has a right to be here.

I resist the urge to pat my pockets and wipe my hands on my pants.

Just breathe. If she's talking, it can't be all that bad, surely. But then the word *murder* comes back and bites me again and again. Ripping at my skin relentlessly. I halt. "Nurse, wait."

She turns around, soft blonde hair sweeping her shoulders. "Yes?"

My eyes drop to the floor and then I muster my courage, gather what I can. "Please, so I can prepare myself…" *So I can be strong.* "Can you tell me how bad her injuries are?"

Words hurt like torpedoes being shot into my chest.

Worst beating she's ever seen.

Collapsed lung. Broken tibia.

Internal bleeding.

Severe concussion from repeated trauma. The nurse then acts out the motion of Kite's head being slammed against a dumpster over and over again, and I think I might be sick. My hand lifts to my mouth as I try to keep the curse words in and the horror out.

She stares at me with a new sympathy. Like I am bereaved. "There's something else…"

Oh God, how could there be anything left?

Hold it together. You have to. For Kite. "Tell me." I steady myself on the wall. This is too much.

"Well… she was *bleeding* when she arrived." The way she says *bleeding* gives it a different meaning than the usual.

"You mean…" My eyes drop. She nods. I knew this. I knew she had her *monthly.*

"Well, we are required to do thorough examinations. We took records for the court case. Signs of previous abuse. Broken bones. Scarring both externally and internally…" I nod along, only half able to listen. But the nurse gets the sense this is not a shock to me. "It seems your fiancée has suffered a great deal of blunt trauma to her abdomen over the past ten years." She twists awkwardly. "Her doctor sent over her records. Seems she had only just visited him on the day of the attack... He was quite forthcoming in sharing his diagnosis..."

I might just melt into the floor since my skeleton doesn't feel capable of holding me up any longer. "Please, Nurse, just tell me what it is."

She shakes her head and sniffs. Wiping at her eyes. "It's such a shame for someone so young, you know? After everything she's had to endure, this seems like the cruelest twist of fate."

I don't know. I don't know what she's talking about. "Nurse," I prompt, my teeth grinding against each other.

"It appears Miss Deere's abdominal scarring has caused adhesions that mean it is highly unlikely she will ever be able to bear children."

My eyes widen and my heart squashes in my chest. Pieces of this jagged and complicated puzzle start to fly from the corners of my eyes, coming together. Revealing a picture. And I think I know, at least I hope I know, why she said *no*. A curse word escapes. "That son of a bitch." The nurse nods in agreement.

Swallowing my anger, I remember why I'm here. What I know I must say to her now.

This is not about marriage or money now.

There are simple words that I can say. Standing straight, I walk to her room.

It is the most heartbreaking truth of our story. While some husbands and beaus might not be able to identify their beloved after an attack, with their face swollen and purple, I recognize Kite straight away. Because as long as I've known Kite, she has always had some degree of bruising. She has always been coming from a beating or heading back into one.

The weight of that realization carves pieces from me.

My fingers grip the doorframe, fingernails digging into paint the color of mushrooms. My eyes rake the room. Kite shouldn't be in this drab, neutral place. She deserves splashes of color, satin, and light. She deserves everything. The world to spin at her chosen pace and angle. The sun to slant and brush her beautiful cheeks. Swallowing a lump in my throat, I find it hard to believe that what she wants is me. When she looks up with strength and fragility, her amber eyes engulf me. As her lip quivers, I move to her side, sheltering her in my arms and covering her with kisses. There should never be space between us. Never be words we cannot say to each other.

"Oh, Kite, Look at you." I carefully survey her. Tears bulge from her lashes and drag down her cheeks. Her lip is held between her teeth like it is holding in a scream. She is broken, but still holding together by pure will alone. "You are so strong. So beautiful." I trace her jaw with a touch like gauze.

Making these strange hiccupping sounds, her ribs rattle like combs. She's allowing herself a fall-apart moment. I edge onto the bed and let her bury her head in my chest and expel all the pain and fear that's been stuck inside her these past few days. I stroke her head like it's made of eggshell, letting her sniff and wipe snot on my shirt. As she pours all her grief into me, I know I can take it.

It's a long time before she calms down, but her breath eventually becomes steadier.

"Where's Frankie?" she asks as I hand her a box of Kleenex.

I hold her hand, trying to get as close as possible without hurting her. "She's safe."

At the same time, we whisper each other's name. "Hiro."

"Kite."

She emits a tiny laugh like one precious strand of steam, and I rejoice. *She can still laugh.* As she starts to speak, I can feel the explanations bubbling below her throat. But she owes me none. There is only one thing that needs to be said. "Kite. You are *all* I want."

Our eyes connect, and sadness brims in hers. I know mine are full of love. "But…" she begins.

Taking her hand, I press it to my lips. "You are, and will always be, enough for me." I keep her eyes, see the warmth creeping in at the edges. The love that we somehow managed to grow out of dust and dirt. "You. Are. Everything. I. Need."

Her chin falls, her eyes on our hands. "Everything?"

"Everything."

I wish I could leave it there, but she presses. And I understand. She needs to be sure. "So, you know about my condition?"

Wanting to be clear, I make sure there is no doubt in her head or heart that I will grow to resent us. "What I know is that you're the strongest woman I've ever met. And even though I know you would make a wonderful mother, if that is not possible for you, I am sure you and I will find other ways to share your love and compassion. And if you decide to share just a tiny part of that incredible heart with me, I'd be the luckiest guy in the world."

She giggles, and I blush for all my gushing. "I'm scared you'll change your mind."

I smile. "You of all people should know how stubborn I can be." Her lips are split. Blackened blood holding them together. "It doesn't matter to me. You're all that matters." I run the tips of my fingers over her cheek to her lips, catching on the broken parts.

Her voice breaks over her words. These utterances crashing like small waves on the shore. "*I* wanted it. It mattered to me. I could see them. I dreamt about our children. And now they're just… gone."

I lean in and gently kiss her stubborn, damaged mouth. "We will fill our house with children. They may not be our own, but that doesn't mean we won't love them just as much."

Again, the tears begin. She needs to grieve what she has lost. She whispers into my salted shirt. "He took this from me, and I can't get it back."

As I take her shoulders, her skin and bones feel as delicate as a bird's. But she is also formidable. I put a small amount of space between us, so I can see her face in all its ruined beauty. "Let this be the last thing he ever takes from you, okay? It ends here."

She nods.

It ends here for Christopher Deere.

But Hiro and Kite are just beginning.

Chapter Forty-eight

Kite

Gentle hands smooth my blanket, and then a palm rests on my forehead while fingers press to my wrist. These hands are not rough from rusty hooks or chipped from chain-link fences.

"He hasn't left your side," sighs the nurse. "It's so romantic."

I watch Hiro, twisted in a plastic chair. He's good at sleeping in tight places. He's just… good. We haven't spoken of marriage again. Those words feel pushed through a keyhole. It's enough that he's here—that I truly understand his love was never conditional on traditional things. He's right. We can make our own family. With the Kings, we're more than halfway there as it is.

I haven't told him about my visit with Mr. Inkham but I will. For once, I feel like we have some time and space to figure things out. Time used to be measured in escaping seconds. Now, despite my collapsed lung, I feel like I can breathe.

"Hiro," I whisper. "Wake up."

He blinks awake suddenly, arms up in defense from imagined threats. It could take a while for him to adjust to a life where he's not always fighting for survival. Biting my lip, I worry about his ties to the tunnel and the Kings. *What if he doesn't want to leave?*

He comes to the bed and takes my hand. "What is it? Do you need something?" His dark eyes are sleepy, his hair crinkled and messy.

I frown. I do. I need Frankie, but at the same time, I'm not sure I want her to see me like this. "I…"

He finishes for me. "You need Frankie, but you don't know if she can handle…" He gestures at my general state. "…all of this."

All of this. All of me folded into a swollen red and purple shape. I nod. "I don't want to scare her."

He sighs. Eyes darting to the corner. To those shadows we've become so accustomed to that are now missing. "Can I say something?" His dark hair ruffles over his eyebrows. His concern so sweet.

"Always."

"She's much tougher than you know. She also understands a lot more than we give her credit for… It may upset her to see you like this, but this is the truth of your situation. She needs to see what he did… and know there is no coming back from it. It will kind of be a final way for her to put *him* to rest."

It sounds extremely harsh. I gulp. "You know he's in prison now."

He nods, eyes narrowing. "I know. It's better than he deserves."

I want to tell him that we could go home, to a real home, but something holds me back. He's said *no* to me so many times. I couldn't bear it if he turned me down again. I also need to be sure it's what I want, so I clutch the news to my chest even as it flaps its anxious wings and tries to get away from me. *I'll tell him. I will...* There's a break in the wings. A feather missing. I'm still not sure *I* want to go home. Not to that home.

"Can you bring her to me?" I ask, eyes glistening.

He smiles, teeth hiding. "Of course."

I don't want him to leave. The second we manage to mend, something else gets in the way.

Trying to settle my nerves, I tell myself it will be okay. We're used to the call of other responsibilities.

He takes his coat and leaves.

And I feel like the threads between us are getting stretched, just a little. Because I want to give Hiro the world, and I'm scared he won't accept it.

He's only gone an hour, but it's enough time for me to have chewed my nails down and started on the skin. A small knock on the door startles me, and I straighten in my bed, trying to look less destroyed.

"Nor-ah..." Frankie sounds like a mouse. It's unusual for her. But then, what must I look like to her? I smile, hurting my cut lip, and I touch it to check it hasn't started bleeding again. "Are you okay?"

Timid feet tiptoe into the room. Messy, fire-lit hair. Smudge of dirt on her jaw. A strong, warm shadow behind her, keeping her safe. For me.

"I'm okay." I catch Hiro's expression of encouragement. It says *you're not okay, but you will be.* I beckon to her and she scuttles across the linoleum floor, her arms landing on the bed. She tries to hug me, and I make a strange squealing noise when she presses too hard on my chest. "Actually, Frankie, I'm not really okay. I'm hurt. I'm quite badly hurt." Those last words are so hard for me to say. I've been the soldier and shield for so long, protecting her from physical harm. But I've also shut her out of the details.

She blinks at me with tears in her eyes, and I don't want to continue talking. Hiro tips his chin, telling me with his eyes that I can do this. He steps away from the doorway, leaving us alone.

"What happened to you, Nor-ah?" She swings where she stands, always in constant movement like a top that perpetually spins. But she's being careful of me. She's growing up. *God, I wish she wouldn't.*

"Our father got very angry…" I start, then stop. Realizing in some way, I'm trying to justify his actions. "I mean…"

Her blue eyes show she knows it all. She just needs me to confirm it. "Deddy hurt you, didn't he?"

I reach for her hands. Our clasped fingers becoming a haven for a new life, free from the terror of Christopher Deere. "Our father really hurt me, Frankie. I want you to understand that he hurt me so badly that the police came and took him away."

"Is he in jail?" she asks, still squeezing my fingers. Her little chest rises and falls as her feet dance.

"He's in jail, and he will probably be there for a very long time." Not probably. *He will. He will. He will.*

She exhales loudly. I can actually feel the relief pouring from her rattling lungs. A sweet breeze carrying blossoms and lilies. "Good. Then we can go home." She crosses her arms over her chest.

My face tightens. *Home.* Home feels far away for me but Frankie's eyes are bright with anticipation and hope. "I don't know…"

She stands on her tiptoes. Leaning over me, a waif with flames for hair and iron for will. "If he's not there, then we can be there. If he's not coming back, then we don't hef to worry no more."

There's a *please* in her eyes. A please I can't possibly refuse. "Okay. When I get out of here, we can go home." And maybe with her help and Hiro's, we can flush the bad air out and fill it with good things. Lost and found things.

When she jumps up, she nearly sends a bag of fluids sailing across the room with my arm attached to it. Biting down to stop from screaming, I press my hand to the vein and tube to stop it from popping out. "And Kettle and Kelpie? And Keg and Krow and…"

I bat my hands. "Calm down. Calm down. I don't know about that."

Her face falls, and she purses her little mouth. "I ain't goin' without Kelpie. I promised he could sleep in ma room."

I exhale through my nose loudly. "You shouldn't have done that."

A wobbly cough makes us both look up. Marie waddles into the room with apologies all over her face. I see a familiar black eye, a single injury to envy. It's of a swing out and an almost miss that I rarely got. If he missed me, he always came back around for extra punishment. I try to relax at the sight of this reminder.

You're safe. You're safe. You're safe. Words I nestle into every available space. Between the blinds, under my pillow, on the windowsill.

I do know that when Marie looks at my face, all she will see is gratitude.

Chapter Forty-nine

Kite

"Marie!" Frankie slams into Marie like she's found the cloud she's been chasing. She squeezes the poor woman until an odd-sounding grunt escapes. Air forced up and out from the pressure.

I raise my broken arm carefully. "Frankie, please stop trying to squeeze all the air out of Marie." She releases her a little, and I see a heave of relief from the plump woman's breast.

She pats Frankie on the head, smiling warily. "It's good to see you, Miss Frances. Where have you... I mean, how have you been?"

Frankie chomps at the air with her teeth. It makes an awful noise, and we both grimace. "I been good. I been makin' friends..." She starts counting them on her fingers. "Kelpie, Keg, Krow... an...an... Kettle!" she shouts through the doorway. I don't know where he's disappeared to. "What's tha name of the new kid?"

Small puffs of pride fluff the lining of my chest at her adaptability. Her reference to the "new kid" like she's an old member of the Kings.

Marie, stunned by all the names and information, clucks her tongue. "Goodness, child. That's a lot of new friends. With some very interesting names."

Frankie nods like a toy on a spring. "It is. It is. It is." She wiggles her fingers. "I hef a new name, too. It's Kricket." She squats down and frog leaps.

Marie laughs nervously. "Kricket suits you very well."

Hiro's head appears in the doorway, his expression dark. Maybe it's Marie. The last time he saw her, she closed the door while I was being beaten with a coat rack.

Small shivers try to creep up my spine and I make a concerted effort to stop them. This is harder than I thought it would be.

I whisper to myself, "You're safe." And tap my heart.

"What's the new kid's name?" Frankie asks, running to Hiro and slamming into him like a quarterback. He stumbles back playfully.

"Krafty," he mutters in a guarded voice.

I was only gone a few days, and there's already a new kid. Frowning, I pick at loose threads on my cast.

Frankie buzzes around the room, too excited to sit. I give Hiro a look, which doesn't go unnoticed by Marie. He sweeps Frankie up, carrying her out of the room.

"Let's see if we can come up with a really keen drawing for your sister's cast." His voice gets further away. I breathe in and out deeply, enjoying in the calm air for a moment.

Marie steps forward, producing a tin of cookies from her large bag. "Here," she whispers. "I made these for you. I know they're your favorite."

When I open the lid, the smell of ginger and butter drags me backward. Presses my back into a Christmas pine tree, needles puncturing my clothes. The ornaments rattle as he approaches, and his hand is already in back swing. Swallowing, I shut the lid. "Thank you, Marie, that's very kind of you." These memories aren't easy to shake. Maybe I'll never quite be rid of them. The important thing to hold onto is the knowledge they are *only* memories. Pictures and plays of the past that will never be repeated. She bows like I'm a princess. Like I should be fussed over and treated. "I want to say…" Her words dissolve. She's so frozen in the way things are supposed to be between maids and masters, parents and children. I was there when she stepped out of that cast once and I know she can do it again.

I'm going to need her help if my plan is to work.

"Marie. You don't need to say anything. I know how hard it was to stand up to him. I know why you didn't in the past. I am forever grateful for what you did. You helped me end it. And… you saved my life."

Tears are forming in the soft, crinkled corners of her eyes. Like dew on curling autumn leaves. "I still want to say I'm sorry. I did wrong by you and your sister. And I will never forgive myself for it. I won't."

Wringing her hands, she stares at the floor. "Please, Marie. Don't hold onto this guilt. It will do you no good at all. If you must hold onto something, hold onto to the good you did."

I reach for her hands. My fingers just brushing the tense ball of fingers.

"Yes. At least he can't hurt you no more." She sets her mouth and chin hard. There is no sympathy for my father in there. "Now, Miss Nora, when are you coming home? I've cleaned the house from top to bottom, so it's nice and fresh for your homecoming."

I'm unsure. Nervous of what Hiro might say. Scared of how I might feel gazing up at those terrible stairs. "I don't know." She looks concerned. Not sure which way to turn. "Marie. Are you still receiving your wages? Is our driver and the other staff?"

She shakes her head. "Don't you worry about that, Miss. We'll manage."

I purse my lips. This new coat of adulthood alighting my shoulders. "I certainly will worry about it. I will speak to Mr. Inkham to have you all paid by the end of the week."

"Thank you, Miss. And then, when you come home, we can set about making the place your own."

My own. My. Own. I *own* the brownstone.

I nod. Still wrestling with the truth. Maybe the only way to rid myself of him is to clear him out. Take ownership of the house and make it mine.

Straightening my bedding, she offers one last thing. "Let me look after Frankie for you while you recover. I promise, I'll take good care of her. She hasn't missed too much school. I'm sure she can catch up."

As if on cue, Frankie coughs and re-enters the room. "I ain't goin' without you." She crosses her arms over her chest. Eyes stormy. Hair raising, anticipating a lightning strike.

I stroke her restless head as Hiro's face reads through emotions like a runaway scroll. "You should go. You can sleep in your own bed. Eat Marie's delicious pancakes."

Frankie shivers, and the lightning is absorbed by the earth. "But what about you?"

I kiss the top of her head. "I'll be right behind you."

She leans into my palm. *I'm always right behind you.*

Chapter Fifty

Hiro

This is where it was always supposed to end. With the rich girl going back to her brownstone and me going back to my life as a King. But when I heard her say, *I don't know about that,* it's like she's clamped a hand around my heart and tugged as hard as she could.

Love is there but practicality leads us.

They say goodbye, but Marie, the round housemaid, promises to bring Kricket back for daily visits. Kite's face swings to mine, physical and emotional pain wreaking havoc on her stretched face. "Will you drop Frankie's things to the brownstone?"

"Sure."

She looks smarted by my one-word answer, but I don't know what to say. Of course, I knew she wasn't going to stay in the tunnel forever. Hell, I knew I couldn't stay there forever. But I was hoping for a little more time.

I watch her expression. There's a new sharpness to her eyes. "Hiro, I need to tell you something…"

I cut her off. "It's okay. You're going back to your home, to the brownstone. You should; it's where you belong." I start packing things that don't even belong to me just for something to do.

Her eyebrows draw together. Her hand shrinks to a fist. "Where *we* belong. You, me, and Frankie." She thumps the mattress weakly. She's still so damaged. "It has to be *our* home, or it's nothing."

"What?" I scrunch a plastic cup in my hand.

She continues to softly thump the mattress in a steady beat like a battle march. "I don't belong anywhere if you're not with me. I would sleep in an abandoned subway tunnel or a cardboard box in a dirty alley til' the end of my days, as long as I'm with you." She gestures wildly, hands still fisted like she's holding onto her words for dear life. I take them and still them, laughing a little at her grim expression and determination.

I chuckle. "That won't be necessary. But I don't know what I'm going to tell the Kings."

A wicked smile breaks across her lips like treasure is hidden behind her teeth. "You can tell them the Kings have a new hideout."

My heart punches out a new rhythm, a 'this can't really be happening' kind of song. *Can I really take what she's offering?* I look into her amber eyes with bright sparks of stardust. They look infinitely stubborn. *I don't think she's going to take no for an answer.*

I lean into her. Our noses touching.

"Are you sure about this? You just said you weren't only five minutes ago." She gives me quizzical look, lips quirked. Eyes dancing like a ballerina.

She pokes me in the chest. "Eavesdropper. I was thinking I wasn't sure if *I* wanted to be back there. It holds a lot of bad memories. I would never leave the Kings. They're my family, I'm not going to leave them behind."

"We'll chase out the bad together," I say goofily, and she giggles.

"I was hoping you'd say that. And there is something else. Someone else we need to talk to..." She watches my face, waiting for something.

When it dawns on me, she laughs loudly, touching her chest when it stings her injuries. "Kin..."

She grins. "Tell your brother to pack his belongings."

I'm weightless, finding myself in an actual good dream. I clasp her hands, kissing them. Looking up, I search for doubt. "You know this will cause a huge scandal. Us living in sin and housing a bunch of street urchins..." I find none.

She gobbles up all the light. This bright, new star shining through her, around her. "I love a good scandal!"

Chapter Fifty-one

Hiro

I have several tasks to perform.

Talk to the Kings. Get Frankie's stuff and bring it to the brownstone. Our new home. Those three words seem impossible, like three animals destined to be enemies all lined up in a row.

I observe my brown hands, turning them over. It has been a while since I've looked at myself as different. That's Kite doing. She's worked her way into my mind, changed things that needed changing and loving all of me anyway.

It may seem strange, but I don't mind the idea of living in sin. I want to marry her, but I want her to be in control of her life first. She needs to run the show. That's the only way I see it working.

Reaching the turnstile, I hesitate with my hands clutching the metal. She's offering me the world and I will make sure I am worthy of it. A man shoves me in the back, and I curve over the turnstile like a folded tortilla. "Move it, Jap traitor."

This is where I should pull my hat down and step aside but change is in the air. I turn around to face the man. "Excuse me?" I stand tall. The man growls and places a hand on my shoulder, shoving me aside like I'm an obstacle, not a person.

"You heard me." He spits on the ground.

I smile. Tipping my hat at him, I say, "I'm a Japanese American. I'm no traitor. I work hard. I take care of my family. I deserve your respect, not your hate."

The jostle of people is making it hard to be heard. My eyes are steel glinting in the sun and my face is proud and strong. I will not hide anymore.

The man's burly fist hits me like a brick. I manage one break-out punch before it goes dark as tar paper.

Cold concrete presses against my face. The rush of blood swirling against my eardrums. Scrunching my eyes, I don't feel the tar-papered thin boards beneath me. The paper-thin boards that felt like an origami box and barely kept the cold air out. I'm not *there*. I am here. Though I don't know where *here* is. I don't want to open my eyes to find army greens and distrusting expressions.

I press my palms to the ground, feeling unfamiliar surfaces which is good.

A voice like popcorn in a paper bag—amused and buttery. "The kid's alive!" Hands clap. Boots tap out warning messages on the floor.

Feet shuffle close by. *Open your eyes.*

"It's a mean trick, Officer." The bars between our cells vibrate as they're struck in frustration. "Putting the kid so close, yet so far away." Papers ruffle. A telephone rings.

As I take a deep breath, the slow ebb of panic builds to a wave. *They have me. They caught me.* It will be over so fast. I have a vague memory of shiny car doors slamming. People discussing my life like it's not my own. *What to do. What to do. What to do.* With the Jap kid. The Nip. The traitor. The spy.

My head whirls as I try to adjust to the white light. Dark wood desks and the disarray of a police station surround me. The cell bars seem to press into my chest and stripe my skin, making it hard to breathe. My jaw smarts, and I lift my hand to it gingerly.

Oxygen is tight. I swallow small gulps of it like it's running out.

The police officer steps closer and squats down. Frowning, he wipes black, floppy hair from his forehead. "You took a pretty hard knock to the head, kid. Just take it slowly."

His words seem kind enough. I know my face is coated with confusion as I try to absorb my surroundings. I'm in the center of a holding cell and there is no way out.

I try to compress my fear, but it does the opposite. Expanding past my body, it fills the room with a dark, hopeless cloud.

Head tipped to the side, the cop watches me with several degrees of fascination, squinting like I'm the bull's-eye of a shooting target. "What's your story?" he asks, filling a cup with water and passing it through the bars. "You Chinese or something?"

I take the cup with shaky hands. "Or something." I don't want them to know my true heritage. I don't want to give them any reason to look into my *story* any further.

Standing, he shakes his head. "No need for the bad attitude, son. I was just curious."

After I place the cup down, I scoot backward until my back is against the bars. The cop turns away from me, and his partner chuckles. "Why don't you get him to teach you some of those Kung-Fu moves. Though, he got knocked out too easily to be a master."

Shadows move in the corner coalescing into the stench of sour, whiskey-stink breath. An arm wraps around my throat before I have a chance to react. I scratch at the arm as it pulls me hard against the bars. "It'd be Karate. He's a Jap," the owner of the arm shouts with hate and disgust. My airway is crushed until I can't even scream while part of me is impressed that this drunk knows the difference between Kung Fu and Karate. "I should know. I've killed enough of 'em." Then they sour.

Maybe this is how it ends for me. Choked by a drunk in the opposite cell. My face the cause; the war the reason.

My eyes start to fade black at the corners like the end of a movie.

The cops scramble to the cell, swinging the door open. The muffled bash and crash of the drunk being subdued flies over my head. The arm finally releases and I fall to the floor, coughing and spluttering and crawling out of reach.

"Marvin, we warned you," the cop says as he cuffs the drunk to the bars. "You just never learn, do you?"

Marvin spits on the floor and sneers. "His kind shouldn't be allowed to jes' walk the streets like they own the place."

The cop shoots me a look I don't know how to respond to. It's sort of an eye roll and it's also like he's bringing me in on it, like he wants me to join him. I just stare, eyes round as dinner plates. I'm waiting for them to make the call.

"He's just a kid, for Christ's sake." He points at me. "How old are you?"

Lie.

"Eighteen, sir." My eyes find the warm corners of the room. I'm so scared he'll know I'm lying that my knees shake.

This is all my bad past gathered in one room. Incarceration is the nightmare that's been chasing me my whole life. I don't know how to act. I don't know who to trust or what's real.

Ignoring Marvin's cursing, the cop slams the door to his cell and locks it. "See, eighteen. Now, I'm not great at math, but even I know he would have been a little kid when the war started. Hell, when it ended, too."

Marvin continues to say horrible things. I know this kind of man. There is no appealing to his rational side.

The cop comes back to my cell and stares. "So, you're Japanese…" He's assessing my face. My clothes. He's trying to make sense of me.

"Half." I pull my knees up, resting my elbows on them. I want to bury myself under the concrete floor. It can only be a matter of time before they come.

"Half Japanese, jeepers. You must have had an interesting life." Interesting? *Hard.*

His partner snorts. "Come finish your paperwork."

My hands wrap around the bars tightly. I pull. Not because I think I can move them but because I need something to hold onto as my world slips down the drain like laundry water.

It was all there.

And now it's gone.

Chapter Fifty-two

Kite

iving in sin. I like the way that sounds.

I run my hands along my arms along hairs that refuse to lay down. The idea that I could have what I want feels so ridiculously good. My smile breaks the cut through my lips, and I taste blood.

The nurse enters, starched and soft, and quirks an eyebrow. "You look cheerful."

I blink away what I think must be tears of joy. They run through the trails already staked and marked by pain, revitalizing parched hopeless places.

I press my finger to my lips, gazing at the droplet of blood coloring my skin. "I am. Very."

She gives me a quizzical look, then leans me forward to fluff my pillow. "Well, I'm glad, dear. If you've managed to find a little piece of joy in this world, you should hold onto it for all it's worth."

I nod, trying to lessen my smile so my cut can clot. *I plan to.*

"Could you please telephone my lawyer, Mr. Inkham, for me? I'd like to meet with him as soon as possible."

The nurse nods. "You got it."

Mr. Inkham looks flustered. His scarf carries hitchhiking snowflakes that melt to water spots as he removes his hat and coat.

I've been waiting for Hiro to return. Watching the door like it's a portal about to close. I know he must have much to organize, but...

I shake my head to clear the bad thoughts, batting at old worry like dusty rugs. *It's okay. You're safe.*

"Miss Deere, how are you feeling? I hope you're well." He talks fast. "What can I do for you?"

I giggle. "Are you all right, Mr. Inkham? You seem a little, er, harried."

He swipes at his face. "No. No. I'm perfectly all right. I'm just following quite a few cases right now. Tell me, Nora, what can I do for *you*?" The way he says it seems meaningful. Like he's decided to step further into my story.

As I explain my intentions, his eyes widen until I think they won't stay in his head, instead they might pop like buttons from a torn shirt. Coughing, he plays with his tie and takes a deep breath.

I watch him carefully for signs this is a bad idea. I see none except acknowledgement that it's a large undertaking. "So... that's it. I need your assistance with the finer details. The legal obstacles..."

"Miss Deere, you do realize you'll be going against what is considered socially acceptable, don't you? People will have strong opinions on what you plan to do. It will make your life quite… difficult. Are you prepared for the consequences?"

I almost laugh and have to cover my mouth, before the absurdity hits him square in the eye. Sighing, I compose myself. "Mr. Inkham, with all due respect, my life up until now has been *difficult*. Nothing about this seems insurmountable. To me, this is the easiest decision. It makes the most sense."

His eyes soften and settle. Getting out a pen, he starts jotting down my instructions and making his own notes. When he's done, he stabs the paper like he's marking the occasion. Pinpointing the day my life truly changed.

The nurse returns, and I ask, "How much longer do I need to stay here?"

She pats my hand. "If you can afford a private nurse to visit you once a day, I don't see why you wouldn't be able to leave tomorrow." I want to climb up her words like a rope ladder out of here, but she puts a finger up to stop me. "Just… let me check with the doctor first."

Mr. Inkham looks up from his paper. "So, Miss Deere, if you would like to go ahead with the establishment of your home as a private orphanage, just sign here to authorize me to begin the process."

I sign what I am told will be the first of many, many papers. He's trying to warn me, but I welcome the work. *Let papers fly at my face, laundry pile to the rafters, plates stack high in our kitchen. I float above it all.*

I shift in my bed. Ready to walk. To fly. "Thank you, Mr. Inkham. Could you do me one more favor?"

"Of course." His body is still, awaiting my request. He's a strange man. One I don't really know but I guess that will change.

"Can you stop by the house and check on Frankie? I worry about her all alone in that big place with Marie." I smile at secrets on wings carrying my mouth upward. "I worry about poor old Marie, too, all alone in that big house with my whirlwind of a sister!"

He nods, not quite smiling. He doesn't strike as me a someone who smiles very much. "Absolutely." He tilts his head. Opens and closes his mouth. Stares at his tie and then looks up. "You know you remind so much of Rebecca sometimes. Before she met your father, she had grand plans to change the world."

My eyes fall.

He stumbles over his words. "Oh, dear. I don't mean to upset you. What I'm trying to say is I think she would be very impressed with the young woman you've become."

I feel a flutter of pride and then it fades. I'm glad he sees something in me that will make him work harder for what I want to achieve. The Rebecca I knew was a shell and barely kept me safe. She did little and caused much. I loved her but she's not my hero. She's not someone I aspire to be. If anything, I aspire to be less like her. I'm doing this for me and the Kings. Not to win approval. In fact, I think to many, it will have the opposite effect.

He leaves in a flurry, same as he entered. He has a lot of work to do.

And so do I.

Changing the world will happen in small, slight turns. I'll be happy if we can change just one street, or even one stoop.

Chapter Fifty-three

Frankie

It feels good to be home and back in my bed. I like my toys. I like rolling around on the carpet. It's soft and warm and if I wiggle enough, my fingers spark and I can shock Marie. I liked the tunnel, too, but it was cold. I hate being cold.

I lie on my tummy, pressing my fingers into the patterns on the floor, waiting for Nora to tell me off. I sigh big enough to fill a hot air balloon. Nora's not here. Nora's all banged up and broken, and Daddy made her that way.

Daddy needs to stay away from here.

I hear a knock at the door and jump up. My feet are springs and I'm a bunny, *jumpin', jumpin', jumpin'* out the door and across the landing. *Jump. Jump. Jump* to the scary stairs.

I bite my lip and hold onto the railing, being more careful coz that's what Nora would want me to be.

I'm being super fast but really careful as I take the stairs two at a time, my skirts flying up like there's a big wind in the reception hall. When I hit the bottom step, I see a man standing there like a funny little statue. His eyes are round, and his hair is squashed down from his hat. He bows to me like I'm a princess, and I give him my best frown.

"I know you," I say, pointing at him as Marie tuts and takes the man's coat. "I seen you a bunch a times." Mommy used to talk to this man when Daddy wasn't home. They'd sit in the front room and whisper like they had secrets. And when I tried to come in and see what was going on, Mommy would close the door on me. I didn't like it one bit.

The man clears his throat, holding out his hand. "I'm Mr. Inkham, your family solicitor. Your sister may have mentioned me before. She asked me to stop by and check on you."

I feel my face puckering up like I've just bitten into a lemon, which I have done before, a lot of times even though Nora told me not to. "My soul… Soul stir?" I shake my head.

"Or you can say lawyer. I handle your family's legal affairs. Does that make sense?" He bends to looks in my eyes. He's giving me that look like Nora gives me when she thinks I've said something I shouldn't have said.

I lean away. "No, I know you from when Mommy was still here."

Marie makes a funny noise, then starts pushing me toward the stairs. "Nothing to worry about here. We're doing just fine. Aren't we, Miss Frances?"

I grip the railing and think about Nora. Marie keeps pushing, and I poke my butt out. Making it hard for her to move me. "I'm fine," I shout. "But Nor-ah's not so good."

The man looks sad. "No, she has been through a lot."

Turning around suddenly, I glare at Marie. "I wanna talk to Mister Ink… Ham."

Marie looks real worried and her face shakes like jello, but Mr. Inkham nods and shoos her away. It annoys me that she listens to him and not me, but at least she's gone.

I sit on the step, patting the space next to me. He looks all uncomfortable like he wants to pee, but then he sits beside me. "What can I do for you, Miss Frances?"

I cross my arms. "It's Frankie or Kricket, but actually, though, don't call me Kricket. That name's special."

He puts his hands on his knees, staring at the door to the outside. "Okay, Frankie. What did you want to talk about?"

"I want to talk about Deddy." He moves on the stairs, breathing slowly like he's getting ready to hold it. I'm not good at that game. "Where is ma Deddy right now?"

His mouth is hard, and his jaw looks tight like he can't swallow. "Your father is being held in a prison."

I tilt my head. "How long will he stay there?"

Mr. Inkham sighs long. "It's hard to be sure but I believe he will be there for a very long time. Your sister's and Marie's accounts, plus that of the policemen, are solid evidence that will be very hard to refute."

I kick his ankle with my bare foot. "Yer using a lot of big words I don't understand. I want to know for sure. I want to know that he cain't ever come back here no more."

Mr. Inkham looks very sad now. Putting his hands in his hair and frowning. "I can't promise anything one hundred percent until the trial is over. The problem is your father is pleading *not guilty*." I scowl at him again, and he says, "He's saying he didn't do it."

This makes my chest hurt and a fire build behind my eyes. "But he did do it. He's been doin' it forever!"

Mr. Inkham nods. "Yes. But he is presumed innocent until proven guilty. Luckily, because he assaulted a police officer, he's been refused bail."

"That's stupid, and what's bail?"

He's trying to be patient with me, but he doesn't seem too used to kids. "He will be held in jail until after the trial."

I need to do something. When I think about Daddy being back in this house or him getting close to Nora again, I feel like

I might explode with worry. "What'd make him hef to stay in jail with no… uh… trial? Like how could we make him one hundred per cents have to stay in there?" I ask.

He turns to me. His eyes have gone really serious. "The only way that would happen would be if your father pleaded guilty. He would have to admit what he had done and accept responsibility for his actions."

Standing, I face him. This seems like a good plan. This is the thing I can do for Nora, when she's done so much for me. "Well, let's make him do that."

Mr. Inkham's eyebrows rise, but he doesn't have the 'no' look in his eyes.

I know Nora would be cross at me for doing this. I'm gonna have to keep it a secret, at least for a little while.

We got to ride in a taxi, then we got out and walked up a long path to a big gray building with fences as high as the sky. My neck hurts from looking up, and I squeeze Mr. Inkham's hand as we walk through gates and doors and more gates and more doors. Until we're standing in a funny room. Kind of like a ticket office.

Daddy looks small. He's dressed in pajamas, and his hair is messy. His face looks scratchy. He is very surprised to see me. He is mad to see Mr. Inkham.

There's glass between us and a telephone. Daddy's eyes are dark and angry, and I try to find him in there. I wave and smile, and he suddenly looks more like he used to on those days when he would give me a kiss and make pancakes. I let go of Mr. Inkham's hand, then scrunch my fingers into fists. That Daddy, the pancake one, never stayed around for very long. I mostly remember the angry one. The hitting one.

Mr. Inkham sits down, picking up the phone. I can't hear what Daddy says, but he looks like he did when he found me in Mama's closet trying on her dresses.

His voice is calm. But that kind of calm someone forces into their voice.

"Yes. I know this is no place for a little girl. ... She insisted. ... This is what it has come to, Christopher, because you can't accept what you have done. ... No. ... I promised you would listen. It's the absolute least you can do."

Mr. Inkham gets up, then lets me sit. He gives me the telephone, and I press it hard to my ear so I can hear better.

"Frances, darling, it's so good to see you." I know this voice. It's at the start of something bad. I put my hand up to the glass to test it. It's pretty thick. And there are people here to save me and stop him.

I think about my words really careful. "Hello, Deddy. I hef come here to ask you to plead guilty to what you did to Nor-ah."

I watch his face change. Eyebrows go up. Cheeks tighten. His mouth is smiling but it's not a real smile, and I feel like I've swallowed a bird and it's trying to peck its way out of my chest. "Frances. Frankie. It's not as simple as they would have you believe... I..."

I spread my hand out over the glass. "Stop. Deddy, please. Please jes stop hurting us. You don't know how to do it by yerself. I know you've tried, but it never works. You need to stay here so we can be safe. You need to let Nor-ah and me be safe."

His fingers go all white around the telephone, coz he's holding it so tight. I think he's gonna yell at me. I think maybe he'll try and smash the glass with the phone, but his hand slowly goes back to pink and his eyes stop being hard and angry.

His neck seems to go all floppy, and his head falls into his hands. And then he does what I thought he would. He starts smashing. Thumping the little table in front of him with his fists. The glass shakes, and I can feel the pounding coming through to the table in front of me. It sends wobbles through my body. He just keeps smashing, smashing, smashing. He's scaring me, and I stand up and turn to Mr. Inkham, who wraps his arms around me and holds me close. I don't want to look at Daddy no more. I don't think I ever want to see his face again.

"You did so well, Frankie."

He takes my hand, and we walk away.

I really hope Daddy listened to me.

Chapter Fifty-four

Hiro

Groaning, the cop slaps a hand over his face. "Ugh! I almost forgot. Your phone call."

Small trickles of hope slide down the black brick walls. I lift my eyes. "My phone call?"

He strides to the cell briskly and unlocks it. Blunt iron. The door swings open, and he just lets me walk out. "You get one phone call. Everyone gets one phone call."

He picks up the phone and holds it out to me, yanking it away when I reach for it. "First, you need to give me a name." I don't know why I say it; it just kind of flies out before I can stop myself. "Hiro Deere," I mutter. The cop scrawls the name on a piece of paper, spelling it correctly, which is surprising, and nods.

"Make sense, I guess. Japanese first name and American second name…" He doesn't get the ridiculousness of his statement. Even if my last name had been Japanese, it would still be American. But that's such a large part of the problem.

His partner grunts. "You idiot, Torres."

"What… what did I say?" He approaches his partner, the spiral cord of the phone stretching, and they start arguing. I take the opportunity to dial while they're distracted. It starts ringing, and the cop speaks into the receiver. "Hi, this is Officer Torres of the 77th. I have Hiro Deere for…"

"Katsutoshi," I say.

Officer Torres sounds out the name slowly. "Kat…su…toshi." Seeming very impressed with himself for getting it right.

He hands me the phone. Kin's voice is like a warm breeze in this freezing hellhole. "Kettle, Kettle, Kettle." Kin clucks his tongue. "What kind of trouble have you got yourself into now?"

His humor dissipates as I explain my predicament. "I'll be there as soon as I can," he says, and I sigh with relief. "Do you know why they're holding you?"

I turn to the cop. "Why are you holding me?"

The cop frowns. "We're waiting for Marvin to sober up, so we can get a statement."

I look at the snoring, slobbering mess that is Marvin and purse my lips. If he's what decides my fate, then I'm in bigger trouble than I thought. "Kin," I whisper. "I'm…"

His voice is too calm. "I know, little brother, but try not to panic."

I'm led back into my cell. Bars were where I started. Maybe that was always where I was going to end.

My eyes droop heavily. My feet have pins and needles as I un-cross them and cross them the other way. I don't know how long I've been here, and I'm starting to wish they'd just throw me in the black car and be done with it already. The waiting is agony.

The stretch of knowing Kite is waiting for me is torture, like I'm on a medieval rack. I reach through the air, close my eyes, and imagine my cheek pressed to hers. Her bottled-star laughs and deep dark sighs.

I lace my fingers across my chest, listening to the throttling snore of Marvin. The bastard who got me into this mess. I want to kick him and then scream at the unfairness of it all for good measure.

It must be nearly twelve hours now. The cops have changed shifts twice, and now I see the same officers I had the day before.

The snore becomes a rumbling thunder, reminding me of lightning chasing black clouds over the desert. Flashes of white illuminating yellow eyed coyotes, frozen like a photo, and then gone by the next strike. The chain-link fence rattled like cheap bells as they tried to dig their way in. Rain evaporating on the cracked, begging-for-moisture earth. My first real home shaking like a house of cards as it was butted by headstrong wind.

I breathe in deeply.

The smell of wet grass. Grateful faces lifted to the sky. It was like that all the time. Searching for a promise no one was making. Hoping this month was the last month. Always disappointed.

Always.

These memories are cross-stitched into my skin.

The creak of greasy hinges slaps me awake. "Hiro Deere. You are free to go."

Blinking, I stay right where I am. Needles and cotton sewing me to the floor.

The knock of wood makes the cops turn around and me nearly smile, though I don't trust it. "You're telling me I came all the way downtown for nothing?"

Kin's imposing shadow is cut into long, proud pieces by the bars I'm still hiding behind. "Kin..." I sigh.

I stand warily, still acting like a caged animal that doesn't trust the offered freedom. I take a step forward, and the cop watches me. Kin watches me, too, dark concern over his features.

"Do you want to stay behind bars or what, Mr. Deere?" the cop asks, confused. Kin raises an eyebrow but doesn't say anything.

I pass the cop, wiping my hands on my pants and staring at the floor. "I… I don't understand. Why am I being released?"

After he shuts the cell gate behind me, he locks it. "Well, we gave up on getting anything useful out of Marvin. So, we went looking for a statement from the ticket attendant. We had some trouble tracking him down after his shift. Anyway, he confirmed what we thought. That old Marvin here…" He points at the stinking, sleeping man, arm hanging from the low bench. "Threw the first punch."

My eyes widen. Still not quite ready to believe I can just walk out of here. "So, that's it? There's nothing else…"

Chuckling, Kin throws his arm around my shoulder. "You'll have to excuse my little brother here. He's never been in trouble like this before. I think he's a little shook up." Kin's wearing an army jacket with his father's medals pinned to the chest. The men nod, looking him directly in the eye. I stand there like an idiot, waiting for it all to turn. For cuffs to snap and sharp words to be thrown. Quick punches and bowed heads. But Kin just shakes one of their hands before saying, "Thank you, Officers. I'm sorry for all the trouble."

They both nod, then go back to their paperwork.

We walk out of the police station untouched, and I can't believe it.

I also can't believe the attitude rolling off Kin's broad back. He seems irritated. Almost disappointed.

The moment we've stepped onto the sidewalk, Kin shakes his head and groans. I flinch. "What, what is it? Are they coming?"

My body tenses. I'm ready for flight.

Kin's mouth sets like concrete, gazing down on me with this serious, knowing expression I don't like. "No one is coming, Kettle. That's the point."

My shoulders roll and tense. My heart twists like a rope swing. Let it go and it'll spin and spin. "What are you talking about, Kin? I was lucky."

He shakes his head, a strange, mocking smile on his lips. I don't like the smile. "Get a clue, man."

My head switches back and forth, looking for a dark alley. My mind falls back to old instincts. "Get what clue?" I ask, tugging on his arm so we can cross the street, but he won't move.

His eyes lift to a small delicatessen on the corner, and he starts hobbling toward it. He ignores my question. "I could use some breakfast. What about you?"

Kin's eyes are connecting with curious gazes. Mine are on my hands, wrapped around the steaming cup on the table. "Look up," he says quietly. My eyes stay low. I can't quite shake the feeling something bad is just behind the newsstand or waiting around the corner. Kin thumps the table. "Look up, damn it!" he demands.

My eyes lift slowly. "What's the matter with you?" I say tersely, hunching down when eyes land on the two of us.

"What's the matter with *you*?" He points at my chest hard, and I freeze. Not understanding why he's so angry.

My butt hugs the edge of the chair as I slink down. "Kin. People are staring. Stop it."

He shrugs. "So what? Who cares?"

"I care. You should care, too."

He exhales noisily and bites into his bagel, chewing slowly and watching me with shadowy, unreadable eyes. Finally, he swallows and speaks, "No. You've got it wrong, brother. I've let that fear go. I don't need to care. No one's looking for me. No one's going to lock me up and throw away the key." He's talking too loudly, and I shrink. "You need to let go of your fear."

Meekly and without much conviction, I say, "I have."

He chuckles in a sarcastic kind of way. "No. You haven't. It rules you. You have a right to be here. To live here. This is your city. Your home."

I want to believe him. I feel like I'm over halfway there, but I can't just drop my shadow in the street. It's going to cling to me. Follow me whether I like it or not.

"But you saw what happened. I got arrested just for defending myself." I shove the proof in his face, but he won't take it.

Kin snorts. "Yeah, you got in a fight. You got arrested, and you were released. They treated you like any other idiot who got in a fight in the subway. Welcome to America, buddy." He puts on a harsh Yankee accent.

I try to expel the last little piece of barbed wire that's been living inside my throat, scraping out a small round space. "You done?" I ask, kicking his good leg under the table.

Kin straightens. "I'm never done. I'm like a zombie. You can keep shooting, keep putting me down, but I'll always get back up. I'll keep on comin' and comin'…"

I finally smile, breaking the tension. "All right. All right. You can let it go now."

Kin takes another bite of his bagel, then spits crumbs across the table as he asks, "Can you?"

I'll try. I'm trying. This battle is long and I'm not sure I'll ever stop looking over my shoulder. But I have learned that the world can be fair. *On occasion.* The most I can offer is that. Even as I hunch from perceived shadows and threats, I'll keep walking forward. I won't hide. I won't let it hold me back any longer.

"I hope so," I reply.

He grunts. It's probably not enough, but it will have to do for now.

Light settles over my shoulders. A sprinkling of hopeful dust as I remember I have something to tell him. "Kin..." I start, grinning.

He swipes at his mouth, "What... do I have something on my face?"

Shaking my head, I laugh. A barbed-wire-free laugh.

I hold the news in, savoring it. It's not every day I get to tell someone their fantasy is about to come true.

Chapter Fifty-five

Kite

I hear him before I see him. A rumbling voice followed by nurses giggling. I imagine them blushing and falling all over themselves as he throws them a wink. Kin. I strain for Hiro's voice. And soon enough, I hear him chastising his brother as Kin tries to commandeer a wheelchair. "You can walk. Hop along," Hiro snaps.

Together, they are the bell and the rope. Their absence from each other's lives had left a music-less void. It is wonderful to hear the song again. "Yeah, but I'm going for 'wounded soldier'. This completes the look."

"You want to get girls through pity?" Hiro chuckles.

There's a pause. Another giggle. "I'll take what I can get."

"I guess beggars can't be choosers." Their words are a line I reel in. I pull them closer. Closer.

"Watch it! Who are you calling a beggar?"

They sound happy.

They enter the room. Kin's eyes widen briefly, but he covers his surprise well. Coughing, he limps farther into the room. "Looking good, Kite, though I don't I think much of your outfit." His eyes go up and down animatedly.

Staring at my hospital gown, I drag it up to my throat. "Kin, I'm so glad to see you," I gush.

Hiro comes in behind him, his eyes a little beveled from tiredness. He gives me a quick smile, and my heart flips like a coin. "Where have you been?" I ask.

With his eyes sweeping the floor before rising to meet mine, I spot the pain there. He takes my hand. "I'm sorry I took so long," is all he says. It is enough for now.

I want to lean into him. I want to take his face in my hands and kiss him, but Kin's watching us, amused and unapologetic. This self-congratulatory expression on his face. "This..." He smiles wide and points between us. "This makes me very happy."

Hiro strokes my hair, ignoring his brother. "Kite, I have something to show you."

I gulp. His eyes are a mixed oil painting of hope and happiness, dread and anticipation. A collage of past hurt and a free future. He pulls a newspaper from his back pocket. Kin suddenly becomes very interested in the view outside my window. As my eyes scan the headlines, they water from fear. I've not known much good news in my life.

I can't find what he's trying to show me. He places a finger on the small headline, right at the bottom of the page.

Lawyer Confesses to Attempted Murder. Judge unmoved... There are more words and a lot of numbers. Years. *Years and years.* I have stopped breathing and my body is frozen in shock. I mouth the words over and over. My hands shaking as I grip the edges of the paper.

My eyes slide to Hiro, who's watching me with care. Waiting for a cue. "How?"

He shrugs slowly. "I don't know."

I let the paper fall to my lap. "Does this mean I don't have to face him in court? That he'll just stay in prison now?"

He nods. "I think that's what it means, yes."

"Oh."

Kin groans. "You two are the absolute worst at celebrating." He hobbles over and slings an arm around us both, though very gently around my shoulders. "This is a *good* thing. A very good thing."

Is it? It is. Of course it is.

I'm waiting for the news to sink in, but it keeps bouncing on the outside of my head and can't find a way in. It just seems so impossible that he would plead guilty.

Hiro says what I'm thinking. "Just give her a second, all right? This isn't easy to accept. It's like you're asking her to believe in fairies and cotton-candy clouds when all she's known is torn wings and hard concrete."

Kin sniggers. "Sometimes I forget how sensitive and poetic you are."

I giggle. I do want to believe in those things. "I do need a moment to get used to the idea…" I stare down at my healing hands. My arm cast that Frankie scribbled on. Large loopy letters spell her name and mine. Kite and Kricket.

Kin smiles with a regal nod. "Just not too long. We have more important things to discuss—like where my room is. I need first floor, southern-facing windows…"

Hiro punches him lightly in the arm. Everything is light. Lighter. Lightening.

Like the sun on its way up.

It will find its way in. Slowly. It starts with a small smile and a little hope.

Chapter Fifty-six

Hiro

Kelpie slams into my leg, clamping on like a monkey to its mother's back. His blue eyes are full of street stories. Scavenging victories. Scrapping wins. His face is smudged with grime, and his hair is knotted in places. I try to scruff his hair, and my hand gets caught in the mess of curls. "What have you been doing in the last two days, rolling in the mud, rubbing tree sap in your hair?"

Kelpie snaps his teeth. "Did you bring food?" He has that scrounging, hungry look. His fingers are waiting for something edible to be pressed into his palm. He skirts my legs, assuming I have a bag behind my back. I don't.

"I'm sorry, Kelpie. I don't have food but I have something better." I squat to his confused face. His eyebrows look darker since they are crusted with dirt, giving him a Marx-brother kind of look.

He tilts his head. "Nothing better than food in my belly." He pats his stomach, glancing around at the other boys. They are creeping closer like shadows over a dying fire in the forest.

I straighten his dirty collar with a smile. "I have some pretty neat news." I'm so nervous that I'm stalling. I'm worried they won't go for it. I wouldn't blame them if they didn't trust my words. These kids have traveled here on the backs of broken promises and raised fists. It's not in their nature to believe in fairy tales.

Krow slopes toward us. "Where's Kite?" he asks suspiciously, then he flaps his hand around eight-year-old height. "And the little one who can't sit still."

How to start... I tap my chin. The smell of wet stones and dirty clothes is a homely scent, but it was one we always hoped was temporary. I stand, bringing Kelpie under my arm. He nuzzles me. "I'm sorry I haven't been back in a couple of days. A lot has happened. Some good things, and some not so good things."

Krow leans in. "Are they all right, Kettle?" His fists tighten. We lose kids all the time, but it never gets easier. The idea that we may not have to lose anyone anymore breaks sunlight over my head.

"Kite's father got to her." The Kings seem to draw in one breath and hold it, and I follow quickly with, "She's okay, but she was badly hurt. Kricket wasn't hurt."

Kelpie frowns. His little body shaking so I hold him closer. "And the good thing?" Keg whispers.

These words feel like the orange in an autumn leaf. Beautiful but so brief it's hard to be sure one saw it. "The good thing is they caught him. He's in jail, and he'll be staying there for a long time."

The boys scoff. Krafty laughs, short and blunt. "Yeah, sure thing. Pull the other leg. He's in *jail*."

I take a step forward, bringing myself to the center of this doubting circle. "It's true."

Krow shakes his head sorrowfully. "You know that doesn't happen. Even if he's there now, he'll get out and it'll just make him angrier. Shit like this doesn't happen to kids like us."

Blowing air through my pursed lips, I glance at the sky. I understand where they're coming from. They're not used to things going even slightly their way. *Why would they believe it?* "I know this is hard to believe, and I haven't even got to the best part yet. Kite has inherited the entire family fortune and she wants you all to come live with her... in her brownstone uptown."

Krow turns away from me, kicking a loose stone. It ricochets off the wall. Lands on someone's bed. "It ain't April Fool's. Quit messing around."

They know more than survival. Things like the crack of a belt or the crunch of a fist in their guts. That's all they know. Their eyes tell me they want to believe me. But they can't. History holds them back with strong, violent hands and cold, cold nights. "Kings!" I shout. "I need to you to trust me. Have faith. I know it seems unbelievable that good could happen to us, but sometimes you just have to take a leap. Now I'm not going to force you. But if you believe in me and the Kings, then pack your stuff and come with me. The Kings are finally getting a castle."

Some kids' fates seem to be set in stone. Some find the wild, free street life suits them. Other kids have been waiting patiently, hopefully, for someone to scoop them up, stroke their heads and tell them *you're home now. You're safe, and I'm going to take care of you.* Many have lost their trust, and there's no way to get it back. It's shed like a cicada skin, leaving a tougher hide in its place.

Despite this, three quarters of the Kings stand in a huddle, bags and pillowcases slung over their shoulders. They have equal parts of hope and doubt in their eyes. But they're trying to believe in me. *Me.*

I sweep my eyes one last time over the tunnel. I try to memorize the ornate, theatre style lighting and the way the golden stones rise like a wave. I feel surprisingly okay. I don't mourn it. This place served us well for years, saving us. It has done its job, and now it can be a resting place for others in need. I hand it over. I hand it in.

I'm ready to go home.

We are a spectacle as we walk down the snow-scattered street, looking like Snow White's dwarves. *I'll have to do as the princess.* I snort, and a woman with a dead animal draped over her shoulders audibly gasps and quickly trots across the street. She starts skidding on the icy road, and I run to help her. Her haughtiness and pinched face make me laugh as she accepts my help, and then bats down her clothes like she's trying to get the homelessness stink off her clothes.

I'm dreaming of a hot bath. It is the number-one luxury I have been thinking about since this all started. That and holding Kite, feeling her permanence in my arms.

I jog back to the Kings, my feet used to the slip of ice. They stand in the street looking lost, like pieces on a chessboard awaiting a move. They're used to the spaces between the buildings. Here on the sidewalk, passing cascading staircases hemmed with curling wrought-iron balustrades and men and women in suits and fur coats, they seem so out of place. Small doubt starts to creep in but then Kelpie grabs my arm and tugs. "C'mon, Kettle. I cain't wait to see Kricket!"

Leaving uneven tracks in the snow, we traipse down the wide streets that will be leafy, tree-lined come spring.

We turn the corner onto Kite's street. Krow smirks, knocking my shoulder. "Which house is hers?"

One block down, we reach the bottom of the stairs to Kite's brownstone. I glance around at the boys. We're a muddy puddle on this clean street.

This is going to be a challenge.

Chewing on my lip, I turn to them, taking my cap off and making them do the same. I eye each boy, trying to say without saying that they need to be well mannered and respectful. They all give me a solemn nod. Caps in hand, we climb the stairs.

A challenge worth facing.

I take a deep breath, my finger hovering over the buzzer. My chest is filled with clouds and ocean foam. This doesn't feel real. I lean down to Kelpie. "Hey, little man, can you do me a favor?"

Kelpie nods seriously. "Whatchya need, Kettle?"

"Pinch me."

Chapter Fifty-seven

Kite

"Ouch!" I hear on the other side of the door. "Well, I guess I asked for that."

Wringing my hands nervously, my body sways a little. Kin winks at me as he manages to appear casually confident, leaning against the hall table. Frankie swings from the bottom of the stairs, grinning. This feels unreal. "Frankie, Kricket…" I beckon with my bruised fingers. She bounds to my side, knocking my hip. I plant my feet. *I am strong. I am safe. I am…*

I shake my head. "What's tha matter, Nor-ah?" Frankie asks, tipping her head up to me.

"I just… This just… It feels a little like a dream." I feel a pinch at my elbow, and I jerk my hand away. "Ouch!"

"There. Now ya know yer awake." She nods once and gallops to the door while Kin chuckles, already a comfortable installation in this home.

Frankie throws open the door, and there he is. *Hiro.* Staring down at his arm and rubbing it. "You didn't have to pinch me so hard, Kelp…" He glances up. Our eyes meet, and it's like the heat rises, and I think I might evaporate to steam.

I open my arms; they shake and bow like rigging in a storm. But I strengthen with every step he takes toward me. "Welcome…" He looks a little scared and a lot relieved. Like he's just realized, as I have, that this *is* real. And it's ours.

The boys stream around us, awestruck but certainly not struck dumb. The house rumbles with noise as they run their hands over the polished wood. Poke at the heavy curtains. Marie opens the kitchen door, and the smell of beef potpie lures them. She barely has time to press herself against the door as they squash through the opening and disappear. I hear Kelpie say, "May I please have a slice of pie, Madam?" And I giggle, covering my mouth.

Kin limps away, Frankie following. He mutters something like, "Lovebirds," and shoulders the door open.

We stand on the black and white tiles, two breaths between us. He closes the gap and takes my hand, pulling it from where it lingers over my mouth. Gold on the horizon of a dark blue sea. "Welcome…" I start again. He brushes his lips over mine. There is a pain to his movements. I feel it, too. We have to believe it. We have to let go. "…Home."

His kiss is soft. Like a nervous step over the threshold. But he whispers against my mouth, "It's good to *be* home."

We're given less than sixty seconds before the Kings pour back into the foyer. Marie chasing them with napkins, begging them to use cutlery. I smile. We have much to teach them. That alone brings a bubbling effervescence coursing through my body.

Kin's deep, joyous laughter fills the space. He taps his cane loudly on the tiles. *Clap. Clap. Clap.* "Just had to check it was solid. That I wasn't dead and floating on a cloud."

Hiro slaps his brother on the back. "I can't believe it either."

This makes me happier than I ever thought I could be. Giving this to the Kings, to Hiro, makes me feel so light I could fly. Opening my arms, I close my eyes. This house has never sounded so full. Bursting with excitement and love.

Hiro wraps his arms around my waist, pulling me into his chest. His mouth at my ear. "Last chance to take it back." He's joking, but there's a twist of realness to his words. Like me, he's still struggling to believe. He's still waiting for the earth to shake and crumble. For the solid things to give way and the dream to pitch in with it. This will take time.

I lean into him. Let his lips brush my ear. His nose burying in my hair. "Never."

Never. Never. Never.

Kin tsks loudly as he hobbles past us. "Sinful. Positively sinful, you two." We bounce apart. *Always* this small distance between us the size and shape of a wedding ring. Then Kin lifts his cane, pointing to the sky. "Now, if you would be so good as to show me to my room…"

Chapter Fifty-eight

Kite

We're folding into a family. Our corners rough and jagged. Nothing is neat. Nothing meets where it should, but for me, its imperfection makes it close to perfect. *These weeks* have been close to perfect. Listening to the shift and snore of boys sleeping in the playroom, I ease the door open a crack and count their heads. A warm smile creeping over my lips.

The window is ajar, and I pad between the beds to reach up and latch it closed. The inky sky gives promising twinkles of light through thready clouds. The snow lacing the trees can return to beautiful. No longer dangerous.

The boys are tucked in with blankets around their ears. I let my hand drift over their toes as I leave the room, thinking about schools and uniforms and how they're going to fight me. And I can't wait.

Through Frankie's closed door, I hear Kelpie and her whispering to each other. Secrets of children. Dreams and grand plans. I knock lightly on the door. "Sh! You two need to go to sleep."

They giggle, and I roll my eyes. Little *chipmunks*. I hear furniture dragging across the floor, and I have to go inside.

"What on earth are you doing?" Kelpie is pushing his bed to the foot of Frankie's. I touch my chest and try to contain the laugh that wants to escape, because they look so earnest and guilty at the same time. It bangs against the bedpost, and they huff.

"There." Frankie dusts her hands, appearing terribly grown up. "That will do nicely."

I point at the beds, ordering them in. "Right now, both of you under the covers." I kiss them both goodnight, praying they'll get some sleep.

As I leave, I feel a compression in my chest. It almost feels like jealousy. Thinking how unfair it is that they can share a room, yet Hiro and I cannot.

I huff. This is the fifties. I'm a modern woman. Yet, there are some things I can't seem to compromise. And if I'm honest, some things I desperately want.

Bare feet across a landing that used to feel like an unsteady bridge or an unsafe crossing. Now it's just a landing. It thunders with children's feet. It softens nighttime trips to the bathroom.

Sighing, I push open the bathroom door.

A splash of water hits the tiles as Hiro, who is lying in the bath, suddenly pulls his limbs into his body in an effort to cover himself. My mind etches a vision of his wet torso into its pages, and I quickly turn around. "Oh my God! Hiro, I didn't know you were in here."

Water moves as he shifts in the tub. "Well, you didn't knock." He sounds amused. Not embarrassed. *I* am embarrassed. "Can you… er… pass me a towel?"

I pull a towel from the hook, then walk backward slowly with it in my hand, my feet stepping in puddles. He takes it, and

I hear him rise from the water. My thoughts whirl like a tornado. My cheeks feel like red hot coals. "Are you…"

Hearing the water draining, I turn as he's wrapping the towel around his waist. I bite my lip. My eyes dancing over everything in the room, avoiding his gaze. He reaches for a hand towel and rubs his hair. It sticks up at all angles, his face fresh and flushed from the hot water. His eyes feel like a branding iron in the way they rest on me. I touch my heart. It bangs against my chest like a child caught in a closet. "Kite," he says, walking toward me adorably disheveled and nervous.

"Y…y…yes?" I say, my back pressing against the door. A towel rail digging into my back.

In a rather resigned voice, he murmurs, "Can you pass me my shirt?"

"Oh. Of course. Sorry." I grab the shirt. Press it to his chest. Just wanting to feel the heat of his skin for the slip of a second. He puts his hand over mine, but I dip down and away. Fleeing before I do something I'll regret.

I hear him exhale loudly as I speed down the hallway.

Yes, things are close to perfect. But this last little part, this missing corner, is becoming some sort of exquisite torture.

Chapter Fifty-nine

Kin

Today my little brother turns eighteen. He's officially an adult though he's been acting like one for as long as I can remember. Kettle the responsible one, always thinking about the consequences, though somehow remaining a dreamer.

Leaning on my good leg, I ignore the occasional shots of pain coming from my bad one. I know he watches me for signs. I don't want to give him any worry right now.

Kettle, who is now Hiro as well, and has taken so many steps forward, sits at the grand polished oak table, eyes closed, wary smile. It has served him well to dream. It started small, but it got bigger than either of us could have spun in those dumpster-side stories. All because he was always ready to give someone else a chance. Let new kids in.

I shake my head as a cake covered in candles is placed in front of him. The flames give him a golden glow. He opens his eyes to the decorated chocolate fudge cake with garlands of sugar flowers and blue blobs of sky-colored icing. It makes me laugh, but with this twinge of sadness at the sight of him taking in his *very first* birthday cake. The mix of emotions crossing his face—from overwhelmed to pleased, and then to that expression I've seen so many times. The one where he's counting the number of mouths to feed and how far he can stretch it.

I want to tell him that he doesn't have to do that anymore.

Is it possible that big heart of his got what it deserved?

Almost.

He always said anything was possible. I never believed.

I was so wrong to doubt. Not that I'd tell him. The Kings sing loudly, though half don't know the words. Kite's vulnerable voice sailing over the others. That honey gaze of hers is for him only. *Lucky bastard.* With a snort, I join the last chorus, singing as obnoxiously and as off key as I can.

"Happy birthday to you!" I slug his shoulder, and he gives me a treacherous look.

I put my hands up. "Hey, just be glad I only gave you one. Technically, I owe you seventeen more." I waggle my brows.

I pretend to punch him again, and he ducks from my fist. The flames flicker and melt wax onto the writing. *Happy Birthday, Hero.* My jaw tenses. Of course they changed the spelling, thinking it was a mistake. It shouldn't matter. I pump my fists. *It doesn't matter. Just let it go.*

Kettle sits at the head of the table, just staring at the cake, kind of frozen in this hallmark moment, unsure of what to do. Kite leans down, her cheek close to his. The tension between them is amusing and damn painful, and I chuckle. He smiles, but I can tell he's getting uncomfortable and doesn't know what to do.

I clap my hands. "Hurry up, we're hungry. Blow them out and make a wish." Like a slap, Kettle remembers what he's supposed to do. This tradition is not exactly new; we saw it happen in the camps when an officer celebrated his birthday. We got to sing. We rarely got a slice, though.

He inhales and blows. Kite laughs when he only manages to blow out four candles. "Go on, Kite. Give the poor guy a hand. He's obviously lost the ability to breathe with you standing so close."

"Oh," she mutters. "All right." They both turn scarlet, which I enjoy immensely. I shouldn't, but I've got to get my kicks where I can find them. My leg twinges. A sharp pain shooting through my hip and into my back like a bad telegraph. Shifting, I lean against the door, trying to arrange my face in a *happy birthday* way, not an *I'm in excruciating pain* way.

They blow the candles out together. Eyes meeting electricity sparking and all that mushy stuff. I roll my eyes. Now that Kettle is eighteen, there is absolutely no reason why he can't marry the girl. Though I'm sure he'll find some moral objection to it. Like the money or her mental fragility or some other bullshit.

Kricket shoves her way to the front. "Did you make a wish?"

Crossing my arms over my chest, I smirk. "Yeah, Kettle, what did you wish for?" The way they're looking at each other, the wish is probably not for children's ears and probably involves something like Kite and him alone in a bedroom…

I open my mouth to say just that, but Kite speaks first. "Sh! You don't tell anyone what you've wished for. If you do, it won't come true."

I feel for my brother. I know what he wished for, and it's not as debase and fun as what I would wish for. It's written all over his face that he just wants to be with her. I wish he'd stop tying himself in knots and do it already. Frankie watches him. She touches his arm gently, which is an effort for her, and I can tell she knows what he wished for, too.

Kite picks up the cake, and it's tracked by many pairs of hungry eyes. "I'm just going to cut this up."

Kettle stands suddenly, then wrestles the tray from her hands. "Please. Let me." Always the gentleman.

He walks out of the dining room, warnings in his eyes that I have no intention of heeding. Most of the boys follow him, already fighting over who gets the biggest piece, the corner piece, and who gets to eat the candied flowers.

Kite flops into a chair, skirts puffing up around her, and sighs. She glances up at me. This bruised and stitched-together girl. Half samurai, half geisha. I get why he loves her. They fit together. Star and sky. She stares with wide, worried eyes. "Do you think he liked the cake? I know they spelled his name wrong." Her irritation dives down. "I actually spelled it for them twice over the phone to make sure, and they still got it wrong."

I pull the chair out beside her. Ease into it. In the kitchen, I hear scrapping. Stools falling to the floor as the boys fight over the cake. "I think he loved it." Putting a hand on her arm, I pat it once. She tenses mildly. I see her trying to relax, but it's hard. I understand. She's not ready to let me into that bubble yet. And that's okay. "The fact that you even tried to get them to spell it right means a lot." *A whole lot.*

She swipes at her frizzy blonde hair. "I suppose." Her eyes are downcast. Her hands clasped neatly in her lap. A girl carved from finishing school and beatings. It's a peculiar combination.

"Kite. You've done so much for him. I think he just has a hard time accepting all the…" I gesture around the room. "All of this."

She laughs. Soft and pretty. "Gosh. I haven't done anything compared to what he's done for me."

My eyes hurt from all the rolling. I rub my brow.

Frankie cuts through the crap. "Why hafn't you and Hiro gotten married yet?" she asks.

"I… um… I guess we've been so busy getting the Kings settled and organizing the house that we haven't really had much time to think about it." Her eyes drop. I can tell it's probably all she thinks about. "Besides, I'm not sure he still wants to. He hasn't asked me."

Frankie takes her hand. "Maybe he's waiting fer you to ask him again."

Her amber eyes want and dream just like Kettle's. "I don't think so. I think it's just… not the right time."

"Do you want to marry Hiro?" The kid keeps pressing. I like that she doesn't get subtlety and hints. It makes for fun and awkward conversations.

Kite sighs. "More than anything."

These two are idiots. Too damn polite for their own good. I want to shout it to the ceiling, but I clench my teeth together and stretch my words. "Aaanyway… I think I'm ready to try and eat my weight in frosting." I stand up, limping my way to the kitchen and shouting through the swing door, "You better have left me a corner piece!"

Kricket bounds behind me, leaving Kite swirling greasy patterns on the table with her finger. "Aren't you gonna eat the cake, too?"

I laugh. "The frosting's the good shi…" Kite gives me a warning look. "…stuff. It's the good *stuff.* But hell, I guess if I have to, I could be persuaded to eat some cake, too."

She huffs as I leave the room. She may be even more annoyed once she finds out what I've got turning around in my head. Then again, it might be just what the two of them need.

A swift kick up the *you know what.*

Chapter Sixty

Hiro

I stare at the ceiling, unable to sleep. Shifting under my duvet and feeling the foreignness of warmth. The carpet beneath me is more comfortable than my mattress in the tunnel. The bed is untouched. I prefer the floor. It's what I'm used to. The rose with its swirled, ornate plasterwork mocks me, threatens to fall. Today was a good day. Filled with new things. Unnecessary things. Indulgences. Sugar. And looks that keep me alive and make me want to die at the same time.

But...

I fold my arms over my chest, breathing in deeply. These are things I never thought I'd have. I'm eighteen. I got there. I survived. A few months ago, that would have been enough for me. Just to have got to this point, to have lived this long. But now there are needs and wishes that go unfilled. They make new holes in an already-leaky vessel. They add stars to my night sky. Unreachable light. Light I will always crave and search for.

"Kite," I whisper. It sounds like a sigh. It sounds like the only word I want on my tongue. I chuckle quietly. My hands stretch and crack, and I place them beneath my head. *I'm in deep*.

The door creaks open, my heart flattens, but then evens as the smallest shadow vibrates across the floor. Kricket. She steps into the room, golden light from the landing gracing her shoulders like a fairy cape. Propping up on my elbows, I tilt my head. "You're awfully formal for bedtime. Aren't you, kid?"

Her expression is strangely serene and at odds with the way she walks, pumping up and down on her tiptoes. She has a garland of silk flowers in her hair, and she bows her head. Standing over me, a strong whip of a child, she whispers, "I hef a present for you, Kettle. For yer berfday." She holds out her hand, and I take it. Humoring whatever play this is.

She pulls me down the long, carpeted landing. There are sprinkles of rose petals on the floor, all a little bruised and crushed beneath her feet. They point a path like shells to the beach. They lead to Kite's bedroom door. I stall, my feet lining up like I'm waiting for an inspection. "Kricket... does your sister know you've brought me here?" She shakes her head, a mischievous smile creeping over her peachy lips.

"She's not in there," Kricket mutters while opening the door and shoving me inside with more strength than I would have anticipated. I stumble headlong into the room. When my eyes lift, I gasp.

The curtains flutter from the open window. Candles burn and waver on every surface. It smells like smoke and snow, but mostly it has the sweet, soft smell of Kite. My eyes touch upon the tiny folded stars and cranes and lotus flowers strewn over the dresser, the floor, the bed. I've been teaching Kricket the crane. I hadn't got to lotus flowers yet. My eyes narrow.

The mirror sparkles with reflected light, like she's actually trapped a comet in here and its tail is lying gently across the furniture.

Kricket shoves a shirt and a bowtie into my arms. "Put this on." Her eyes have returned to serious, and she looks like she'll hurt me if I don't abide her wishes. I shrug out of my shirt and put the white one on, quickly fastening the black buttons. The bowtie looks more complicated than origami and I wrap it around my collar, tying it loosely. I have no idea how to do it properly.

Kricket throws me a dinner jacket. I look ridiculous, barefoot in pajama pants and a tuxedo shirt paired with a dinner jacket. But Kricket nods her approval.

She grabs my waist with pointy fingers. Lines me up by the window. "Stand right here an don't move," she orders, pointing at a spot on the floor almost grumpily. I salute and do as I'm told.

Muffled voices on the other side of the door. "Okay, Kin, do you think you know everything there is to know about the plumbing in the basement now?"

Kin's mocking tone is liquid lies. "Well, I thought it was necessary knowledge, you know, in case something goes wrong. You'll need a man to fix things around the place."

I can imagine him puffing his chest out proudly.

Kite laughs daintily. "It took you twenty minutes to tell the difference between water pipes and heating lines. Not to mention the stairs…" Her voice is like rustling corn silk in a field. Sweet and surprising.

"Well, now I know the…" Kin's voice darkens like he has a secret. I step forward, and Kricket slaps her hand on my chest to stop me.

The door opens, and Kin and Kricket whisper, "Surprise!" at the same time.

Kite steps into the room, her hair plaited messily and resting over one shoulder. Her nightdress hangs below a tightly fastened robe. She puts her hand on her heart, gasping like I did at the sight of her room. "What on earth!"

Kin waggles his eyebrows behind her, and I frown. When her eyes meet mine, we are stretched elastic, winding tighter and tighter until she is standing in front of me. I face my palms to the ceiling. "I'm in the dark, too," I manage.

Kin strides over to us, standing at the windowsill, icy breeze reddening our cheeks. He gently places a garland of flowers on Kite's head like a crown. Her chin dips, and she bites her lip. Her lashes are dark and curled and sprinkled with pollen. The flowers hang lower over one ear, and I reach out to tuck them back into her hair. She is more than beautiful. She is the beginning of the universe. Stars colliding.

We turn to the two conspirators, who look very pleased with themselves. "What are you two up to?" I ask.

Proudly, Kricket marches to the window and takes a pre-decided position at the sill. "I'm gonna marry you an Nor-ah. Though I know you call her Kite. So, for the porpoises of the ceremony, I will say Kite. Not Nor-ah. Okay, Nor-ah? Shoot. Okay, Kite?"

We both laugh quietly, getting an irritated look from the little redhead. Kite taps her apricot lips with a nod. "Yes, of course, Frankie." Who points between us, indicating for Kite and me to face each other.

"Dearly loved. We're gonna gather around and marry Hiro and *Kite*." She says the word emphatically. She reads from a torn piece of paper, her eyes running over each word carefully.

My smile is stretching beyond my face. My heart is breaking free from my chest. I find Kite's eyes, and I can tell she feels the same.

Kricket straightens the paper. Points at her sister. "Kite loves Hiro." She waits for confirmations, and Kite nods shyly. Then she points at me. "And Hiro *loves* Kite."

"I do," I murmur, hooked into that honey expression. Waves of warmth crashing over my eyes. A rainbow slow dances over us from the leadlight lamp by the window.

Kricket slaps my arm. "We're not at that part yet." Letting out a groan, she traces the words with her finger. "Ya made me lose ma place." She taps her ear as it crackles and whines.

Kin chuckles beside me, but when I find his expression, it is genuine and encouraging. It's the other side of the ticket. The return trip. He flicks his hand, telling me to turn back toward Kite.

Kricket mutters to herself, then says, "Right! They been worryin' about things that don't need worryin' about. When them being in love with each other is the only thing they should be worryin' about. Well, not worryin'… I mean, thinking about."

In her eyes, I see resolution. I feel it within myself. The kid is right.

I wait to hear a snicker from Kin, but all I hear is a long, deep breath in.

Kricket points her thin finger at my chest. "Hiro, say I marry you, Kite."

These words, though spoken by a child in the middle of the night, carry importance. "I marry you, Kite." I hold my breath for the next part. My heart hinged on what Kite will say.

Kricket swings in her party dress, flashes of pink satin and milky-way light. "Kite, say I marry you, Hiro."

She says it with determination and abandon. With all the pain and scars thrown to the side. I take them. I'll hold them for her as long as she needs me to. "I marry you, Hiro."

Kricket clears her throat. An icy wind pours through the window. Kite reaches up and closes it behind her little sister's head. The cold can't come in. The words won't fly away. "Now join hands." When she curses, Kite draws in shocked breath. "Aw hell, I was s'posed to do that first. Just pretend you were holdin' hands tha whole time."

I can't help but let out a folded laugh, creased in the corners by something big happening right here. In the bedroom of the girl who lived in the fancy brownstone and wanted to fly away.

Whose feet are now firmly on the ground, facing mine. Saying things I am so happy to hear. Things I believe in, wholeheartedly.

Kite pats her sister's head. "It doesn't matter, Frankie. You're doing great."

"Jus hold hands extra tight; that'll make up for it."

We hold hands. They lock together, and maybe our feet lift a little. Like there's still magic left. Still stardust to squander.

Kricket puts her hands over ours. Pushes them down quite forcefully. "I now pronunciate you married!" She presents the simple pewter ring with a star on it I bought at the drugstore. "Stick that on Nor… Kite's finger, please."

I slide it onto her ring finger. It's too big and rolls over so the star is underneath, but Kite gazes at it like it's the most beautiful thing she's ever owned.

Kricket claps her hands, jumping up and down. Kite's eyes are lit like the blazing sun on the summer sea. I grin and she grins, and we can't let go of each other.

Kin mutters something, grabbing hold of Kricket's arm. "C'mon, you little ferret," he says affectionately. I hear them, but my eyes can't stray. They see only the air around her face. The distance from me to her lips.

"But I wanna stay," Kricket moans as she's being gently dragged across the carpet.

"No. You don't," Kin says, pausing in the doorway.

"Why, what's gonna happen?" her husky voice whines.

Kin's chest rumbles with that deep chuckle that comes straight from his mischievous heart. "Because they're gonna kiss." He makes smooching noises, and I'm sure Kricket's face scrunches.

"Ew!" she manages as she's pulled through the doorway and it's latched. The sound pulls the hands from the clock. Time doesn't just stand still. It ceases to be. This moment is purely and endlessly ours.

I wrap my arms around her waist, and she does the same. Pressing close. Eyes alight. Our toes touching. Our hearts winding around each other in a permanent, unbreakable kind of way. It's a kiss free from pain. And it's the best one so far because I know there are so many more to follow.

I *know* that we're right where we're meant to be. Not holding each other together. Just holding each other.

We fall. We laugh. We open.

We are bridged and broken no longer.

"So, what do we do now?" Kite asks with a heart that's full but knows there's more.

I smile. "Whatever we want."

Also by Lauren Nicolle Taylor

The Girl with the Hickory Heart

Mulan meets *The Last Airbender* in this dark fantasy, set in an island nation akin to a wooden Hong Kong.

Two Asian women from warring tribes: Lye, a powerful slave of the Emperor and Luna, a Char defying tradition.

For Luna, the price of peace in a time of war is a heart of hickory. But to have a hickory heart leaves no room for love. When the lives of her three brothers are tied to refugee siblings from the warring tribe, Luna must test the limits of her wooden heart, trust those she's been taught to hate, and now she's destined to destroy.

Acknowledgements

This book was written in the interest of a fresh start. Having felt like I was being creatively restrained for two years, I sat down to write with abandon and freedom. *Hiro Loves Kite* is a reflection of letting go and holding on. Letting go of expectations, of the need to please and holding onto love and the belief that good things can and will happen. What resulted is a representation of real, messy, hopeful love. And the story of two people who must come to terms with the fact that they truly deserve to have that love.

If you take anything away from this novel, let it be that you do deserve good things. I think far too often, when bad things happen, we believe we're being punished. We think, *of course that happened. It was only a matter of time. It's been a bad week, a bad month, a bad year.* We hold onto the negative: Due to trauma, a bad string of events or something else that makes us think that luck is not on our side. When what we should be doing is holding onto the good. It's a rope dangling right in front of our faces, offering a way out of the hole we've dug. But it can be so hard to grasp. The climb looks hard. The rope swings out of range. It's slippery. It burns our hands when we lose purchase. We can't see over the edge and we worry it's more of the same up there.

Take it! Even if you don't know what's waiting at the top. Believe it's good. Or, that once you get out, you'll find the good thing, down the path, around the corner. I promise, it's not out of reach. It's waiting for its moment.

We all deserve happiness. Don't let the world, the universe, the freakin' sky, tell you any different.

Lauren Nicolle Taylor is the bestselling author of The Woodlands series, the Hickory Heart series, and this book, the award-winning *Nora & Kettle* (Gold medal Winner for Multicultural Fiction, Independent Publishers Book Awards 2017), which is the first book in the acclaimed Paper Stars series.

She has a Health Science degree and an honors degree in Obstetrics and Gynecology.

A full time writer and artist, Lauren recently moved from Australia to Canada with her husband and three children for a new adventure. She is a proud hapa and draws on her multicultural background in all of her novels.

Lauren is represented by Golden Wheat Literary.

Find Lauren at www.laurennicolletaylor.com

#NoraandKettle
#HiroLovesKite

www.ingramcontent.com/pod-product-compliance
Lightning Source LLC
Chambersburg PA
CBHW020749190726
48285CB00006B/1945